THE
NIGHT
WEAVER

Other Books by Monique Snyman

Muti Nation

Honors

2018 Bram Stoker Nominee for
Superior Achievement in a Young Adult Novel

THE NIGHT WEAVER
2018 Bram Stoker Awards Nominee
MONIQUE SNYMAN

The Night Weaver

This is a work of fiction. Names, characters, places, and incidents either are the product of the author's imagination or are used fictitiously.
Any resemblance to actual persons, living or dead, or locales is entirely coincidental.

Original Cover Art by Marcela Bolívar
http://www.marcelabolivar.com/about/

Title Treatment by Michael J. Canales
http://mjcimageworks.com

ISBN: 978-1-64548-006-8

Vesuvian Books

Published by Vesuvian Books
www.vesuvianbooks.com

Printed in the United States of America

10 9 8 7 6 5 4 3 2 1

For Manus,
Look, Honey, I did the writing thing again. Yay me!

Table of Contents

Chapter One
A Perfectly Pleasant Town

At the road's end, a weathered ACCESS PROHIBITED sign stands sentinel at a narrow opening to the dark, Maine wilderness. Beyond the sign is an ancient beech tree, its thick branches reaching to the sky. White ash and red oaks flourish behind the tree; flora grows densely around the trunks but never seems to cross the invisible boundary beyond the signpost. The valley farther on is an almost circular basin enclosed within a mountainous range and a radius fifteen miles wide.

The sound of a faint, unnerving scream echoes through the labyrinth of trees. Fear prickles the back of Rachel Cleary's neck. She listens, certain she saw movement even if *nothing* ever moves in the forest. The wind itself seems wary of the place. No critters or birds make the forest their home. There are only trees, flowers, and shrubs. And now, a scream …

An out-of-tune honk startles Rachel back to reality. She pivots. The Honda Ballade is waiting in Mrs. Crenshaw's driveway. Black plumes of exhaust rise as the vehicle idles. In the driver's seat sits the elderly woman, her shock of white hair pulled into a neat bun—*it's God's natural facelift, my dear.* Apart from rouge dabbed onto her cheekbones, Mrs. Crenshaw has made no attempt to hide her age.

"See something interesting in there, Rachel?" Mrs. Crenshaw asks by way of greeting.

"Maybe," Rachel says. "It's probably just my imagination, though."

Mrs. Crenshaw fixes her gaze on Rachel, crow's feet emphasizing the narrowing of her eyes. "Sometimes there are things in there ... *interesting* things." She lets the vague words hang between them before reversing out of the driveway and shifting into first gear. She calls out a deceptively upbeat, "Hop in." Her expression makes it clear that Rachel has no choice but to go along.

Rachel reaches out to find the passenger door already unlocked, climbs inside, and pulls the safety belt over her body. The Honda sputters forward.

"Where are we going, Mrs. Crenshaw?" Rachel asks when it becomes clear her neighbor isn't going to elaborate.

"Shopping," Mrs. Crenshaw says. "My grandson is coming for an extended visit sometime tonight and I haven't the foggiest what teenage boys eat these days."

Rachel's eyes widen. "You have a grandson?"

"I have four grandsons, two granddaughters, and three great-grandchildren." Mrs. Crenshaw glances in Rachel's direction. "Surely I've told you?"

"No." Seventeen years of living across the road from Mrs. Crenshaw—the same woman who'd babysat her, who'd taught her how to tie her shoes, who'd gifted her a ten dollar bill every birthday and Christmas for as long as she can remember—and Rachel never suspected Mrs. Crenshaw had children at some point in her life. "You don't have any photos in your house of them."

"Well, they aren't anything to brag about," Mrs. Crenshaw says, the beginnings of a deep crease forming on her forehead. "Where do you think I go during the holiday season?"

"I don't know. Florida?"

Mrs. Crenshaw shakes her head. "Can't blame you, I suppose. God knows the only time I ever see my children is when I visit them."

"Why?"

"You're curious about all the wrong things today." Mrs. Crenshaw keeps her eyes on Griswold Road. Desolate, as it often is, the road twists and winds through Shadow Grove's undeveloped lands. "Neither Matthew nor Sophie will set foot in this place. They ran off as soon as they turned eighteen, claiming they didn't want to get stuck in a small town like their daddy had. It's my own fault, of course, but it's such an inconvenience."

The conversation halts as they approach Eerie Creek Bridge, its barrier created from slats of wood haphazardly nailed together and painted over in a neutral white. Mrs. Crenshaw leans forward, squinting hard at something beside the road. Rachel follows her gaze to where Maggie Dawson and Eddie Roberts run up the creek bank, giggling all the way, their clothes soaked through. Rachel doesn't look for long, although she has half a mind to shout at them to get a room.

Mrs. Crenshaw turns onto the bridge and inhales deeply, relaxing against her seat as soon as the car crosses into the suburbs of the small town, where boxy, symmetrical homes line the street. Here and there a wrought-iron fence surrounds a property. A decorative balustrade becomes a feature point, setting the fraternal houses on Eerie Street apart. Every garden is maintained—green, lush, and overrun with a variety of flowers—

in accordance with the strict homeowners' association guidelines.

The suburbs are pretty, no doubt, but a tad too utilitarian for Rachel's tastes.

Mrs. Crenshaw slows and turns her car onto Main Road, where colonial buildings have been repurposed to house Shadow Grove's thriving small businesses. Alice's Vintage Emporium, which sells upmarket fashion from yesteryear, is neighbor to a quaint sit-down coffee shop called Café Grove—where the who's who of Ridge Crest High usually hang out.

"Did you notice there isn't a single missing person flyer posted anywhere in town?" Rachel asks, remembering the scream she'd heard—or imagined she'd heard.

"Yes, I have."

A shudder runs down her back. "It's weird, right? I mean, if this was any other town, people would've immediately formed search parties to look for the missing kids. Not to mention, their parents would've approached every newspaper and news station in the state by now. At the very least, we'd have gotten word of there being a Facebook group, or seen posts on other social media sites. Hashtag where are they?"

Mrs. Crenshaw grimaces. "I s'pose."

Rachel places her hands in her lap when Mrs. Crenshaw's response doesn't meet her expectations. Where is the outrage? Little kids are going missing and nobody over the age of eighteen seems in the least bit concerned. In fact, the Sheriff's Department is making it sound like there's a perfectly reasonable explanation for the disappearances. Take, for example, eight-year-old Dana Crosby, who went missing on her way home right after Christmas break. She'd stayed after school later than usual, according to her teacher, because she'd received detention for speaking out of turn.

A day later, when folks were becoming antsy about Dana's safety, Sheriff Carter released a press statement implying the girl was prone to throwing temper tantrums and running away when she didn't get her way. She was, presumably, a troubled young girl, and she would, most likely, make her way home when she was good and ready.

Two weeks after Dana Crosby supposedly threw a tantrum and ran away, four-year-old Eric Smith was snatched out of his mother's backyard around dusk. His mother said he'd been playing in his sandbox, driving his cars across the snow-capped sandy hills he'd created.

"I only looked away for a second, I swear!"

Mrs. Smith's public breakdown in Café Grove hadn't changed the town's indifferent outlook on the situation.

Somehow, Sheriff Carter convinced the poor woman that her son had been taken by her estranged husband. He'd even gone so far as to tell her Eric's father was well within his rights to take their son because there weren't any explicit custody terms in place. The logic behind his proclamation was flawed, but Eric's mother didn't officially pursue the matter any further.

Two months later, as winter began to thaw and the world renewed itself in spectacular fashion, twelve-year-old Becky Goldstein, an avid birdwatcher and budding artist, vanished near Eerie Creek. Her sketchbook was found on the creek bank a few days later, a drawing of an evening grosbeak still unfinished, along with her binoculars and pencils.

"There is no evidence of foul play in Becky Goldstein's disappearance. We have reason to believe she ran away from home after we found and read her diary, which explicitly states: 'I wish I could live in New York forever. One day, if I'm ever brave enough,

I'll run away and live beneath the lights with an artist.'"

Becky Goldstein, contrary to Sheriff Carter's statement, was not the runaway type. Rachel should know because she'd babysat her on occasion. The girl came from a good home—her grades were outstanding, and she didn't hang around with the wrong crowd as everyone was led to believe. The girl was an introvert, happiest whenever she had those binoculars against her face, sure. But Becky wasn't socially inept either. She had plenty of age-appropriate friends who didn't get into any trouble. Furthermore, those diary entries Sheriff Carter loved to quote were the shared fantasies and dreams of every prepubescent girl in today's society. No names were mentioned, no plans were made, no way had she left everything she knew and loved behind.

Then nine-year-old Toby Merkel was gone, followed by six-year-old Michael O'Conner.

One after the other, kids vanish into thin air, and every single time Sheriff Carter finds a reason *not* to investigate their disappearances.

There were other incidents, of course, and other cover-ups unrelated to the mysterious disappearances, but the issue of the missing children is the most disconcerting matter now.

"You'd be out there looking for me if I went missing, right?"

"You know I would, dear." Mrs. Crenshaw's tone doesn't leave room for doubt.

Rachel gulps down her emotions, grateful that someone, anyone, would remember she existed if she's ever taken against her will.

An awkward silence stretches between them as Mrs. Crenshaw maneuvers her vehicle around the park, heading for the Other Side of town, which is no more than a euphemism for the so-called less-desirable residents and businesses in Shadow Grove. Hidden away from the tourists' eyes, trailers and smaller houses stand alongside steelworks and other closed down factories, just beyond the now-defunct train station. Ashfall Heights—a neglected, solitary apartment building, built just before the Great Depression when a mediocre population boom made the town council worry about a future housing problem—stands nine stories high, and is mostly surrounded by undeveloped wilderness.

The Other Side is also where the more popular chain-stores find themselves.

Rachel says, "You know what Sheriff Carter said when I asked him about what he's doing to find the missing kids? He said if anything's amiss, it doesn't fall into his jurisdiction anyway." She picks at her thumb's cuticle with her index finger, a nervous habit, and barely feels the sharp pain as she digs too deep and draws blood. "What does that even mean? What's the deal with Bulltwang Bill al—"

She cuts herself off, realizing her mistake.

"Who now?"

Rachel's face warms. "Sheriff Carter."

Mrs. Crenshaw's lips tug into one of her secretive smiles, then vanishes. "Have you spoken to your mother about any of this?" There's both sympathy and regret in her voice.

Rachel barks a humorless laugh. "Every time I bring it up, she changes the subject."

Mrs. Crenshaw exhales loudly, shaking her head as she turns onto 7th Avenue and drives into the chain supermarket's parking lot. She parks in one of the empty spaces nearest to the automatic sliding door. The Honda's engine wheezes from the six-mile drive, rumbling with gratitude when she turns the key in the ignition. Mrs. Crenshaw's knuckles are white from gripping the steering wheel, liver spots paling quickly and wrinkles smoothing.

Maybe this issue is affecting her more than she lets on?

"I don't get it," Rachel says. "There's likely a kiddie-fiddler on the loose, possibly one with a tendency to kill his victims, but people aren't freaking out. What's wrong with this town?"

"It's not my place to tell you why this town is the way it is." Mrs. Crenshaw sounds older than her seventy-two years; her icy blue eyes hold too much wisdom for one person to have collected in a single lifetime. "What I can tell you is that when I struggle to understand the present, I tend to study the past. I try to piece things together by sifting through the chaos.

"The usual avenues hold no answers, though; libraries, archives, even digital sources have been manipulated to help with Shadow Grove's long-term rebranding plan. If you want answers, you're going to have to get creative and dig real deep. You'll need to find unaltered history.

"If I were you," she continues in a conspirator's whisper. "I'd find my clues where the really old stuff is kept—"

"I'm *not* breaking into the museum," Rachel interrupts.

The old woman cackles like a witch, her frail shoulders shaking underneath her silk blouse. She releases her grip on the steering wheel, visibly relaxing. "I should hope not," she says between her fits of laughter. "No, sweetheart, I don't mean the museum—it's under town council control anyway. Listen to me: when I struggle to understand the *present*, I tend to study the *past*. I try to piece things together by *sifting* through the *chaos*."

Rachel frowns.

Mom always hides the Christmas presents in the cluttered attic, near the trunk with the box of old kitchen utensils in it. Does she mean Dad's old stuff?

"The attic?" she asks, unsure.

Mrs. Crenshaw raises her hand and touches her index finger to her nose, eyes gleaming with mischief, before she reaches between the seats to find her purse.

Relieved, Rachel releases her seatbelt. "Was that so hard?"

Mrs. Crenshaw opens the driver's door. "Instead of sassing me, run ahead and get us a shopping cart."

"Whatever happened to bribing me with ice-cream to do your bidding, huh?" Rachel tuts and shakes her head, hiding her smile with a forced frown.

"I think there are laws against that type of thing now," Mrs. Crenshaw responds under her breath, making Rachel laugh as she walks off to find a shopping cart.

Chapter Two
Small Town, Big Problems

After spending the better half of an hour listing the disappearances in chronological order, Rachel comes to the conclusion that her detective skills aren't nearly as good as she'd hoped, and her natural talent for research only goes as far as the available information. Nevertheless, she's certain there's more to the story. Call it instinct or wishful thinking, but an inexplicable gut feeling tells her those children were taken for a reason.

The reason is *important.*

"But why?" she asks herself, frustration threatening to overpower her determination. Any answer would do at this point. She's been putting off a trip into the attic since the previous evening, not completely in the mood to rummage through generations of accumulated junk.

Her attention moves toward her bedroom window and the gleaming forest beyond, where emerald leaves glitter in the mid-morning sunlight. The world outside is as quiet as the house itself—motionless, devoid of life. The forest always reminds her of a graveyard, unsettling in its solemnity. These days, it also *feels* different, like something is watching … waiting.

Waiting for what?

Rachel shudders, uneasy at the thought. She pushes herself out of the chair and crosses the room. With a last, quick assessment of the area outside, she shuts the curtains and stands there, fabric clutched in her hands.

What if something is watching me? What if it's the same something that took the children? What if I'm next?

Rachel talks herself out of peeking through the crack between the drops of thick fabric.

Be reasonable. The kids who've been taken were between four and twelve years old. You're seventeen, Rachel. You're too old.

The creepy feeling is replaced with a frisson of intense fear.

Still, what if I'm wrong?

"Nope. Nope. Nope."

Rachel turns on her heels and heads for the door, repeating the word under her breath until it becomes an irritating mantra she can't stop uttering. She makes her way through the hallway, toward the staircase, and descends two steps at a time to put as much distance between herself and the window. By the time she reaches the first floor, she's ready to sprint across Griswold Road, toward the safety of Mrs. Crenshaw's house.

She uses too much strength to pull the front door open and the momentum drags her off balance. Before she can begin to understand what's happening *outside* her own mind, a shriek tears out of her as she locks eyes with an unexpected, auburn-haired stranger, his fist still raised to knock against the now-open door. Rachel clamps a hand over her mouth to stifle her cry of surprise. The guy lowers his fist.

He's tall, towering over Rachel's five-six, and brawny enough to make her not want to mess with him. He doesn't appear to be much older than her. She'd wager he's nineteen or twenty, maybe. His icy blue eyes have a familiarity she can't seem to pinpoint. It's as if her fear has rendered her deduction abilities moot, leaving her completely defenseless.

"Ye look like ye have the devil chasin' after ye," he says, peering around Rachel to study the area behind her. He turns his attention back to her. "Nan asked if ye wanted to come plant some eggs with us. I'm not sure what the old witch meant."

"What?" Rachel's confusion is muffled behind her hand.

"My Nan—" He gestures across the street to Mrs. Crenshaw's house with a thumb over his shoulder.

Rachel slips her hand away from her mouth as her mind connects the dots. Those ice-blue eyes belong to Mrs. Crenshaw, and that particular shade of auburn-colored hair is similar to her own. There's no doubt in who he is, weird accent or no. "Oh. You're Mrs. Crenshaw's grandson?"

"Aye," he says, sighing. "Are ye comin' then?"

She steps outside the house and pulls the door shut behind her. Whatever it is Mrs. Crenshaw wants them to do is infinitely better than being alone, especially being alone in a house that's being watched by … well, by whatever is inside the forest.

They walk down the porch steps, Rachel leading the way. Silence hangs over them, one full of unasked questions like: 'What's your name?' and 'Sorry for the freak-out, but did you perchance see someone peeping through my bedroom window on your way over?' Before she can ask him anything, Rachel spots Mrs. Crenshaw in the distance, near the forest entrance. The old woman sits in a lawn chair, beneath the shade of a faded pink umbrella, her sunhat on her head and the bottle of sunblock within her reach. She looks so tiny these days, so much tinier and more delicate than she was a year ago.

"I'm Rachel," she says to the herculean guy when they reach the lawn. "Rachel Cleary."

"Nan said as much." He pushes one hand through his thick, wavy hair. "Dougal Charles Mackay." He pronounces his name *Doogle Charls Meckeye*, melodic vowels and throaty consonants rolling off his tongue.

"Nice name." Rachel crosses her arms just to do something with her hands. He tilts his head in her direction. The warmth of a blush comes without warning, heating her cheeks. She clears her throat and says, "So, what exactly are we going to do at Mrs. Crenshaw's?"

He shakes his head, hair falling over his forehead. "I dunno. Somethin' about plantin' eggs."

Rachel frowns, struggling to decipher his words. "Planting eggs?"

"Aye."

"As in, she wants us to dig a hole and put a chicken egg into the ground?"

Dougal purses his lips as his brow furrows before he slowly nods. They reach the sun-bleached asphalt. He looks toward the forest entrance, to where his grandmother sits, before his gaze slips to study the road.

"Weird," Rachel says. "Mind you, your grandmother always occupied my time with odd activities."

"What's taking you so long, Dougal?" Mrs. Crenshaw shouts. She stretches her neck to look over her shoulder. "Stop dawdling and fetch the basket of eggs on the kitchen counter and the shovel at the back door. We have a lot of work to do today."

"Lord, help me," Dougal says, speeding up.

Rachel snickers as she watches him go.

"Are you sassing me, boy?" Mrs. Crenshaw asks in a stern voice, the same voice Rachel used to fear as a kid. "Don't think you're old enough not to get a paddle to the butt!"

"I wasn't sassing ye, Nan," he says loud enough for her to hear.

"You'd better not be. Also, you can tone down on the Scots already. I've heard you mocking your mother's accent enough to know you can speak passable English," Mrs. Crenshaw calls as Rachel hurries to the old woman's side, glad not to be on the other end of this particular conversation. "When he sulks, I can barely understand him."

"I was having some trouble in that department myself," Rachel concurs.

"You'll get used to the accent after a while, but I can't say the same thing about the bagpipes at five o'clock in the morning. I swear, whenever I go up to Scotland, his father plays those damned bagpipes on purpose just to get on my nerves."

"Please tell me Dougal doesn't play bagpipes."

"*That* miscreant? Ha. He doesn't have a musical bone in his body, thank the heavens."

Rachel sighs in relief.

"Listen," Mrs. Crenshaw changes her tone to match the seriousness gleaming in her eyes. "I'm sure you've noticed or have already suspected, but it deserves mentioning anyway. You and Dougal are *not* to get romantic in any way."

"The hair kinda gave it away," Rachel says.

"Good," Mrs. Crenshaw says. "I'm yet to broach the subject with him about you two being related. Hopefully, Sophie got around to it before she put him on the plane."

"Don't worry, Mrs. Crenshaw," Rachel says, unable to keep

herself from grimacing at the mere thought of her and Dougal being anything more than friends. "He's not my type anyway."

"Keep it that way." Mrs. Crenshaw glances over her shoulder again. "Dougal, what's taking you so long?"

Dougal appears on the porch, holding a basket filled with eggs in one hand and a shovel clutched in his other hand. He crosses the distance, sets the basket beside the chair, and plants the shovel's blade into the earth. He leans on the handle, waiting for direction.

"Now we can plant some eggs." Mrs. Crenshaw rubs her hands together.

Dougal opens his mouth to protest—or ask a question—and Rachel gestures for him to stop by waving her hands around behind his grandmother's back. If there's one thing she's learned about Mrs. Crenshaw, it's that when she's in one of these moods, it's best to keep quiet and go along with her whims. Dougal shuts his mouth but raises an inquisitive eyebrow at Rachel instead.

"Dougal, you're going to dig some holes. They need to be about one foot deep and a yard apart. Begin at the edge of the MacCleary property and work your way to the end of mine, past the ACCESS PROHIBITED sign. Rachel, you're going to *carefully* put the egg into the hole and cover it with soil. Don't plant a cracked egg. Be gentle with them." She claps her hands, signaling the beginning of the workday, one in which she won't be participating.

Rachel stands, grabs the egg basket, and falls into step beside Mrs. Crenshaw's sullen grandson.

"Is Nan always like this?" Dougal asks when they're out of earshot. "Ye know her better."

"Not *always*. She tends to get peculiar around this time of year, but it's not harmful or malicious—just strange."

For the most part, the MacCleary land is relatively big but remains unused. The border of the property follows one curve of the mountainous range holding the forest, the rocky terrain steadily becoming a steep cliff looming over the farthest edge of the property. Across Griswold Road, the Fraser land is a mirror image, laid out in an identical way against the other curve. The only difference is the houses' façades and the additions built in the past to accommodate the growing families. Both families had been large once.

When Rachel and Dougal arrive at the border of the MacCleary property, he tests the ground with the shovel. The blade penetrates the soft soil with ease but stops when it slams against a rock hidden within the earth. He wiggles the shovel around to loosen the rock from its hold, before moving the first bit of ground to the side.

"About eight years ago, around the time my dad died, your grandmother came over with a boxful of saucers and a crate of milk," Rachel says.

"Whit wey?"

"Huh?"

"Why?" Dougal clarifies.

"Oh. Well, Mrs. Crenshaw doesn't tell me why we do half the things we do. It's easier not to ask questions when it comes to her eccentricities. That day, the two of us filled the saucers with milk and lined them up in this exact way. I told her all of Shadow Grove's stray cats would come over and we'll never get rid of them again, but she shushed me and told me to get back to work."

Dougal stops his shoveling, his expression turning concerned rather than curious. "Did the cats come?"

"No, but each and every one of those saucers was empty the next morning." Rachel picks the first egg out of the basket. "That hole looks deep enough."

Dougal grunts in affirmation and moves a yard over, giving Rachel enough space to start her part of the assigned work. She scrapes the loose soil over the egg, covering it as instructed, and picks out the next egg. The process is repeated a couple of times, the silence between them growing again.

"Mah maw—" Dougal begins but stops himself. He clears his throat, cheeks reddening. "My ma used this place as a threat when we were weans, tellin' us if we were naughty, she'd send us to Nan."

"Doesn't sound like much of a threat," Rachel says. "Granted, you flew across the ocean to plant eggs, so it seems like your mom doesn't make empty promises."

His lips curl up into a sheepish smile. "Aye. First time she's followed through, too. She isn't like Nan."

"Nobody's like Mrs. Crenshaw, I assure you. She runs this town."

"I believe ye. Nan's the only person my da's scared of; says the fair folk don't come near the house when she visits."

Rachel can't contain her smile as she imagines Mrs. Crenshaw ordering large Scottish men around and having them obey her. If anyone can do it, it's that tiny, old lady, after all.

Their conversation continues, the topics leaning toward the mundane. The almost rhythmic dig-plant-cover-repeat soothes Rachel's worries from earlier, back when she'd been alone in her bedroom, and slowly Dougal becomes chattier. Sweat trickles between her shoulder blades as the sun reaches its apex, her muscles ache from the unnatural exercise of having to plant eggs along the invisible border.

When they reach the ACCESS PROHIBITED sign, around one o'clock in the afternoon, Mrs. Crenshaw is nowhere to be seen. In her place sits a tray, though—a jug of lemonade and two tall glasses, along with a plate stacked with sandwiches.

"Time for a wee break." Dougal's relief is evident. He stabs the shovel's blade into the ground and holds a hand out for Rachel. She contemplates his offer, studying his calloused palm, before accepting the help. He pulls her to her feet, looking deep into her eyes, and says, "I understand why Nan's fond o' ye."

Rachel swallows hard. "It's probably because she helped raise me."

Dougal releases her hand, and she moves toward the lawn chair. "Yer not what I expected, Rachel Cleary. I thought ye might be one of them spoilt American lasses that talk too much and do little else."

"That's mildly racist," Rachel says.

"Only mildly? Och! I'm already losin' my touch."

She laughs as she pulls the insect net off the tray, picks up the lemonade, and pours them both a drink. He accepts a glass and takes a seat on the grassy lawn, stretching out beneath the umbrella's shade.

"So, how long are you staying?"

"Nan didn't tell ye?"

"I didn't even know Mrs. Crenshaw had kids or grandkids until yesterday."

Dougal exhales loudly through his nose. "I got lifted for stealin' a car."

"I only understood about seventy percent of that sentence.

Try again."

He rolls his eyes. "I went out to the pub, got really wasted, stole a car, and wrapped it 'round a tree," he explains slowly, his brogue still there but his enunciation better suited to the untrained ear. "Ma decided then and there I wasn't gonna end up like my cousin, who's servin' time in a Texas prison for somethin' or other. So, she bought me a one-way ticket to Shadow Grove and said I was gonna finish high school here, under Nan's keen eye."

"Wait, you're still in high school?"

"Aye, I'm seventeen," he answers. "Ye thought I was older?"

"Yeah."

Dougal shrugs and reaches for a sandwich.

"Was it bad? The accident, I mean."

"Aye," is all he says.

She takes a sip of her lemonade, enjoying the sweet coolness running down her dry throat, hoping it'll keep her from being rude and blurting out the questions she's dying to ask.

Their respite is interrupted by a rustle—no more than a dry whisper of foliage moving around, but it's enough to catch them both off guard. A sudden gust of wind rushes from the forest's entrance, chilling the sweat clinging to Rachel's body. With the wind comes the sound of laughing children. Ethereal echoes blow onto Griswold Road. Rachel snaps her attention toward the fleeting shadow, moving from one tree to the next, hiding. She searches for whatever lurks just beyond her sight, scans the edge of the wood for a trace of any kids who might've snuck inside the infernal place to play.

Rachel stands from her perch on the lawn chair's armrest, ignoring the way her bones click from misuse. Her muscles scream for mercy as she takes a step forward, examining the trees ahead and the spaces between them.

Dougal is by her side a moment later, staring into the dense woodlands where the sun barely penetrates through the thick canopy of leaves.

"Did you hear that?" she asks.

"Sounded like weans playin'," Dougal says. "Did ye feel it?"

First the faint scream yesterday, and now this? She doesn't want to admit the truth, not to a person she's only met, but she can't deny her unease anymore either. The way her hair stands on end, how her adrenaline spikes.

Her fear increases.

"Yes."

Without looking her way, his tone too casual under the circumstances, he asks, "If ye don't mind me askin', why did ye look so scared earlier?"

"There's something wrong with the forest," she whispers. "It's waking up."

Chapter Three
Lie In Wait

It takes a lot of persuading to get Dougal out of his grandmother's house. A lot of pleading—*It'll be social suicide if he doesn't come tonight*—explaining—*A barn bash is just a little get-together to kick the summer off, and it's the perfect time for Dougal to get acquainted with people from Ridge Crest High*—and promises—*I'll make sure he's home by midnight, Mrs. Crenshaw, I swear*—were involved. Mrs. Crenshaw relented after a while, but only because Rachel timed her nagging to the old woman's favorite TV show.

By the time they leave, the darkness is absolute. Vantablack replaces the starry backdrop; the moon is no more than a sliver of gray in the night sky. An uncanny quiet surrounds the car as it passes the Eerie Creek Bridge, and a heavy silence fills the space inside. Rachel keeps her car steady on Griswold Road, the headlights brightening the long, white line on the asphalt. Beside her, Dougal stares out the passenger window, studying the abyss rushing parallel to the road. His pensive expression reflects in the window, while he taps his fingertips against his temple in rhythm to an unheard song. He smells nice—his woody aromatic cologne wafts through the air and fills the interior of the car. His freshly washed hair is tousled, brushed up, collapsing slightly to one side.

He's dressed simply, too: a black tee, just tight enough to show off an athletic physique underneath his clothes, and a pair of loose-fitting jeans. It's more than enough to make a good impression at the first barn bash of the summer.

The girls of Ridge Crest High won't be able to keep their eyes or hands off him.

Rachel shifts in her seat, attention returning to the road.

There are at least six barn bashes every summer, and none are small affairs. It's the only way for Shadow Grove's teenagers to unwind after the long year and the only way to have some fun in this dreary small town without having to go into the city.

This particular barn bash is hosted by the affable Eddie Roberts.

"Do you play any sports?" she asks, shattering the silence.

Dougal turns away from the window and says, "Rugby. It's like American football, but without the paddin' and helmets."

"I know what rugby is," Rachel says, smiling. "We don't have it at Ridge Crest High, though. How do you feel about trying out for football next year instead?"

"No. I won't live it down if my mates hear I'm playin' shite football."

Rachel removes a hand from the steering wheel to scratch her cheek, thoughtful. "Okay, how do you feel about lacrosse?" She glimpses him raising an eyebrow in her peripheral vision. "Never mind."

She flips the indicator and slacks off as they come up to the Roberts' farm.

"I get it. You're anxious, but you don't have to be. People around here are generally nice, sometimes painfully so," Rachel says. "You're clearly used to a certain degree of popularity, which is why I'm going to give you a few tips. Firstly, I suggest you don't call football 'shite' in public. Secondly, don't tell *anyone* about the weird chores your grandmother makes us do. Neither of those things will win you any points at Ridge Crest High, believe me."

"Nan's strange, I know," he mutters. "What else?"

"I'm not going to stop you from getting wasted or high, but I'm going to ask you to please not overdo it. If you throw up in my car, you're paying to get it detailed. Also, there's some mouthwash, gum, and hand sanitizer in the glove compartment if you need to freshen up on the way home."

"Och! Yer makin' me sound like an alcoholic." He chuckles under his breath, shaking his head.

"That's not what I meant—"

"Aye, I know, Rachel."

She clears her throat, pulls her lips into a thin line as she searches for the gravelly turnoff. "There's one last thing. After I've introduced you to some people, ditch me. It'll be in your best interest."

"Whit wey?"

Rachel sighs. She spots the barn in the distance, centered in a corona of artificial light, which casts a glow across the multitude of vehicles parked near the massive sliding door. She maneuvers the car off the asphalt, gravel crunching beneath the tires.

After another long moment, she finally says, "Let's just say people like me enough to invite me to their parties, but they'd prefer it if I don't show up. Do you understand?"

Dougal shrugs. "I s'pose."

"I like it better this way, too, okay? I'm friends with everyone and no one. It keeps my socializing to a minimum, which means

I can focus on getting into my dream college and as far away from this town as I can."

Dougal gives her a curt nod.

"Good—"

"Doesn't mean I'm gonna ditch ye the first chance I get," Dougal says. "Yer my ride home, after all."

Rachel smiles as she parks in the first available spot, a brief walk from the entrance. She grabs her purse and climbs out, wondering why she isn't greeted by seductive vibrations. Barn bashes are notoriously loud; the night air is usually full of rhythmic beats and electronic screeches. Not tonight, though.

Dougal slams the passenger door shut, and Rachel presses the key fob to lock the doors.

"Seems quiet for a party," Dougal says, walking up to Rachel's side.

Rachel doesn't respond, although the sentiment is mutual. Together, they head toward the barn entrance. No colorful, flashing lights sweep around inside to set the mood. Instead, the barn is brightly lit. Somberness in place of juvenile joviality.

"We simply can't sit by and do *nothing*." Greg Pearson's booming voice escapes the barn, shattering the night's uneasy silence.

When Rachel reaches the door, she sees him standing on a makeshift stage, addressing almost the entire Ridge Crest High student body. His hair is styled perfectly, blazer sleeves are rolled up to his elbows, and his politician-in-training face is severe as he looks his peers in the eyes. They sit on bales of hay, positioned in rows in a half circle around the stage.

Rachel grabs Dougal's arm and leads him to an empty space in the back of the barn, beside a redheaded girl whose name she can't recall.

"What's going on?" Rachel whispers to the girl as she takes a seat on the hay.

The girl stretches her neck to reach Rachel's ear and says, "Astraea Hayward literally vanished into thin air this evening, in front of witnesses."

"The girl who works at Alice's Vintage Emporium?"

"Yuh huh," she whispers back.

"These are our brothers and sisters, our friends, who're at risk." Greg's voice reverberates through the silent barn. "*We* are at risk. It isn't our responsibility to keep ourselves—and each other—safe, but it's obvious the adults aren't worried about our safety or wellbeing any longer."

Whispered conversations break out as each person talks to those beside them. On the other side of the barn, Francine Gilligan, a brunette with bright green spectacles, raises her hand, but quickly pulls it down again. After glancing around the barn, she frowns, then sits ramrod straight and raises her hand high. Greg points to her and she stands, but trembles.

"My sister says all the children can hear whoever it is outside at night, calling to them, beckoning them to follow." Dark crimson blossoms on the apples of her cheeks. "I don't let her sleep in her own room anymore because my parents brushed off her concerns, and I'm not willing to lose her because some freak's going around town kidnapping kids."

"Keith said the same thing to me," Ronald Stevens, the Ridge Crest Devils' quarterback, adds. "My kid brother doesn't have an imagination, man. He's not making this up."

"Maybe the kids are just scared because they don't understand where their friends are?" Jolene Chambers says. She looks around the barn, searching for supporters of her theory.

A few nod in agreement.

"It's paranoia, nothing else."

"Tell that to my cousin," Bianca Novak stands up, looking straight at Jolene. "Jasper told me there was something out there targeting little kids."

Whoa. Eleven-year-old Jasper Novak is a bona fide genius.

"He's scared out of his mind."

"Jasper's scared of his own shadow," someone shouts.

A few kids snicker in response.

Bianca sneers as she searches the barn for the heckler. "His anxiety doesn't invalidate his fears."

"Maybe the kids are simply coping with the prospect of being snatched by turning this whole thing into a local legend," Jolene says, shrugging. "It wouldn't be the first time a legend was born from fear."

"So, what? You think we should stand back and do nothing?" Bianca says in a high-pitched tone. "Or maybe you'd like us to wrap the little kids and hand them off to this—"

"That's not what I said!"

"Bianca, I think what Jolene was trying to say was that we need to consider all the options," Greg interjects. He turns his attention to the entire assembly, and says, "While I'm sure we're all vigilant these days, we do need to start looking for the already-missing children. The sheriff's department did a half-assed job the first time around, so I propose we form search parties and do the job properly."

"While we're at it, we should come up with a kidnapping prevention plan or something," Bianca says.

Greg nods, flashes one of his diplomatic smiles, and says,

"This is the type of proactive thinking we need right now. Yes, good!"

Ideas are thrown around the gathering, opinions are voiced, and it's all very civilized.

Too civilized.

The anger inside Rachel builds. This nasty business has forced teenagers into adult roles. Barn bashes aren't supposed to be town meetings. Teenagers aren't supposed to be talking about instigating an unofficial curfew and finding lost children.

"Our purpose in life, at this age, is to get into trouble and enjoy our youth," Greg says.

"Did anyone search for the weans in the forest?" Dougal asks.

The low-level conversations stop and everyone stares at Dougal. Their eyes narrow in judgment at the stranger who's invaded a semi-private meeting.

He reluctantly stands.

"Who are you?" Greg asks.

"Dougal Charles Mackay," Dougal answers, unperturbed, fearless.

Curious gazes move to Rachel, asking for an explanation. It's almost as if everyone knows she's dragged him here, like she's the one responsible for the interruption. Technically she *is* responsible, but this jumping-to-conclusions thing sucks.

Rachel groans as she stands beside Dougal, and says, "Dougal is Mrs. Crenshaw's grandson. He's originally from Scotland and will be attending Ridge Crest in the fall."

"In that case, nobody goes into the—"

"Aye, nobody goes into the forest, I've heard, but what if they're in there?" Dougal interrupts Greg's sorry excuse. "Rachel and I heard somethin' in there today which sounded an awful lot like weans playin'."

Greg shakes his head. "Outsiders aren't usually familiar with the forest and locals won't be caught dead on Fraser and MacCleary lands. It's not possible. If anything, the kidnapper has the children stashed somewhere on the other side of Shadow Grove. My money's on them being held captive in, or nearby, the junkyard."

"I need more clarification on your reasoning, Greg," Rachel says. "Come to think of it, I've asked you before why nobody's searched the forest and you gave me the same runaround."

Greg shrugs. "That's *your* families' lands. *You* search them if you suspect there's someone hiding in there."

"Ye can't possibly mean ye want a wee girl to search the forest by herself. How big is that area, anyhow?"

"The land area has an approximate radius of fifteen miles," Rachel's automated response is accompanied by a deadpan tone. It won't make any difference, though. When it comes to the forest, Shadow Grove's residents don't want to believe it's part of their town.

Dougal gestures to her as she makes his point for him. "What if Rachel actually comes across someone in there? Never try to save a drownin' man if ye can't swim, eh?"

"I didn't suggest Rachel search it by herself," Greg says, brow furrowing as if he's still figuring out where Dougal's accent is from. "The forest is on your family's land, too."

Dougal's amicability dissipates as he stares Greg down from across the barn. Greg, who is much shorter and less muscular than the Scotsman, doesn't budge. The tension builds between the two. Dougal's fists clenching by his sides, his teeth grinding.

The cords in his neck become more prominent as anger changes the color of his face to bright red. If Dougal decides to beat some sense into Greg, nobody's going to be able to stop him.

"I'll wait for ye by the car," Dougal says to Rachel, already turning his back on Greg.

"No need," she says, glancing in Greg's direction. "I'm in no mood to argue with a hypocrite tonight."

"I'm not a hypocrite, Rachel."

"Oh, but you are. You're talking about saving missing children, which is admirable, but you have no issue with sending me and Dougal into the forest by ourselves," Rachel snaps back. "Why is that, huh?"

She doesn't wait for one of his lame answers. Rachel motions for Dougal to walk around the bale of hay, following him closely. Inquisitive gazes sear into her back as she exits the barn.

Typical Greg. He's always preaching about how we can be better, how we should be stronger, how Ridge Crest High's students should be unified. He's always charming the masses with his diplomatic smile and oh-so-important vote-winning causes, but when the time comes for him to get his hands dirty, he's always got some stupid excuse. Worst of all, people actually believe those excuses.

"Idiot," she grumbles, directing her key fob toward the car to unlock the doors. The lights flick on and off, and the beep sounds.

They walk in silence to the vehicle, both seething at the same person. For Rachel it's more than just Greg's inability to be logical—it's their history.

"That guy's beggin' for a beatin'," Dougal says over the rooftop, opening the passenger door.

"You're telling me." Rachel climbs inside, closes the door,

and pulls the seatbelt across her body. "Greg wouldn't have listened to anything we said about the forest, because he's been brainwashed into believing it's out of the town's jurisdiction. My advice to you is to make peace with the fact that Shadow Grove is a cesspool of ignorance before it drives you insane."

Rachel turns the key in the ignition and reverses onto the gravel road, turns the steering wheel, and slowly moves back to the Roberts' farm entrance.

"We heard them, Rachel. They're in there ... somewhere."

"Yes, but ordinary kidnappers don't go around advertising their hiding places with creepy recordings of children." Rachel keeps her gaze fixed on the gravelly road. "We can't go in there until we've figured out what we're up against."

Dougal grumbles an affirmative.

On the surface, he might be a hot-tempered delinquent, but Rachel isn't blind or dumb.

Dougal Mackay is a kindred spirit. He's the hot to her cold, the yin to her yang.

Possibly a real friend?

The night seems to fold in on itself, growing darker and more claustrophobic the farther they move from the barn. The headlights struggle to illuminate the road ahead, fighting and losing its battle against the encompassing night. Time seems to pass slower than usual, too. It's as if the car wades through thick, black ink, inching forward into the unending void. Only when she spots the two stout brick pillars, situated on either side of the farm road, does reality dare to intrude in this surreal darkness.

She flips on the indicator, grateful to be leaving the Roberts' farm, and makes a slow turn back onto Griswold Road.

"Tonight feels wrong," she whispers more to herself than her companion. "It makes me wonder if the sun will ever shine again."

"It's as black as the Earl o' Hell's waistcoat." Dougal's voice is low, contemplative.

Rachel fails to swallow the bitter taste of fear coating her tongue. She grips the steering wheel tightly, her knuckles turning white from the force. If she lets go, will she float away into oblivion? Anxious to get somewhere safe, she accelerates gently—not so much as to go over the speed limit, but not so little as to offend the foreboding night searching for its next victim.

"Now just hold on, Rachel," he says. "Yer goin' a wee bit fast."

"I'm under the limit," she counters, unnecessarily impatient with his backseat driving.

He shakes his head. "I can't see a thing, and I doubt ye can see much better. Slow down, 'fore ye bump into somethin'."

"What?" she snaps, her attention leaving the road.

Dougal's eyes widen. Annoyance and anxiety dance across his pale facial features as he stares ahead. "Slow. Down," he repeats each word individually.

Rachel opens her mouth to argue.

Horror suddenly chases away whatever other emotions he'd harbored two seconds earlier. "*Stop!*"

Rachel slams down on the brake before her eyes return to the road. The wheels lock. Rubber and asphalt battle it out. Tires screech as she tries to gain control of the situation, fighting the steering wheel to keep from slamming into either the cliff on one side of the road or going over into the Eerie Creek on the other side. The back of the car proves too heavy for the sudden stop and swerves clockwise.

A moment turns into a lifetime as the headlights swoop across a hunched-over figure in the road. A blue-faced hag peers out from beneath a filthy, torn cloak, which seems to both absorb and dispel the darkness surrounding her. Thick, chapped lips pull into a snarl and reveal rusty nails where teeth should be. A warning or a threat? Rachel can't tell. Those gleaming eyes, on the other hand, are filled with menace—promising a painful end if ever their paths cross again.

The dark world around her disappears in a flash.

A deathly pale arm takes over her entire line of sight, lying limply on a gritty floor. Scarlet splotches surround the limb, black in the grim lighting, and rotting pieces of flesh rest in coagulating pools of blood. Rachel's gut twists further as her view broadens. It's as if the camera's zoomed out, giving her the full, gory picture of the arm—a child's arm, torn off at the shoulder—and surrounding it are other putrefying body parts, ripped to shreds, gnawed on in places by rats and …

Oh my God!

The glazed-over eyes of a young boy, no older than five, stare back at her. He wears an ugly, unnatural sneer because half his face is missing. Entire patches of his hair are gone, specifically around the cracks in his skull. Worst of all, there's no body attached to his scrawny neck anymore.

Rachel wants to look away, but her eyelids can't shut, and her body is frozen in place. She wants to scream, but her vocal cords don't work either.

As quickly as she was thrust into the nightmarish hallucination, she returns to reality.

The car's nose moves sideways from the momentum, and the hag disappears. Only then does Rachel realize Dougal's arm is stretched out in front of her, holding her in place against the seat, and his other is braced against the dashboard in the event of impact.

Impact doesn't come.

When the car comes to a complete stop, they're facing the Eerie Creek Bridge and the vehicle stands horizontally across both lanes of Griswold Road. Rachel's labored breathing and stinging eyes are the first signs of shock. The fear of almost running someone over because she wasn't paying attention is going to give her a few sleepless nights. That hallucination may take years to process.

Dougal's voice intrudes as he pulls his arm away. Rachel turns to him, watches his lips as they move. The words are muddled and nonsensical, but the exotic sounds roll off his tongue, captivating her even if she can't make head or tails of what he's saying. He undoes his seatbelt and climbs out of the car, shouting into the night as he walks to the same area where they had seen that *thing*.

She somehow composes herself enough to reach a shaky hand to roll down the window.

"Get in the car," she manages to say without breaking into tears. "Dougal, please get back here."

He spins around and continues his incoherent ramblings, gesturing behind him as he makes his way to her door.

Rachel wipes a strand of hair away from her forehead and hooks it behind her ear. "I don't understand you when you go full Scots," she says, her voice sounding calmer already. Her mind's a mess, though. She could've killed someone!

"Move over," he says, waving her off with one hand and opens the driver's door.

She stares at him, surprised.

"Och, away ye go already!"

She unclicks her seatbelt and shifts across the space to take the vacant passenger seat for herself, still shaking, unable to calm her racing pulse.

"Seatbelt," he grumbles, shifting the seat back to make enough space for his legs, and fixes the mirrors to his liking. Rachel pulls the seatbelt across her body, whispering an apology he doesn't seem to hear as he rights the vehicle on the road.

She notices his rapid breathing, the lines of concern etched into his forehead, the penetrative glare constantly searching the jet-black night outside the windshield. It's not anger nibbling away at his mood but rather fear. Dougal, she decides, wears fear the same way her mother wears her new shapeless dresses—it just looks so horribly unnatural.

"Ye wanna know what yer dealin' with in this town, eh? Why the weans are gettin' nicked and the night is so dark?" Dougal asks without taking his eyes off the road ahead, without waiting for an answer. "This business isn't the doin' o' no psychopath, Rachel. Shadow Grove's got itself a Black Annis lurkin' about."

Chapter Four
The Forest With No Name

Black Annis," Rachel says loudly to rouse the sleeping figure sprawled across the single bed.

Dougal jerks to awareness, his snoring cut short.

"Black Annis, an English variation of the bogeyman figure, is said to be a blue-faced crone with white teeth and iron claws," she continues. He props himself onto his elbows and groans from the effort. "If folklore is to be believed, Black Annis is prone to stealing children through open windows and then she eats them, because why not traumatize your kids with threats of being cannibalized when they don't want to take a bath, right?"

"What's the time?" Dougal reaches up to wipe the sleep from his eyes.

"Seven o'clock." Rachel leans back against the doorframe, scanning through the printed pages in her file. "I'm not saying this fairytale character is real, but after what we saw last night, it's difficult to deny we saw *something*."

"Can ye get out of my room and come back at a holier hour?"

Rachel glances up from her file, contemplates the request, and responds with a simple, "No."

Dougal groans louder. He falls onto his stomach and pulls

the pillow over his head.

"My dad used to be a historian who specialized in The New Nation era, but in his spare time he enjoyed researching Shadow Grove's history," she starts again, undeterred by his muffled retorts. "When he died, my mom boxed all of his stuff up and stored it in the attic. I never so much as thought about his old research until your grandmother nudged me in that direction the other day."

"Get to the point already." Dougal flips onto his back, one arm covering his eyes. "Please."

"Don't rush me," she says, pulling out a printed page and closing the file. "Anyway, after you left last night, I decided to go up to our attic and poke through Daddy's old journals. There is a *lot* of information stored in those boxes, too much for one person to go through in a few hours, but just as I was about to give up on my search, I stumbled on an odd doodle in one of the margins. It resembles what we saw on the road." Rachel pushes away from the doorway and crosses the room to show Dougal the crude drawing.

He sits up to study the sketch and exhales through his nose. "Aye, that's a Black Annis, all right," he confirms. "What's a historian doin' with a drawin' of her?"

"Good question," Rachel says. "Get up, get dressed, and come help me find out."

"It's seven o'clock on a Sunday mornin'," Dougal whines as he gets out of bed, his reluctance evident in the way he forces himself to the closet in the corner of the bedroom, feet dragging, shoulders sagging, hair tousled from sleep. Dougal is clearly not a morning person, but at least he's not mean about it.

"It's not like you have anything better to do," Rachel says, retreating from his bedroom. "Don't take too long. It gets especially stuffy up there during the summer," she calls over her shoulder as she makes her way downstairs to wait for him.

Fifteen minutes later, years of undisturbed dust swirls back to life as Rachel and Dougal enter the cluttered attic, much of which flies up her nose and settles in her lungs. The stagnant air is stifling, thanks to the summer heat. Dust motes dance in the weak sun rays penetrating the grimy, arched window. Stacks upon stacks of boxes lean precariously against the walls, pieces of antique furniture stand about. It's a maze built out of lost and forgotten things, several generations' worth of crap and treasures.

"It's a bit of an obstacle course up here." Rachel inches around a wardrobe dating back to the 1920s. "Mind your head," she says just as a hard thump sounds behind her. Dougal says something she can't understand, probably cursing the low-hanging Halloween decoration she'd ducked beneath in time. She giggles. They pass the creepy dressmaker's mannequin that stands beside the empty cello case and an old military trunk with faded bold lettering along the side. "Both our families have a tendency to hoard."

"Yer tellin' me Nan's attic is in a similar state?"

"Worse," Rachel says over her shoulder. "Your grandmother isn't the sentimental type, though, so don't be surprised if she decides we need to clean up *that* mess just to keep busy. Consider this a fair warning."

"Och!"

"Indeed," she says, finally coming up to the clearing she'd made the previous night. Close to fifty boxes surround the cramped space, with *Liam's Stuff* carefully written on their lids in permanent marker. She spreads her arms wide. "Here we are. The boxes aren't marked by year, but my dad had a sorting system for his journals." Rachel bends to retrieve a journal from the open box, flips it around, and points to the number scrawled in blue ink on a large label in the right corner. "In this journal's case, my father was working on something that occurred in 1792, during the year 2006, and this number here shows it's the second journal pertaining to that particular section of his work." She opens the journal to a random page, scans it through, and finds a similar number in the notes. "My dad also used this system to refer to other journals. It's not exactly the most rational system, but it worked for him."

Dougal grimaces. "All right."

Rachel moves to the spot beside the open box and sits. "Pick a box and start going through the journals."

"Ye want me to read history journals?"

"I doubt you'd find it very interesting, but if you want to read through hundreds of journals about The New Nation era, be my guest."

"Very funny," Dougal says as he takes a seat across from her. He pulls a box closer and opens the lid. "What are we lookin' for?"

"Something like that doodle I showed you. Just page through the journals and see if you can find anything out of the ordinary. You'll recognize the oddity once you come across it," Rachel says, scanning through the journal filled with crisp handwriting in blue ink. "Daddy didn't trust computers. He said it rendered his research, which he deemed a cathartic ritual, impersonal. The only time he used a computer was when he worked on his dissertations."

Dougal pulls a random journal out of the box and opens it to the first page. He scans through words, turns the page, repeats the process. Before long, he says, "Do ye want to talk about it?"

"There isn't much to say, is there? Greg is probably considering how to make your life hell at school next year, but if you—"

"I don't care about haver."

She looks up from the journal in her lap, eyebrows rising. "Haver?"

"Nonsense," Dougal clarifies.

"I'm not sure I'd classify Greg's temper tantrums as nonsense, especially when he's nursing a bruised ego," Rachel says, casting her gaze to the journal once more. She turns the page. "Greg's not an enemy I intended to make in this town. He's the …" Rachel runs her fingertips across the faded brownish splatters on the sheet, bled through from the next page. She flips through the journal until she finds a large splash of dried rust-colored ink.

"Greg's the what?" Dougal presses.

Rachel pushes the journal beneath Dougal's nose. "What do you make of this?"

He scratches his cheek, studying the blob, nails scraping across his unshaven chin. "Looks to me like dried blood. Yer dad must've had a nosebleed at some point?"

"Only crazy people will sit over a journal and allow a nosebleed to go unchecked. My dad was sick, not mad." She frowns, tracing the edges of the splatter with her gaze. "It *could* be blood." But there's no indication as to what caused the blood to flow so freely. It's probably nothing, she decides, and moves on.

They work through the boxes of journals, while the clock

ticks on and the summer heat rises. A few apparent oddities are found in the hundreds of written pages, and those books are set aside for further inspection at a later time, but for the most part the journals are unremarkable.

One of these remnants of her father's life dates back to the early 1990s, when Liam and Jenny were mere acquaintances. The journal, belonging to her teenaged father, mainly revolves around his day-to-day experiences at Ridge Crest High. A class schedule is crudely drawn on one page, and a few hasty, typical teenager notes are scribbled down on other pages. The most interesting part about this journal is a brief account of when her father snuck into the forest. He doesn't say much about his trip—in fact, it reads like a secret government file where entire sentences have been blocked out with black marker—but the contact details for someone called Misty Robins are in the corner, the words *In Case of Emergency* written below her number. Rachel doesn't recall ever hearing the name Misty Robins, and finds it suspicious that someone who isn't related is listed as an emergency contact. It could be nothing, but Rachel plays it safe and sets the journal into the High Priority pile.

In the meantime, she relays macabre tales of Shadow Grove to its newest resident.

Cursed land, cursed bloodlines, accursed life in the middle of nowhere.

She tells Dougal about the Siren's Pit, located near the abandoned train station on the Other Side, where a hundred or so corpses were buried after an influenza outbreak in the early days—*Not enough hands left to do all the grave-digging by the time the influenza outbreak ended*—and about how Henry Henderson took the opportunity to get rid of his nagging wife when nobody was paying close attention. Speaking of the Henderson family, she goes on to relay the tragic tale of Vince Henderson and his killing spree almost two hundred years after his ancestor committed the initial crime. Rachel mentions how only Justin Henderson survived his father's descent into madness—*Thank heavens he got a full ride to attend college three states over.* Once that's over, she moves on to tell Dougal about the horrifying history of the Eerie Creek Sawmill, built in conjunction with a large lumber company back in the late 1700s, and how immigrants decided to come to Shadow Grove for work—*They flocked here to begin anew and died in droves for no apparent reason.*

Rachel offers Dougal a soda then, because he's gone green in the face. As soon as he's taken a few sugary gulps to replenish his strength, she picks up with the morbid story of Timothy Bentley. The young preacher had settled in Shadow Grove in the early 1910s, bought the old remains where the first church in town had stood—*It burned down during another tragedy*—and rebuilt God's house from the ground up with his own two hands. People liked Timothy Bentley so much that his pews were full every Sunday, from the first day that the church opened its doors to the day he met his end. He took a bad fall down the stairs into the church's cellar, injured his spine, and lost his speech some way or another, and the rats had literally eaten him alive. Or so the story goes.

Moving back to recent events, she tells him about Arsenic Annie's special recipes at the school's cafeteria—*Her food is to die for, seriously*—and recounts the harrowing facts she's gathered about the missing children. With this, Rachel catches Dougal's complete attention. He listens intently, the journal in his lap all but forgotten.

By eleven o'clock, the sweltering heat drives them out of the attic and toward the nearest fan, located in the living room.

"This town is strange," Dougal says, rolling the cold soda can across his forehead to rid himself of the heat.

"Honestly, you haven't heard the half of it," Rachel says. "My dad *loved* researching Shadow Grove's dark history, especially the type of stuff the town council's been covering up or rewriting for the sake of tourism."

"Did he tell ye anythin' about the forest?"

Rachel grimaces. "Daddy only ever told me that the forest may be Fraser and MacCleary land on paper, but it's never belonged to either of our families. We're just guardians."

Dougal frowns, takes the soda can away from his face, and pins Rachel to her seat with his penetrating gaze. "We need to go in there, ye know? We need to go look for those weans 'fore Black Annis decides to eat 'em."

"After everything I've told you about this town, the tragedies and horrors, you're still on this Black Annis bandwagon? There are a lot of monsters out there, Dougal, and none of them are make-believe."

"Aye, but this time the supposedly make-believe monster is the real threat," he says. "Ye can't deny we both saw her."

"Did I almost run a bizarre-looking old woman over last night? Yes. Does the stranger resemble my dad's doodle? Perhaps. Then again, even out here we get our fair share of drifters, and one coincidence is hardly enough reason to go into a panic." Rachel stands and stretches her legs. "However, if it will make you feel better, I'm more than willing to go into the forest and put your fears to rest."

"Ye want to go now?"

"We might as well." Rachel brushes away the hair sticking to her neck. Her skin is slick with sweat, but her muscles beg for movement. "In this heat, we'll suffocate in the attic. Your grandmother won't be home for at least another few hours, and I have no idea when my mom's coming home, so we really ought to break a few rules while we can."

Dougal stands from the armchair across the room, a mischievous grin playing in the corners of his mouth. "Now yer speakin' my language. Let me just go put on my hikin' boots." He crosses the living room, his strides long and powerful.

"Grab a water bottle while you're at it," she says as he passes. "If you faint, I'm leaving you behind."

"Och, yer worse than my ma and Nan put together," Dougal says over his shoulder, his grin now fully developed. "See ye outside in five minutes."

Rachel battles against her own smile as she makes her way to the kitchen to fill her water bottle.

If today had been any other day, going into the forest wouldn't even have entered her mind. She had never harbored a secret, inherent need to explore what lies beyond the ACCESS PROHIBITED sign at the end of Griswold Road, and she definitely wouldn't have embarked on the journey by herself even *if* she had wanted to go in there. After yesterday, Rachel feels somewhat more rebellious. Dougal's company, as much as she hates to admit it, fuels her desire to be more than the goody-goody Cleary girl who has never so much as broken curfew.

She makes her way to the front door but stops to regard the umbrella holder. An inexplicable urge to take one along, in case it's needed, overwhelms her in an instant. Rachel picks out her favorite one from the lot—an indigo umbrella with silver embroidery on its edges and stars carved into the wooden handle.

It had once belonged to her great-grandmother, Alice Green, a woman who'd had big dreams but found herself in a "delicate situation" before she could leave Shadow Grove. This particular umbrella had been a consolation gift from Alice's new husband, a proud father-to-be. Rachel isn't sure whether her great-grandmother had liked or hated what the umbrella represented—possibly the latter—but the uniqueness of the piece is undeniable.

Rachel exits the house, swinging the umbrella as she walks up to where Dougal stands in the middle of the road, a patched-up backpack over his shoulders and a baseball bat leaning against his leg.

"Took ye long enough," he says loudly, fumbling with the backpack shoulder straps. When he looks up, he tilts his head. "Why are ye bringin' along a brolly?"

"Brolly?" Rachel asks.

"Umbrella."

"Oh, it felt like the right thing to do." Rachel shrugs. "Why are you bringing a baseball bat?"

"Felt like the right thing to do," he answers, taking the baseball bat by the handle and raising it into the air. He rests the sleek, wooden club against his shoulder, and says, "Ye ready then?"

With a curt nod, she faces the imposing forest entrance. Despite it appearing devoid of life—not a single leaf rustles in the unholy heat, no birds chirp from the trees, no critters scuttle across the earth—common sense beckons her to stop being so foolish before she gets herself killed. Whatever reservations she may have about this expedition, however, are overruled by her desire to impress the foreign boy with her faux fearlessness. Every step closer to the forest sends a shiver up Rachel's spine, which in turn makes the hair at the back of her neck stand on end. She grips the umbrella's handle with all her might as they near the signpost.

Rachel hesitates when she sees Dougal halting a step beyond the invisible line. He visibly shudders but quickly composes himself.

"I'm still alive, Rach," he says without looking back. "No need to be scared."

"I'm not scared," she retorts, stubbornly stepping across the boundary.

Something akin to electricity runs over her skin, tickling her nerve endings and momentarily washing away any and all thoughts. Rachel cannot subdue the shudder making its way through her system nor the surprised intake of breath. Beyond the brief discomfort, nothing else occurs which can be classified as out of the ordinary. She continues following Dougal, carefully stepping across the wildly overgrown forest floor. Tree roots protrude in large arcs from the earth and low-hanging branches stretch toward each other, intertwining overhead. Sunlight barely penetrates the thick canopy of lush green leaves, creating a gloomy atmosphere the farther they walk from the entrance. There's an unfamiliar freshness in the air, woody and ancient and untouched by man. The forest is silent, though. Quieter than a deserted cemetery.

After about ten minutes, Dougal asks, "Ye still all right back there?"

"Yes, but let's not get too carried away with exploring. Last thing we need is to get lost in here," Rachel says to Dougal's back. "Also, I doubt it's a good idea to wander around too long."

"I was thinkin' along the same lines," he says over his

shoulder. "Don't worry. I'll protect ye if need be."

"I don't need protection," she says.

His breathy chuckle reaches her ears. "Yer so easy to wind up."

"Keep it up and I'll show you how easy it'll be to knock you down."

"With yer brolly?" Dougal continues laughing.

Rachel raises the umbrella and gently pokes him between his shoulder blades with the sharp wooden tip. "You don't know what I'm capable of with this *brolly.*"

Dougal glances at her over his shoulder, a cheeky smile on display. "So there's some bite in that bark after all."

She lowers the umbrella when Dougal faces forward, swinging it to and fro with each step. They don't speak much thereafter, the uneven ground demanding their full attention as they traverse the still woodlands, but she can't shake the feeling of being watched. Like the previous day, while she was in her bedroom making sense of the dilemma which had befallen Shadow Grove's children, she is overcome with the sensation that her every movement is being tracked. Rachel soon notices a change in the air, too, like pressure building before a great storm erupts.

Alarm bells go off in her mind and her worries are reinforced by a muted crack sounding somewhere behind them, somewhere in the distance.

Rachel stops, listening for any other telltale sound, while Dougal walks on.

The almost imperceptible rustling of foliage, like an immense weight slowly pressing down on dead leaves, releases a small amount of adrenaline into her system. She spins around, searching for the stalking presence.

A shapeless shadow flits across her line of sight, moving from one tree to the other. Shadows shouldn't scare people, but this one doesn't act like a normal shadow. It seems almost intelligent, calculating—a hunter incognito.

Rachel's flight or fight response kicks in; the former being the more rational choice. She turns around and sprints to catch up with her companion, dodging branches and jumping over roots. Brambles scratch at her bare legs. The rustling behind her becomes louder, more persistent, following her move for move.

"Run!" Rachel shouts as she comes up behind Dougal, hurdling over another high tree root to overtake him.

She hears his initial confused outrage, followed by an almost girlish shriek. Rachel doesn't look back. She forces her legs to pump faster, unable to relinquish her grip on the umbrella—her only weapon if things turn dire—and continues to dodge, jump, and duck nature's obstacles. Dougal's footfalls quickly join hers, his backpack slapping against his body with his movements. Soon, he's ahead of her, glancing over his shoulder from time to time.

"Crisscross," he shouts.

"What?"

Instead of repeating himself, Dougal crosses in front of her, heads farther into the woods, keeping his pace. She does the same, heading to the other side and narrowly avoids running straight into a tree.

"Again!" The way his voice echoes through the forest, like they're in an outdoor amphitheater with magnificent acoustics, doesn't make sense.

Rachel does as she's told and crosses back to his side, this time ahead of him.

"We need to try and double back," she shouts in passing.

"Good luck wi—" Dougal's sentence is cut off by a crash behind them. The ground shakes, leaves rustle, air rushes. He glimpses over his shoulder again, and the blood drains from his face. "Don't look back." Panic laces his words as he speeds up.

Rachel pushes her body harder, ignoring the burning muscles in her legs, to try and keep up with him. Her labored breathing is quietened by a second crash, louder and closer than the previous one. It takes every ounce of her willpower not to look back.

"Split up?" Dougal shouts the question as they crisscross paths again.

"No!" Rachel's response is fast and thick with justified fear. "Just run."

They keep running through the awakening forest, blindly making their way deeper toward its dark heart. Violent cracks and hollow crashes boom throughout the area. The earth continues to shake, the air churns and grows heavy. Whatever is chasing after them is remorseless in its destruction, chaos personified.

Eventually, the sounds become fainter before the unsettling quiet descends over the forest once more. Not wanting to tempt fate, Dougal encourages her to keep on running with a: "Ye can do it," or a, "C'mon, Rach, just a wee bit longer." Rachel goes on, but her speed falters and her energy reserves deplete. She settles into a jog, gasping for oxygen.

"I can't," she says, stopping. Rachel rests her free hand on her knee, greedily sucking air into her lungs, and plants the umbrella's tip into the ground. Cuts and bruises mar her exposed arms and legs. Her legs are covered in angry, red welts in some places while tiny beads of blood well up where her skin is broken.

A thin film of sweat coats her body. "I can't," she repeats, shaking her head.

"Drink up."

A water bottle comes into view and she realizes she's lost her own somewhere along the way.

Rachel casts a look up at Dougal, who doesn't look to be in much better shape. "What about you?"

"I've got an extra bottle in my backpack," he says, offering the bottle again with a small shake.

She accepts the bottle, unscrews the cap, and takes a sip. The water wets her swollen tongue and coats her dry throat, slowly soothing away the pounding headache forming behind her eyes. Rachel takes another gulp of the water, then another, managing to thank him in between her desperate breaths and swigs. Meanwhile, she wonders how long they had been running, and what they had been running from in the first place. She has no answers to those questions.

Dougal moves toward a nearby red maple tree, removes his patched-up backpack, and leans against the trunk. He rummages around inside and takes out a second water bottle.

"What was that?" she asks, using the back of her arm to wipe the sweat from her forehead. "What did you see?"

Dougal unscrews the bottle. "There are no words for what I saw, but if I had to describe it … We were bein' chased by Death." He closes his eyes and drinks deeply, chest rising and falling in quick repetition. When he pulls the bottle away, Dougal sighs. "Somethin' close to Death. I don't know for sure, but it felt that way."

Rachel grimaces, walking around in a circle to survey their surroundings. They've stopped in what looks like every other part of the forest. All that stands out is the rotting tree trunk overgrown with moss and the strange formation of trees beyond it. There, hidden behind another red maple, four birch trees have grown together, trunks and branches twisting around one another to create a thick, natural arch. She steps across the rotting tree trunk, head tilting as she studies the odd feature encircled in a variety of mushroom species.

"Dougal," she says, walking closer to the arch. "You need to come check this out."

If Dougal hears her, she doesn't catch his response.

Rachel takes another step closer, mesmerized by the bone-white birch trees against the green backdrop. Another step forward brings her to the edge of the mushroom circle. She's almost certain the overgrown grass is greener within the circle, just one shade darker, just a bit lusher than on the outside. She crosses the mushroom barrier and is greeted by a now-familiar sensation that runs across her skin. The electricity is more intense, crackling instead of tingling like before. This time, Rachel doesn't give it too much thought. The birch arch seems to act like a magnet, pulling her closer and closer, and for reasons she can't comprehend, she yields to the silent call and places one foot in front of the other.

A single word is etched into the bark of the twisted arch, the letters irregularly spaced across the middle: Harrowsgate.

She stares at the word and raises a hand, reaching out to touch nothing.

But it feels right to reach out, as illogical as it might be, and touch the nothingness.

She's certain the air ripples as her middle finger presses against the area located between those trees. Rachel withdraws her hand slightly. Curious, she unfolds her fingers and places her whole palm against the air. Along with the indistinct ripples comes a faint resistance. Rachel pushes harder against the unseen obstacle, struggling against midair.

"What the hell?" she whispers, pressing as hard as she can with one hand.

The air doesn't budge.

Rachel pulls away, her frown deepening with confusion as she looks at the empty space between the birch trees.

"Fine, let's do this the hard way." She hooks the umbrella over her wrist and places both hands up against the stubborn area. "Come on," she says through gritted teeth as she leans up against the invisible blockade, pushing at it with all her might. Muffled, distant yelling comes from behind her as the air finally shifts beneath her hands, moving away almost like bricks without concrete keeping them fixed together. Then there's a heaviness, like something's holding onto her shirt and pulling her back.

Rachel looks over her shoulder as the barrier evaporates beneath her touch, far too quickly for her brain to send the correct signals to her body, and she meets Dougal's fear-filled blue eyes as they fall forward together.

Chapter Five
Reckless, Ruthless, Relentless

An audible pop is followed by white-hot pain shooting through Rachel's body as she lands shoulder-first on a hard surface. Before she can come to grips with the throbbing in her bruised shoulder, the numbness running down her arm, or even the unfamiliar surroundings, fingers dig into the soft flesh of her upper arms and manhandle her back onto her feet. A cry of agony rips from her throat, the sound bouncing off stark walls and uneven floors. Tears fill her eyes as those fingers grip her tightly, brutally. A solid figure shoves her forward and Rachel almost trips over her own feet. Those hands keep her upright and push her onward, forcing her forward.

The roughhewn floor is pockmarked from neglect. Liquid festers within the cracks and holes like pus-filled sores. It stinks of mildew and old blood. The stone walls seem to shine as water trickles down from the arched ceiling, gathering in the angles between the floor and wall. There are no windows to allow fresh air and light inside, only a yellow glow coming from a narrow corridor leading out of the chamber.

"Let go o' me!" Dougal's voice rebounds, thick with dread and hoarse from screaming. "Rachel!"

Rachel struggles against her captor, trying to twist around

and out of the hands—more like forceps—keeping her subdued. Her abductor squeezes her shoulder. Stars blind her, and she sucks air through her teeth to counter the pain. A chorus of unfamiliar voices joins in with Dougal's echoing shouts. Laughter and catcalls, taunts and jeers. It's an overwhelming uproar that sounds like the inside of a prison, but the dimly lit, dank surroundings give the stone room the appearance of a medieval dungeon. The incomprehensible circumstances make it difficult for Rachel to focus on anything other than her confusion and pain. Her survival instincts begin to kick in, forcing her to fight back instead of being a benevolent, reasonable human being.

She pulls her good arm forward, bends it upward, and drives her elbow into the body behind her with as much power as she can muster. The *oomph* comes first, before the hands lose their grip on her arms. Rachel spins around, kicks out at her attacker's shin, and throws an almighty punch without aiming. Her fist collides with a chin, making the bones in her hand vibrate. The guy goes down. Not wanting to lose her chance at escape, she sidesteps the lanky man who's thankfully still stunned, and finds Dougal putting some distance between himself and the much larger specimen attempting to restrain him.

She scans the chamber. Her umbrella lies a few feet away, within reach. She rushes toward it.

"Run, Rachel," Dougal shouts from the scuffle with his oversized opponent.

Instead of running, Rachel picks up her umbrella, swallows hard as she walks up behind the man overpowering Dougal, and pulls back her weapon. A satisfying, hollow thwack resounds through the stone room as her umbrella connects with the man's temple. It's enough to make the attacker go limp. She watches him crumple into a heap on the unhygienic floor and kicks him once in his ribs for good measure. Rachel looks up at her red-faced companion, who's now busy catching his breath.

"Where on God's green Earth are we?" Rachel asks as her attacker runs away, most likely to raise the alarm. She doesn't expect Dougal to answer, but he raises a finger, indicating that she wait.

"Fair folk lands," he says.

"That means absolutely nothing to me," she says. When he doesn't answer, Rachel says, "Dougal, can you please elabor—?"

"Fae. Faeries. Fair folk," he explains as he walks past her to pick up his discarded baseball bat, which had rolled across the chamber and stopped against the farthest wall. "We're in the Fae Realm, Rachel."

The nervous titter she involuntarily releases earns her a reproachful look. "That's absurd," she says in a high-pitched, panic-filled voice. "That's completely ludicrous."

"Aye, it is," Dougal says, making his way toward the semi-conscious attacker. He pushes the end of the bat against the guy's shoulder. The man's eyes flutter open, his determination and disdain plain as day. "How do we get back to our world?"

Rachel walks closer to look at the man. Dressed in an official-looking uniform of some kind, he stares at Dougal. She can't make out the exact colors of his attire or see much of his face in the gloom either, but he doesn't appear to be the type of person who goes around assaulting kids for fun. His gaze moves to meet Rachel's as she comes up beside her companion.

"How do we get back to our world?" Dougal repeats in a threatening tone.

"I don't know," he says, turning his attention back to

Dougal. "We were just making our last rounds before the next rotation starts when we heard rolling thunder coming from in here, and there you were. Two kids sneaking around in a forgotten part of His Majesty's dungeons."

Rachel shakes her head, blinking a few times to try and snap out of this crazy dream.

Urgent footfalls belonging to multiple people resonate from somewhere beyond the chamber. "Where are we exactly?" Dougal asks, ignoring the approaching commotion.

"Telfore, Orthega." The man turns his gaze to meet Rachel's once more. "I thought we'd gotten rid of your kind."

"*Excuse me?*" she asks, specifically offended by *your kind*, which could've been directed to any number of things: her Irish ancestry, her gender, the insane belief that somewhere in her lineage women made pacts with the devil and had been convicted of witchcraft and heresy. The list went on.

Dougal wraps a hand around her wrist before she can lose her temper, and he leads her through the opening in the wall, into the narrow corridor she'd noticed earlier. Rachel lengthens her strides to match his walk, but she soon finds jogging easier to keep up with him.

Situated every ten feet apart, wrought iron sconces are mounted against the walls, holding lit torches. Flames flicker and their shadows dance as they hurry down the corridor, which stretches on for a good while before it suddenly curves and ends in a steep, winding staircase carved from rock. There is no railing. No precautions had been made during the building of this place to keep people from falling to their deaths. Dougal, who's clearly not concerned over the architectural defects, walks to the staircase at a brisk pace. Every now and then he glimpses over his shoulder, looking past Rachel to see if anyone's following them.

"We shouldn't go up," she says before Dougal can begin his ascent.

"But—"

"Did you see those guys' uniforms?" she interrupts him as she looks down the dark spiraling staircase, where a void waits to devour anyone who dares enter. "There are more where they came from. I'm pretty sure if we go up, we'll be caught, but if we go down…"

"Sewers," he finishes her train of thought and nods before beginning his descent into the pit.

She hurries after him, ignoring the heavy footfalls and the authoritative shouts growing louder behind them, focusing on her own footing in the pitch-black darkness. With one hand pressed against the wall—a false sense of security if ever there was one—she feels her way to safety.

They accelerate as the footsteps become a distant, bad memory.

Down …

Down …

Down …

It grows colder the farther they travel. Dampness coats the walls and covers the palm of her hand. The stench of sewage becomes more obvious; the sound of rushing water promises freedom. Perhaps, if their luck holds out, there is a slim chance of getting out of this mess alive.

Her mess.

They're done for unless they find a place to hide or find a way back to the forest soon. Adrenaline is the only reason their exhaustion hasn't caught up with them yet, and hers is already depleting.

She reaches solid ground as Dougal raises his bat and slams it down against a metal gate—a metal gate that hinders their escape to safety. The loud *clang, clang, clang* as he rhythmically beats down on a rusty lock can barely be heard over the roar of the stream beyond, but the mere idea of someone hearing the clamor and coming after them doesn't sit well with her.

She looks back, the darkness obscuring any sign of their pursuers. How long do they have? Impatient, she turns back to Dougal as he sorts out the obstacle with brute strength.

Clang, clang, clang.

"Come on," she says, anxious to get out and away. "Come on, Dougal. Put your weight into your swings."

"Yer welcome to take over," he snaps back. Annoyance, or fear, twists his features and colors his skin red. Dougal raises the bat and slams the rusted lock again.

A final *clang* rings before the gate squeaks open. Relief washes over her. She says a little prayer of thanks as they escape into the underground tunnel, where a speck of light is visible in the distance. Apart from the platform, which is hardly wide enough to fit them both comfortably, the rest of the journey is a treacherous one. Water laps at a rocky ledge—broad enough for a single person to carefully walk upon—and kisses the eroding walls.

Rachel follows the hesitant Dougal through the tunnel. Sludge squishes underfoot, sticking against the soles of her shoes, squelching so loudly her stomach churns in disgust.

Time seems to pass slower than usual, like it's working against them, but the speck of light becomes larger and brightens up their surroundings.

"Halt!" a voice booms over the rushing water.

The command is quickly followed by a barrage of arrows being released, arrows that fly every which way and narrowly avoid hitting their intended targets. Warning shots, no doubt.

"Are you crazy?" Rachel shouts at them, heart pounding hard as she speeds up. Their response is to let loose another few arrows, which cut through the air and pin into the walls around them. "We're just kids, you morons!"

Dougal stops, cautiously turns to rest his back against the wall, and bites his lower lip as he studies the stream below. "Can ye swim?" he asks when she closes in.

"Yes," she says without deliberating on her answer for long. Only afterward do the consequences of his question dawn on her. "Oh, no, Dougal."

"Deep breath," he says, taking her hand.

"*No*—" Rachel's scream is lost to the darkness as Dougal pulls her off the ledge.

They break the water together, which envelops them both in a cold, raging embrace. The icy water slams the air out of her lungs, and she loses her grip on Dougal's hand as the violent current drags them downstream. She panics. The tempestuous, dark waters roll around her, making it impossible for her to figure out where the surface is located. Oxygen. She wants to breathe so bad. A hand grabs her by the collar and tugs her backward. She kicks, trying to get away and swim upward—or where she assumes up is—but Dougal's body slams into her. All she wants is to break through the murky water and inhale. The river roils suck her deeper into its shadowy depths. Rainstorm debris and manmade waste toss together in the underwater rollercoaster. Tread water turns to mud. Something prickly jabs into her side, gouges at her clothes, before moving past.

Then, without reason, the water gives way and gravity takes hold again. Gone is the floating. Gone is the tumultuous water. The end of her inexplicable fall is softened by luscious, emerald-green grass. The darkness is replaced by the bright afternoon light, a welcome sight after scurrying around like rats in the sewer. Sputtering and coughing, too weak to begin coming up with an explanation for this wicked trip, Rachel lies on her back and stares through the forest's canopy of leaves. Beside her, still gasping and wheezing, Dougal is on his hands and knees. She watches him grab fistfuls of grass, retching up the filthy water. His strength gives out and he lies down, breathing hard.

Shivering, Rachel sits upright, reaches for the umbrella between them, and drags it closer. She laughs weakly through chattering teeth as she inspects the family heirloom, and finds it in perfect condition, aside from a few muddy splotches covering the umbrella's canopy.

"I don't know what yer laughin' about." He turns his head to face her, cheek pressing against the grass. She ignores his criticism, fumbling with the clasp keeping the material wrapped around the shaft. "We were almost murdered thanks to ye."

She casts her eyes to the white birch arch standing ahead of them, benign. "*I* got us out of that place, remember? If we'd have gone up, we'd never have seen daylight again."

He props himself onto his elbows and looks at her in disbelief, blue eyes scanning her features. Without saying a word, he sits upright.

"Okay, fine. I accept responsibility for getting us there—wherever *there* is—but you have to give me credit for the rest. I did save your life … twice. Just like you saved mine, although I'm not happy about the way you went about it."

"Yer talkin' a lot," he grumbles. "I don't like it."

"I don't care whether you like my talking or not. I'm freaking out here, sue me," Rachel snaps back. "The fact that I'm not hyperventilating right now is amazing in itself. I mean, first we get chased by a shadow, which probably destroyed a huge part of the forest and, God forbid, our homes. Then I get assaulted before I have to swim through heaven-knows-what because some idiots were shooting arrows at us—"

Dougal interrupts her rambling with an outburst of his own, speaking in the same language he'd used the previous night when they had encountered the Black Annis. He stands and wanders off to where he'd left his backpack before their underground adventure.

She hurries to her feet, rushes after him, and asks, "What is that anyway?"

"What?"

"The language you're speaking. What is it?"

"Gaelic." He busies himself with the backpack to avoid looking at her.

"Oh," Rachel says, pushing the mechanism of the umbrella up to dry the fabric.

Dougal's surly silence rolls off him in waves as he pulls the backpack on and walks back the way they had come earlier.

She follows, grimacing from the overall aches and pains, and trying not to pay too much attention to the squishes of her sodden shoes every time she takes a step.

When the silence becomes unbearable, she says, "Quick question: If I had said I couldn't swim back there, would you have left me behind?"

"Aye," he says without looking back.

"Brutal," she mutters.

"I'm not very keen on ye right now, Rachel. Ask me again tomorrow."

Rachel doesn't know how to respond, simply follows him as he retraces their path through the forest, keeping a watchful eye on their surroundings. The trees are as dense as she remembers them, the brush hardly disturbed after their race through the woods. The quiet encircling them is visceral, as usual, but the smell of their unexpected swim lingers no matter which way she turns. Thankfully, the sun is out, and the day is hot, even in the gloomy forest, which helps to dry her clothes and the umbrella. Her shoes, however, are a whole other matter.

"Sorry for goin' off on ye," he says after a while, his tone low.

"It's all right. I'm sorry for getting us into that place," Rachel says in turn, picking up speed to walk beside him. "Friends?"

"Yeah, but don't go steppin' into faerie circles again. Next time, I won't follow ye through." Dougal affords her a weak smile.

"Fair enough," Rachel says, smiling back at him. "Remind me again, what's a faerie circle?"

"Och! Didn't Nan teach ye anythin'? The mushroom circle was a faerie circle, Rach," he explains. "It didn't act like I expected it would, what with the birch arch and all yer pushin' to get through, but usually a faerie circle takes ye to the Fae Realm without any extra hurdles."

She purses her lips together. "I didn't know," she whispers.

"Aye, I know. If ye had, ye would've figured out sooner why Nan's been makin' ye do weird stuff over the years." Dougal shifts the backpack on his shoulders. "In the old days, folks used to leave gifts for the piskies in order to placate them. My da told me about it when I was a bairn."

"Piskies? You mean pixies, right?"

"Aye, pixies," he says. "Our egg plantin' yesterday was s'posed to appease the fair folk in some way, too."

"Judging by the day we've had, I'm going to just say it didn't work."

Dougal makes a show of sniffing in her direction and his face scrunches up in revulsion. "Ye can say that again."

"You don't exactly smell like a bouquet of daisies either," she says, swinging her umbrella around to dry it faster. "Speaking of bad days, what are the chances of us running into any more trouble on our way home?"

Dougal's humor evaporates and his features smooth into a blank expression. He scans the forest again, his body becoming stiff as it readies to deal with a threat as soon as it's detected.

He swallows, and whispers, "I don't know. I hope none."

The forest changes in appearance as they walk; ancient trees seem to have been ripped out by the roots and thrown across the path they had trodden earlier, leaving them no other option than to take the long way around. In some places, smaller flora specimens are crushed beyond recognition, whereas younger trees are damaged by the falls of the bigger ones. It looks like a warzone, like forgotten mines were triggered and had torn apart the earth itself.

She feels a pang of guilt for ignoring the ACCESS PROHIBITED sign, but the guilt soon turns into concern for her hometown, for the people who live there, for the children who are gone. Is this what they're up against? Is this unseen entity, this monster with the strength of a bulldozer, the crux of Shadow Grove's problems?

Rachel can't begin to answer these questions, but she's almost certain her dad, Liam Cleary, can.

Chapter Six
By The Dying Light

Upon their return from the forest, Griswold Road is a flurry of activity. The sheriff department's cruisers' red and blue lights flash in timed intervals, casting an eerie glow over the grim gathering of townsfolk who litter the lawns of both houses. As dusk swells into existence, the heat never relinquishing the power it holds over the world, a distressed Mrs. Crenshaw and Jenny Cleary stand together in the shade of a tree, two lonesome figures amidst the chaos.

Rachel's heart drops to her stomach at the commotion and then does a flip when Mrs. Crenshaw spots them near the forest's ACCESS PROHIBITED sign. The old woman's concern turns to rage in an instant—a frail lady changing into a warrior queen. Gone are the ailments of age, gone is the amicable façade.

"We're in so much trouble," Rachel says as they cautiously approach the road together.

Mrs. Crenshaw takes several footsteps away from Rachel's mother, who wears a blank expression and stares past her toward the forest. Those who are present turn their gazes toward them, relief rather than annoyance filling the air. It's strange, though, oh so very strange that a crowd had gathered outside their houses—possible search parties, if Rachel's reading this scene correctly—in a matter of hours, whilst those poor missing children were never afforded the same luxury. Rachel doesn't mention it to Dougal, doesn't have the courage to utter a single word with Mrs. Crenshaw marching their way, but it's unnerving to imagine her life meaning more than innocent kids' lives.

Why?

"You two better have a damn good explana—" Mrs. Crenshaw almost shouts. She cuts herself off as she draws closer, her nose wrinkling as a pesky breeze blows past them. "What is that smell?" She looks them up and down, now clearly upset by losing her momentum, and runs her hand through her white, loosely braided hair, which isn't her style of choice. "Go get yourselves cleaned up immediately. We'll talk about this excursion of yours when you don't smell like sewage."

"Nan—"

"Don't give me lip, boy. Move."

Rachel watches as Dougal hurries toward the house. He dodges the curious onlookers by cutting across the lawn and slipping around the side of the Frasers' property. She makes her way to the house across the street, gripping the umbrella handle tightly in her fist, defiantly marching through the whispering crowd to reach the front door.

"You and I are going to have a good long talk about responsibility, young lady," her mother says when Rachel passes.

Rachel's response is no more than an indignant snort. The hypocrisy of her mother's words, the very tone she uses, doesn't deserve more than belligerence. Responsibility. Ha! She makes her way up the porch steps, sets down the damp umbrella, and kicks off her ruined shoes. She escapes into the house without a word.

If Jenny wants to talk, if she suddenly feels like it's time to act like a parent again, Rachel decides it's only fair that her mother listens to the long list of complaints she's compiled over the past few months. Period.

Her wet hair hangs over her shoulders and down her back, now several shades darker and infinitely curlier, thanks to the long shower she needed to get rid of the persistent smell. Water drips onto the black, white, and purple geometric carpet, protecting the hardwood beneath. Rachel sits cross-legged on her bedroom floor in the yellow artificial light that shines down from the ceiling, dressed in her favorite pajamas and robe, and scrolls through her emails and Instagram timeline. From the look of things, she hasn't missed much; a few holiday photos, some passive aggressive status updates on Twitter, a handful of spam emails, and a few texts from a number she doesn't recognize—first asking where she is and then whether she's all right.

A knock on the door startles her out of her thoughts, followed by her mother's irate words. "You're grounded for two weeks."

"For what exactly?" Rachel calls back.

"Insubordination."

Rachel rolls her eyes, tosses the phone over her shoulder, which lands on her pillow with a dull thud, and stands from the floor. She crosses her bedroom and opens the door, searching for her mother in the hallway. It's only natural for her to want to contest the unfair punishment, considering she and Dougal hadn't even *technically* left their families' properties, but her mother isn't there. Deliberating, it seems, is out of the question.

The public remark her mother made earlier, about them having a "good long talk about responsibility" won't come to fruition.

She slams her door shut, hard enough to rattle the window, and makes her way to her desk. A few of her father's journals are scattered across the surface, open at seemingly random pages. Her own notebook, which she's been using solely to find a pattern to locate the missing children, sits atop her closed laptop. Rachel takes a seat in her swivel chair, opens the notebook, and looks at the progress she's made. It makes for depressing reading, especially since she hasn't found a single lead to get to the bottom of this frustrating mystery whatsoever, apart from the Black Annis running about town.

She picks up her pen and adds Astraea Hayward's name to the growing list, her age and the information surrounding her disappearance—*Vanished into thin air on Main Road, in front of witnesses.*

She glances at her father's journal, where the Black Annis is doodled in the margin, and sets her notebook aside.

There's more to the sketch than meets the eye, but what? She flips to the first page of the journal and reads through her father's notes, which mainly revolve around the Eerie Creek Sawmill. There isn't anything salacious about the research her father had done. The journal delves into the history of the lumber company that agreed to enter into the partnership with Shadow Grove's leaders. There's a brief overview of the possible malpractices the lumber company was allegedly involved in—child labor, unsafe working environments, fraudulent behavior. Otherwise, it's maddeningly tedious.

Rachel stands and walks over to her bed, lies on her side, and continues reading. There are a lot of facts to sift through, boring facts. In this particular journal, her dad doesn't touch on the subject of the tragedies that had befallen the sawmill's owners or workers, but the entry on the last page does hold promise.

The apathy shown regarding the missing child laborers, some as young as ten years old, during this turbulent time in Shadow Grove's history, is perhaps the most appalling part of the Eerie Creek Sawmill Saga. For two years prior to the fire that would ultimately end the partnership between the town and the lumber company, at least fifteen children disappeared. Is this the work of a serial killer? We may never know.

"Oh." Rachel sits upright on the bed. She rereads the last part of the journal, eagerly searching for more, but the tantalizing tease begins and ends with the paragraph in question. "This has happened before," she whispers her revelation out loud, heart racing as she rushes back to her desk and finds her own notebook.

She copies her father's entry word for word, adds the citation for future reference at the bottom of the copied paragraph, and places the journal to one side of her desk. Rachel picks up the next random journal and repeats the process, hoping to find something else that could help her in the search for those missing kids.

Long hours pass as she wades through useless information about farming methods used in Shadow Grove and how they've changed throughout the town's history. The dull read weighs down her already leaden eyelids, exhaustion after a day of bizarre adventures promises a deep, dreamless sleep. Rachel absentmindedly strokes the soft bedding as her ever-narrowing eyes move across the page, while the pillow supporting her neck gently caresses her cheek. Comfortable, inviting, her resolve to continue reading ebbs until it finally dissolves. Sleep drags her out of the waking world and into blissful nothingness.

Sometime during the night, the temperature plummets. The wind howls as it rushes from the forest and enters the town. Leaves whisper as the wind picks up, the air becomes heavier, clouds gather over Shadow Grove as a storm rolls in. A long, low rumble rouses Rachel from her slumber. Her eyes snap open at the sound, and an incandescent light fills her bedroom for a few milliseconds.

One Mississippi ... Two Mississippi ... Th—

Peals of thunder interrupt her counting. She sits upright, mind muddled with sleep, and wonders if her mother had been the one to turn off the lights or if the storm had blown a fuse. She looks around her dark, undisturbed bedroom, still in the darkness. Aside from the gossamer curtains waving violently as the wind penetrates her room, nothing is out of order. Rachel doesn't recall opening the window since the previous day, when it'd felt like someone—*something*—was watching her.

Lightning cleaves the night sky in half; a clap of thunder rattles the heavens.

She pushes the journal off the bed as she gets up, and it lands face-down on the floor. Her robe's belt drags behind her as she saunters to the window. Yawning, she rubs the sleep from her eyes with the back of her hand. A persistent scratching and a *click, click, clicking* noise—not so loud as to truly hinder a heavy sleeper but loud enough to bother someone who wants to reach their dreamscape again—sounds just outside the window. Rachel pushes the curtains out of her way, battling the swathes of fabric which billow wildly as another gust of wind makes its way through, and comes face-to-face with the stuff of nightmares.

The creature's most noticeable feature is her blue-hued skin tone, and although her rusty nail-like teeth are without a doubt a menacing sight, it's those eyes. With a single glare of those midnight-colored eyes, even Death would surrender his scythe to the Black Annis outside Rachel's window.

Metallic fingernails glint regardless of the absent moonlight—and tap against the glass pane, once, twice, before dragging downward to create a shrill screeching noise that reverberates in the very roots of Rachel's molars. The Black Annis pushes away from the wall and comes into full view. Hanging there, suspended in midair, a satisfied smile spreads across her inhuman features. Then the black cloak, which is not at all filthy as Rachel had assumed the previous night, wraps around the Black Annis' emaciated form, protecting her from the downpour. Rachel suspects the cloak to be sentient as it curls closer to its mistress on its own. Tighter and tighter, restricting like a python.

Whispers ride on the wind. Distant childlike voices, gleeful, as if they're on a playground, swirl into existence around the crone. The soft voices become louder until it sounds like the children are playing right beneath Rachel's bedroom window. The Black Annis' cloak suddenly shoots open and spreads out farther. Impossibly, it somehow fills Rachel's entire line of vision, revealing a collection of ghostlike faces stacked one upon the other and side by side. Chubby-cheeked cherubs avert their hollow gazes to stare at the Black Annis, forced smiles twisting their features horrendously.

The cloak continues unfurling to the sides and the tally keeps climbing as new faces appear. Even if Rachel wanted to study each collected child, in search of the missing children of Shadow Grove, there are simply too many to count.

"What *are* you?" Rachel's words slip out of her mouth of

their own accord, her voice awestruck instead of fearful. Her hands tremble and she feels unsteady on her legs, but curiosity overrides every other sane option.

The question seems to intrigue the Black Annis rather than anger her. Good thing, too, because she drifts closer to the window again, midnight eyes never straying far from Rachel's position.

"The Night Weaver," the Black Annis says without moving her lips. The cloak curls inward again, slowly retracting until it looks like a regular piece of clothing.

"Are y—you from Orthega?" Rachel stutters.

The Night Weaver's face changes to indicate scornful derision.

"Yes." The word is no more than a fleeting thought, a whisper on the wind.

Feeling brave, Rachel asks, "Did you take the children?"

Lightning flashes in the background. A horrible smile crosses the Night Weaver's face, which seems younger now, almost vibrant. Apparently, her expression is answer enough, because the disembodied voice doesn't reply.

Rachel narrows her eyes, anger substituting curiosity and fear. "Give them back," she hisses, her hands balling into fists, even though there's little to nothing she can physically do to retrieve the kids from this otherworldly creature.

The Night Weaver's smile widens. What can only be described as excitement glimmers in those midnight eyes. She floats backward, away from the window, her retreating figure becoming smaller and less visible as the night swallows her whole.

Rachel rushes closer to the window, screaming into the night, "Give them back! Give them back!"

"Come get them."

The final, distant whisper reaches Rachel just as the storm breaks properly and the rain turns to hail. She grabs the windows' handles and pulls them inward, locking them quickly. The hailstones ricochet off the glass pane, pinging as they hit.

Enraged, Rachel spins around and finds her mother standing in the doorway, wide blue eyes set in an ashen face. There's no telling how long her mom's been lurking in the door or how much she's heard. Rachel wants to ask, but whatever courage she's had during her meeting with the Night Weaver has left her. Standing up to some make-believe monster is cake in comparison to confronting Jenny Cleary.

Her mother blinks, as if coming out of a trance, and looks away from the window to meet Rachel's gaze. For a seemingly endless minute, the two of them stare at each other. This rift between them, which seems to have become infinitely wider and deeper since her dad's death, is amplified by the inability to speak openly. These days, the awkward silence is a constant feature in their relationship, and it keeps Rachel from moving closer.

A sudden shift in the atmosphere throws Rachel off guard. The tight, forced smile spreads across her mother's face, blankness glazes over her eyes. There's nothing maternal about the expression, nothing soothing or familiar in the unusual response.

"It's late, sweetheart. Better get to bed," her mother says, her tone sounding far too robotic to pacify Rachel's late-night fears.

Before Rachel can react, Jenny Cleary turns on her heels and slips back into the dark hallway, heading toward her bedroom on the other side of the house. Whether either of them will sleep again tonight, Rachel can't say for sure, but she has no misgivings over how this episode will be dealt with in the future.

Chapter Seven
Wither Away

Being grounded during summer, according to Rachel's mother, usually means spending the duration of one's punishment slaving away in the library, either cataloging new titles or shelving returned books. Sometimes, if Rachel's deemed reformed after whatever bad behavior landed her in trouble in the first place, she's allowed to read children's books to the kids who came for Story Time. Other times, particularly if her mother is in a bad mood, Rachel is sent to the archives located in the dingy basement—otherwise known as The Literary Graveyard—where she has to capture the old library cards' information into the updated electronic library system.

Rachel expects things to play out as they normally do in these situations—getting dragged out of bed at seven o'clock to accompany her mother to the library—but this time she wakes up without assistance. She rolls over and sees her digital alarm clock blinking 08:04 AM. Shocked, Rachel shoots upright on her bed.

"Mom?" she calls out.

When nobody answers, she climbs out of bed and cautiously makes her way to the partially open bedroom door. Rachel sticks her head out and looks around the empty hallway, half hoping her mother will rush into view, still getting dressed because they both overslept. Nothing stirs.

Rachel steps outside her room and treads softly toward the staircase landing. She leans over the crooked wooden banister and peers to the foyer, glimpsing the front door from the corner of her eye.

The quiet is deafening; the loneliness is palpable.

She swallows hard, blinking away the heartache threatening to spill onto her cheeks.

Rachel makes her way to her mother's bedroom, finding the door slightly ajar. She pushes it open and finds the floral white and red bedcover pulled tightly across the mattress. The matching curtains are still shut against the struggling sun, which barely brightens the overcast morning. The wardrobe doors are spread wide, and even from her angle, Rachel notices the shelves' bareness. She walks deeper into the room and spies those ugly dresses her mother has been wearing lately. They hang together in solitude, taking up so little space yet unmistakably all-consuming. Khaki, ochre, dove-gray, gunmetal, black, the dresses are pushed to one side of the wardrobe with their matching pairs of sensible shoes lined up beside one another at the bottom.

The pieces of clothing that assert the real Jenny Cleary's personality are missing—leather pants, skinny jeans, flower-patterned blouses, and statement pajamas, all gone. Even the lilac cocktail dress, the one her mother only ever wore when they went to visit her father's grave, is gone.

Rachel walks over to the dressing table, where her mother's jewelry box stands. She carefully opens the lid to peer inside and sighs in relief. Every family heirloom her mother occasionally wears, every piece of jewelry her father ever bought, is still neatly stored within. She closes the lid and steps back, searching the room for anything else out of sorts.

Apart from the vacant bedside table, where a stack of smutty romance novels usually make their home, nothing else seems wrong. Yet everything *feels* off. It's almost as if her mother, the mother Rachel loves no matter how tenuous things are between them, is slowly disappearing.

She makes her way back to her bedroom, back to where her phone sits on the nightstand, and dials her mother's number. The phone rings for a while before the familiar voice answers.

A single word slips out of Rachel's mouth, tinny and childlike. "Mommy?"

"Yes, dear?" her mother says, almost sounding inconvenienced by the intruding call.

"Where are you?"

"At work. Why?" A hint of concern laces her voice, mixed with something else Rachel can't quite put her finger on. "Is everything all right, Rach?"

"You said I was grounded," Rachel says, picking and scratching at her thumbnail's cuticle.

The silence is full of confusion, pregnant with doubt.

"I don't recall grounding you."

"So, just to be clear, you're telling me that I'm *not* grounded?" Rachel asks, not entirely sure if she should be happy or concerned over having her sentence reduced to time served. Concern, however, seems like the appropriate response to the news. Her mother isn't the type of person who simply forgets about manners. In fact, as fun and carefree as Jenny Cleary used to be at times, she never waived a single opportunity to teach Rachel the importance of responsibility, consequences, and good behavior.

"Are you feeling okay, sweetie? You're not making any sense," her mother says. "Should I come home or—?"

"No, no. I'm fine," Rachel quickly replies. "I probably just had a bad dream or something. Never mind. Have a nice day, all right?"

"Okay, you too."

"Hey, Mom, before you go. What did you do with the lilac dress? The one Daddy bought you just before he died?"

"Oh, I donated it to Goodwill, along with some other clothes which were taking up space." The nonchalance in her mother's voice is staggering.

"Are you serious? You said I could have it one day. I was going to wear that dress to prom."

"Yes, well, I've been doing some soul searching lately and I'm just not that person anymore. Speaking of which, we should tackle your closet next. I mean, how can we expect the world to respect us if we don't respect ourselves enough to cover up, right? Anyway, let's talk about it tonight."

The call ends abruptly, without the customary 'I love you', which her mother always insists on delivering at the end of a phone conversation.

Rachel sits down on her bed, spent, staring at her cell phone's blank screen and wondering if she's somehow lost her mind over the past few days. Plausible as the insanity theory sounds, it doesn't explain her mother's inexplicable personality change. That dress was more than just a dress—it's the last gift her mother ever received from her father.

She remembers how her dad had pored over the internet, searching for the perfect present to commemorate their tenth anniversary. How many hours had he spent calling shops across the country to find that special something-something to show his undying devotion? Her father didn't go out in search of a dress per se; he'd essentially been looking at jewelry prior to the daddy-daughter outing one spring morning. But when Rachel, only eight years old at the time, spotted the dress hanging in the storefront window at Alice's Vintage Emporium, they both instantly knew not even diamonds would top it. They were right. Her mother's expression when she received the lilac dress, packaged in a white embossed box and tied with a periwinkle-colored ribbon, was one of pure joy.

Doesn't this dress just scream: 'I am Jenny Cleary?'

Up until now, the sentimental value alone made it a priceless garment in the Cleary household. Not to mention the actual monetary worth of the dress—an authentic 1950s silk dress with a brocaded bodice, in mint condition—could bring in a small fortune on eBay.

The dress was one of a kind, like her mom used to be, and now they were both gone.

Rachel wipes a tear away from her cheek as she sets the phone down beside her. She sits for a few more minutes, pushing away her emotions. Composed, Rachel stands and goes to the closet to pick out the day's clothes. There are, after all, more crucial matters to attend to than a damn dress and a body-snatched mother. No matter how selfish she wants to be, those things are trivial in comparison to finding the missing children.

Twenty minutes later, Rachel finds herself knocking on Mrs. Crenshaw's door, already formulating an excuse to see Dougal—apparently her only ally in this battle against an entity that shouldn't exist outside of folklore. The front door opens, and the old woman appears—lips taut, frown lines prominent, eyes saying she's none too happy to have Rachel on her doorstep.

The reason Rachel has concocted for her visit flees from her mind and all she can do is *um* and *ah* as Mrs. Crenshaw chastises her with a mere glare.

"He's not here," Mrs. Crenshaw says, somehow figuring out the purpose of Rachel's visit through the muddled words. Her voice is calm and soft, the quiet before a storm. "I got him a job at Farrow & Sons for the summer. The boy's good with his hands, I hear, particularly with machinery. He's off fixing a tractor on the Kempner Farm with Joe Farrow. It's always best to keep troublemakers' minds off trouble, away from temptation, you understand?"

"Mrs. Crenshaw, it wasn't Dougal's fault. I became curious about why nobody ever goes into the forest, and he didn't want me to go in there by myself."

"For seventeen years you hardly glimpse at the forest, but as soon as he comes along you go off on an adventure without giving it a second thought."

"It's not like that—"

"Oh?" she interrupts, unconvinced. "Look, if Joe doesn't work him half to death today, and if he's still able to walk across the road to see you, I'll tell him you were here."

Rachel nods in understanding, whispers her thanks, and turns to leave.

Behind her, Mrs. Crenshaw sighs loudly. "What's the matter, Rachel? You didn't rush over here to test my patience, I'm sure."

She turns back to look at the woman, the closest she's ever had to a grandmother, and says, "You wouldn't believe me if I told you."

Mrs. Crenshaw opens the door wide and takes a step back,

allowing her to enter. "Try me," she says.

Rachel enters the house and makes her way into the living room. A pair of tawny-colored armchairs, both covered in granny-square crocheted afghans, sit across from an outdated television. The boxy relic with its bunny-ear aerial should be in a science and technology museum, but Mrs. Crenshaw doesn't want to get rid of it. She always says her TV is more reliable "out here" than some fancy wall-mounted flat-screen, although Rachel doesn't recall their television ever giving them problems. The taupe-colored sofa, where mismatched patches are displayed like badges of honor, sits against the wall across from the large window overlooking the street. A threadbare carpet with a strange pattern covers the hardwood floor. Rachel knows this living room almost as well as her own bedroom.

Meanwhile, she considers the ramifications of telling Mrs. Crenshaw everything. A prolonged vacation at the Hawthorne Memorial Wellness Center, a mental institution established by a rich businessman back in the 1970s to hide his killer son from the authorities, seems like the most probable outcome. Maybe her mother would be merciful and send her off to a holistic retreat for troubled teens? Doubtful, but a girl can hope. There is a slim chance that Mrs. Crenshaw will believe her, in which case Rachel would have two allies to help her find the missing children. Is it worth the risk?

She selects the most believable piece of the story to share with Mrs. Crenshaw, particularly the part about her mother acting stranger than usual and allows the story of how they got to this point to pour out of her. Bottled up feelings are released in the process; all the angst and disappointment and confusion. Mrs. Crenshaw listens, her face unchanging as the torrent of words and emotions is released. Rachel sucks in a deep breath as she comes to the end of the weird tale, and realizes she was speaking so fast that half of what she said probably didn't make much sense.

"All right." Mrs. Crenshaw doesn't appear like she's ready to call in professionals to force Rachel out of her house, so that's a good sign. "I did notice some ... *things*, like the absences and evasiveness, but I had no idea it was this bad. How long did you say this has been going on?" she asks.

"The worst of it's been going on for about a year now," Rachel says, running her hand over one of the patches on the armrest. "I'd like to blame Sheriff Carter for Mom's weird behavior, but the truth is she was acting dodgy before he started coming around. What do I do?"

"First off, you don't *do* anything," Mrs. Crenshaw says, sitting forward in her favorite armchair. "Adults don't tend to listen to children, even if children are more perceptive. If you confront your mother while she's in a bad place, the issues you've raised will only be brushed aside and the tension between you will escalate. Let me speak to her."

"You'd do that?"

Mrs. Crenshaw raises one of her eyebrows, her way of saying, "Duh."

"Thank you, Mrs. Crenshaw."

Mrs. Crenshaw sits back again, and says, "Your mother isn't the only adult who's been afflicted with this strange behavior. Iris Pearson looked rather bland at church yesterday—gray seems to be all the rage with those uppity peacocks lately. I was more concerned over Andy Rawson, though. He was running his mouth about a woman's place while we were heading out of church and there were quite a few menfolk who seemed interested in his Old Testament views." She clucks her tongue and shakes her head. "I'll have to look into this before a mass hysteria of some kind takes hold of the entire town."

"Like the one back in 1811?" Rachel blurts out. Mrs. Crenshaw tilts her head, the corner of her lip pulling upward. "I've been going through Dad's old journals. He said something about a mass hysteria in 1811, revolving around Shadow Grove's farming methods through the ages. Talk about bland."

"Your dad was smart enough to hide the truth in plain sight. Honestly, how many people would be interested in reading a journal about farming methods?" Mrs. Crenshaw inhales deeply. "The mass hysteria in 1811 wasn't exactly a mass hysteria. It was more like an epidemic of grief that set over into fear, similar to the Salem Witch Trials. Of course, nobody got burned at the stake in Shadow Grove, but it was heading that way fast. If I recall correctly, the townsfolk went after the mayor of the time. They dragged him out of his house, tied him to a donkey, paraded him down Main Road, and then strung him up in front of Town Hall. The ravens pecked at his decaying corpse for weeks."

"Geez," Rachel says. "For what? Why were they so afraid?"

Mrs. Crenshaw shrugs. "Hell if I know. Change, maybe? Unlike your father, mine never searched for the root cause of a problem from years gone by. He just liked to tell me the stories," she explains. "That tidbit is a tad too grim to make it into the official history of Shadow Grove, by the way, but ..."

"But?" she asks when Mrs. Crenshaw doesn't continue.

"You're friends with the Pearson boy, aren't you?"

Rachel shrugs, muttering, "Meh."

"Well, are you up for a recon mission?" she asks. Rachel sits quietly, then nods. Mrs. Crenshaw scoots to the edge of her seat, leans forward, and says in a conspirator's whisper, "Only a few people have access to the town council's archive—a couple of Shadow Grove's founding families. If you want to get more information about what's happening—unedited history that's been redacted from public record—you could ask Greg to take you there. It may save some time with your research; it may even have some information your father couldn't get his hands on."

Rachel averts her eyes to the carpet, fumbling with her hands. She wonders if her mother is capable of senseless violence now that she's developed a Hyde-personality. The *absolutely* that pops into her head, answering her unasked question, doesn't sit well with her. Infiltrating the Pearson house and using Greg to gain access to an archive Rachel hadn't known existed until now is Mrs. Crenshaw's way of pushing her in the right direction, helping her come to the bottom of the mysteries plaguing Shadow Grove. If Rachel's assumptions are correct, the archive could contain knowledge to help her mother return to a semblance of her old self and may even shed some light on the Night Weaver's location. The problem, she realizes, is that Greg isn't stupid enough to fall for pretty lies or hollow threats. They're far too similar and much too competitive *not* to recognize each other's usual tricks.

"While you're in the Pearson household, you should also check to see if Iris is behaving oddly," Mrs. Crenshaw says, interrupting Rachel's thoughts.

She needs a solid plan if she wants to convince Greg—a plan so simple he wouldn't expect her of anything untoward. If she goes to him and starts making demands, he'd never allow her into the archive.

Rachel grins as an idea takes shape in her mind. "It won't hurt to try, right? Not if it's for the greater good." She stands, ready to follow the new lead to the end. "Let's see if I'm lucky enough to pull this off. Do you have any other hints or tips?"

"Keep that umbrella of yours within reach," Mrs. Crenshaw says, her tone conveying a serious, secretive advisement rather than a general suggestion. "It may rain later on."

Rachel frowns, purses her lips, and nods. "Noted. Anything else?"

Mrs. Crenshaw makes a show of thinking as she reclines in her armchair. "Nothing comes to mind right now, but I'll let you know if that changes."

Chapter Eight
The Grim Realities Of Growing Up

Pearson Manor, the biggest colonial-styled residence in Shadow Grove's wealthiest suburban neighborhood, possesses an almost aristocratic quality due to its Georgian-inspired architecture. The Palladian grandeur with minor Baroque influences, better suited for the British countryside than a nowhere town in Maine, is further emphasized by a long gravel road, which is flanked by extravagant topiaries and well-kempt lawns with striking, sprawling gardens. It ends in a moderately-sized circular drive, surrounded by flowerbeds in full bloom.

As Rachel makes her way to the front of the house, where columns are topped with a decorative pediment, she repositions the rolled-up map under her arm and pushes her free hand through her loosely curled hair. Taking her time to cross the distance, she smooths down her cropped denim jacket and straightens her short, white sundress, which flaps carelessly in the slight breeze. The large black door with the brass knocker centered at eye-level comes into full view. The point of no return looms. With a deep breath, Rachel reaches out and uses the knocker to alert the Pearson family of her unannounced arrival.

She waits a while before trying again. Three knocks in quick succession.

A few agonizing moments pass before the door unlocks and is opened wide. Greg wears a startled expression. A small part of her revels in catching him off his guard. He's as dressed up as ever—faded jeans, a button-up shirt, blazer rolled up to his elbows, and hair perfectly coiffed. Another part of her dreads having to go through with the deceit.

"Did you get my texts?" He runs his gaze over the length of her body.

"What texts?" she asks, genuinely surprised by the question.

Greg composes himself and suspicion takes over. He folds his arms and leans with his shoulder against the entranceway. "Your mother came looking for you here yesterday after you disappeared with that foreign guy. She asked me to send you a text, so I did."

She remembers the text messages from the unrecognizable number. "That was you?"

Greg nods, dipping his eyes ever so faintly to look at her long, bare legs.

"Also, *why* would my mom come looking for me here?"

"Your guess is as good as mine," he says. His stormy gray eyes return to hers.

"That only explains the first text, though."

"If something happens to you, I'd have no academic competition whatsoever. Can you imagine how boring school would be if I was pretty much guaranteed the valedictorian title?" Greg says. "By the way, your mom's in the pool house with the rest of the mom club."

Rachel tilts her head and says, "What?"

"Do I need to spell it out for you?" The frustration obvious in his tone and the exhaustion is clear in his face. "There's a congregation of moms in the pool house," he says slowly, almost patronizingly. "Your mom is with them."

"Why?"

Greg shrugs. "They've been coming over here for months, sometimes more than once a day. Anyway, if you're not here about the texts or about your mom, then why are you here at all?"

Rachel glances at the edge of the rolled-up map protruding from underneath her arm. "Can I come in?" she asks, not wanting to tell him the half-truths while they are out in the open.

He sighs loudly, pushes away from the doorway, and steps aside to grant her access into the large house with its mezzanine foyer and oblong windows. A crystal chandelier hangs from the double-high ceiling, illuminating the entrance hall. Turn-of-the-century furniture is accented with expensive vases, tasteful paintings, and framed photographs. Rachel walks over to the traditional console table standing against the wall and studies the large photograph of the Pearson family. Mr. and Mrs. Pearson are both smiling happily, wearing casual beachwear, while Greg and his brother are making goofy faces at the camera. Greg was maybe nine or ten when the picture was taken, and his fraternal twin brother—Luke—was still alive.

"Are you done snooping or would you next like to see Luke's room?" Greg asks in a deadpan voice. "It's exactly the way he left it, you know? A holy shrine my mother can't bring herself to dismantle."

Rachel turns to look at him, wide-eyed and heart panging with sorrow. Once upon a time, the three of them had been inseparable. Luke was the more daring, sociable twin, who pushed Rachel and Greg to their limits. Greg, sensible and cautious, used to be the voice of reason.

She remembers the summer the three of them visited the

Pearson horse ranch, up in Winterville. They couldn't have been older than eleven at the time, and although Mrs. Pearson was well aware what type of trouble they often got themselves into in Shadow Grove, she never expected them to "borrow" horses and go on a joyride through the mountains. Rachel vividly recalls how Luke had pushed them to go farther and farther, away from any civilization in the sparsely populated town, while Greg had tried to get them to turn around.

Luke had gotten them well and truly lost in the wilderness that day.

When they had reached a brook near the foot of The Pinnacle, Luke hadn't hesitated to strip down to his underwear and jump in. Greg had been wary. It'd taken a lot of goading, some chicken clucking, and calling him a scaredy cat before he joined them in the bubbling brook. Splashing away, trying to catch fish with their hands, and sunning on a nearby rock. They had played for hours in the water while the sun moved across the sky.

When night drew closer, Greg had begun to worry about bears, mountain lions, murderers, and hypothermia. Typical Greg stuff.

Luke, the boy with the devil-may-care attitude, had said, *"Well, it won't be a worthy adventure if there isn't* some *danger, Greg."* He'd pulled out a lighter from his back pocket and flicked it until a flame had danced in front of his face, and the grin he'd been wearing grew larger. *"Let there be light."*

Greg had become infuriated with his brother's chilled outlook on life, and they had argued long and hard while the three of them had built a fire. Eventually, they had lain under the stars, talking about unimportant things, feeling invincible and free for the first time in their lives, until they'd fallen asleep side-by-side-by-side.

Luke had been the lynchpin that kept them together, the mastermind of all their escapades. So, when he died the year before they headed to high school, from meningitis of all things, Greg had withdrawn into himself. He didn't want anything to do with anybody in a social setting, least of all Rachel. She suspects it's because she reminds Greg of the brother he's lost, the antics they once had and the ones Luke will never be part of, but she can't be certain.

Then, during their sophomore year, Greg flourished into an ambitious social-climber and seemed to join every club Rachel belonged to—from the debate team to the track team—just to try and beat her at whatever she excelled at. It still boggles her mind trying to fathom what his motivations were for turning into such a prick toward her.

Against her better judgment, forgetting about the intricacies of her plan to persuade him to sneak her into the town council's archive, Rachel steps closer and raises her free hand to press her palm against his cheek. He doesn't recoil or look angry at the invasion of space. Instead, Greg closes his eyes and leans into her touch.

"I miss Luke, too," she says in earnest, stepping a bit closer. "He was my best friend."

Rachel drops the map to the floor. The hollow thump as it lands on the polished wooden floors is succeeded by the sound of subdued rolling. She raises her arm to wrap around Greg's neck, wincing from the pain persisting in her shoulder. Greg wraps his arms around her waist and pulls her tightly against him, resting his chin on her crown. The herbal smell of his cologne invades her nose as she rests her head against his shoulder. She tries not to let her emotions get the upper hand as her mind wanders to the what if's. How different would things have been if they had mourned Luke together?

They stand there for what feels like forever, holding on to one another for dear life.

"Before this gets any more awkward than it already is, you should either feel me up or let me go," Rachel eventually whispers to lighten the mood.

Greg's real laugh, not the diplomatic chuckle he employs in public, comes out as a breathy snigger. He releases her slowly and she puts some space between them. Rachel rolls her shoulder a few times to loosen up the bruised muscles, scowling from the obdurate pain.

"You okay?" he asks, studying her.

"Yeah, it's a battle bruise I picked up yesterday," she says, gradually lowering her arm. "That actually brings me to why I'm here." Rachel bends to retrieve the map. "Is the dining room free for us to use?"

"My mom is redecorating a few rooms in the house, the dining room and office being amongst them, so we'll have to use the desk in my study. Unless—" He pushes his hand through his hair, the indecisiveness obvious. "The kitchen is free if the idea of being alone with me in my apartment doesn't appeal to you."

"Should I be concerned about being alone with you in any type of setting?"

"No."

"So, what's the issue?"

Greg grimaces, shakes his head, and walks through the foyer. He turns into a long corridor, which branches off to the guest toilet and a storage closet and ends in an adjoining bachelor apartment.

Rachel walks into the apartment's open-plan living room where a black leather sofa is situated in front of the mounted flat-screen TV. Beneath the TV, game consoles are displayed in the chrome and glass entertainment unit. Rows of games line the open drawer, categorized by genre and alphabetized by title. A granite kitchen island separates the living room from the kitchenette, where two barstools are stationed. Through a narrow hallway that leads out of the living room, three doors stand open. Two, she knows, are bedrooms, and the other is a full bathroom.

"When did you move in here?"

"A few years ago," Greg says, opening one of the kitchen cupboards. "Do you want something to drink?"

"It depends on how good your coffee-making skills are," she says, walking over to the kitchen island and setting the map on the cold surface.

Greg looks over his shoulder and blindly takes out a glass mug. "I convinced my mom it was time for her to get a new coffee machine, so I liberated the old one."

"In that case, I'll have a coffee, please." Rachel leans on the island and looks around the kitchenette. All the necessary appliances are present—fridge, stove, microwave, coffee pot. "No dishwasher?" she asks.

"I come from money, but I don't rely on it as heavily as people think," he says, hauling over a Tupperware container. "Choose your poison," he instructs and walks back to the fridge.

Rachel opens the container, which is filled with coffee capsules, and pokes around to find a flavor. She chooses the caramel latte flavor and sets the capsules on the granite island.

"The second text was because I worried you'd gotten hurt in the forest. I wasn't serious the other night about you going in there; you just rubbed me the wrong way."

Rachel finds Greg staring down at her, soda in hand. "Yeah, well, I wouldn't advise anyone else to go in there. Dougal and I were almost killed."

"I'm sorry," he says, picking up the capsules from the counter. He heads back to the coffee machine, which whirs to life as the water percolates and gathers. "Did you find anything? Maybe some trace of the missing kids?"

Rachel pushes the container aside and pulls the elastic band off the map she'd brought along. She spreads the paper across the island and uses the container to hold down one end. As Greg returns to her side, Rachel points out the approximate distance of their travels the previous day. "We didn't even go in a third of the way," she says. "We also didn't find any clues relating to the kids, but they're in there. I'm sure."

He exhales through his nose. "Do you want me to rally the troops and send them to their deaths?"

"No, but I do need your help."

"I'm not Luke, Rachel," he says in a firm tone, pointing at the forest on the map. "That place scares me senseless for reasons I can't explain. Only a fool would go in there thinking they'll come out alive."

"I'm not a fool and I'm not asking you to go in there," she says, mimicking his tone. "Leave the actual rescuing to me and Dougal. We will retrieve the kids from the forest when the time comes, but we can't make any rescue attempts until we have enough information. That's why I'm here. I need your help with the research."

"What research?"

Rachel tells him the facts she's gathered during her independent investigation, omitting anything remotely unbelievable so he won't laugh her off. The others may have mentioned some type of bogeyman stalking the town, but there's no knowing if he would accept it as truth. She answers his questions as they come up, nothing too intrusive but important nonetheless, like how she knows this unpleasant history of Shadow Grove is cyclical and from where she's gotten her information. Rachel can see him contemplate her words. They might've grown apart over the years, but Greg still loves solving problems, even more than she does.

"Unfortunately, the library books are riddled with made-up history about our town, and my dad's journals are incomplete. I have no idea where to find unedited historical accounts pertaining to the era, and without it I can't verify my assumptions." Rachel sighs and takes a sip of her coffee, which he'd brought over. "I can't go into the forest without knowing what we'll be up against."

He sits quietly, contemplatively, before he says, "You've heard about the town council's archive, haven't you?"

"Maybe."

More silence. "Okay," he says. "I'll see what I can do, but there are two conditions." Greg holds up two fingers to emphasize his terms.

"Of course," Rachel says in a matter-of-fact tone, earning a shrewd grin from Greg. "What are your conditions?"

"The stuff I get my hands on can't leave this house. You'll have to come do the research here."

"Doable," she says, nodding in agreement. "What's the other

condition?"

His grin evaporates and he lowers his hand, spreading his fingers out on the granite island. He averts his gaze, a frown forming on his forehead. A battle is waged behind his stormy eyes. She waits patiently for his words to be formulated.

"I need you to find out what's been happening with our mothers. They're acting … odd," he says without making eye contact. "Today, I've already gotten three texts from girls attending Ridge Crest High who say their mothers cleared out their closets. What the hell do they expect me to do about it? I've got enough trouble dealing with my own mom these days, not to mention everyone's looking my way to find the missing kids." His frown deepens. "Can you help me with the mom club?"

Behind him, through the kitchen window, she sees the numerous gray-clad women exiting the pool house. Rachel knows her mother would soon see her car parked outside, and she'll either text to find out why she's here or come looking for her in person.

"We have a deal," she says, lifting the coffee mug to her lips and swallowing the remainder of her drink. She fishes her phone out of her jacket pocket and quickly types in Mrs. Crenshaw's number. She holds up a finger to Greg, signaling for him to wait before she lifts the phone to her ear and listens as the call goes through.

"Nancy Crenshaw speaking," Mrs. Crenshaw answers.

"Mrs. Crenshaw, I need you to do me a big favor, please."

"Yes?"

"Remember how I told you this morning my mom threatened to clear out my closet?" Rachel asks.

"Yes."

"Well, I'm going to do something crazy and force her to retaliate in earnest. Would you be so kind as to go into my room and save whatever clothes you can from my closet? I'll try and keep her occupied for as long as I can. Thirty minutes tops." Rachel glances at the kitchen window again and sees her mom and Mrs. White walking out of the pool house together.

This is a new, unforeseen development.

Jenny Cleary and Rebecca White have been rivals since high school, back in the 1990s. Rebecca—who happens to be the notorious Vince Henderson's younger sister—used to steal Jenny's boyfriends through spreading gossip and telling lies. Apparently, things got really bad between them when Rebecca set her sights on Jason White.

Rachel has heard the story before, about how her mom had been going steady with the captain of the football team for close to two years when suddenly, two days before their senior prom, Jason White dropped her like a piece of toast—butter-side down. In steps Liam Cleary, the slightly dorky but always sweet boy who'd been pining over Jenny ever since they were in middle school, to save the pretty cheerleader from humiliation. Rachel knows her parents loved each other deeply, had witnessed it firsthand, but she also knows Jenny Cleary despised Rebecca White for what she'd done.

Seeing them together definitely doesn't sit well with Rachel.

"Sweetie? Hello, are you still there?" Mrs. Crenshaw's voice interrupts her musings.

"Sorry. Yes, I'm here."

"Anything you want me to save in particular?"

"Just take what you can and hide it for me at your house, please. Also, keep your sewing machine at the ready, because I'm going into full rebel-mode for however long it takes to get my mom back," Rachel says.

Mrs. Crenshaw laughs. "Okay, dear. Be careful."

"See you soon." Rachel ends the call and stands up from the barstool. She places her hand over Greg's hand and smiles. "I'm sacrificing a lot by doing this. In fact, my whole wardrobe is on the line here, so you'd best keep up your end of the bargain or I swear I'll make you regret it."

Confusion crosses his expression. "What are you up to?"

Rachel leads him to the sofa, before gesturing for him to sit. He does as he's told, though she's sure it's only because he's not been able to put two-and-two together yet. She walks over to the apartment's door and opens it a crack, listening for any sign of the women. Some muffled conversation comes from the belly of the manor. Rachel rushes back to the sofa.

"Aside from losing her fashion sense, what other odd behavior has your mom displayed?" she asks, sitting down beside him.

"Nothing. Absolutely nothing," Greg says. "*What* are you doing, Rachel?" he repeats, watching her as she takes off her jacket and unbuttons the first couple of buttons on her dress.

"I'm staging a shocking scene for our parents to walk in on," she says. "Take off your shirt."

"*What?*" he drags the word out, still unmoving.

"Stop worrying and do what I ask." She tosses her jacket aside carelessly, kicks off her shoes, and unbuttons one more button for good measure. Then, Rachel lifts her hands to her head and musses her hair.

Greg grumbles under his breath as he pulls off his shirt and drops it onto the floor. "People are going to talk. I hope you know that."

"You're far too worried about what people say," she responds, assessing his torso from her position. Smooth skin, lean and muscular physique. Oh, yes, Greg Pearson certainly has grown up. Whether he's realized it himself, however, Rachel doesn't know. Greg keeps quiet about his romantic life in general so she can't use it against him—the same tactic Rachel has employed during her high school career.

"You do have a plan, right? This isn't one of your tricks to get back at me for some reason?" Greg asks.

"Mrs. Crenshaw says the mass hysteria of 1811 ended with the lynching of the mayor. My thinking is this: if we can focus our mothers' energies on preventing teenage promiscuity, then maybe we can save a life or two. When this stunt is over, and I'm being dragged out of your house, just get on the WhatsApp group and inform everyone that they should suck up to their parents by following the new rules and doing chores or whatever—"

"That'll go down well," he interrupts Rachel.

"*Anyway,*" Rachel continues. "Form a fake Bible study group, something our moms will approve of, so I can have access to your house again. Like I told Mrs. Crenshaw, I'm going full-rebel, and my mom's probably going to do everything in her power to make me change my ways. Or so I hope."

Greg sighs. "Is there any specific information you need me to obtain?"

"Everything you can find about the kids that went missing during the Eerie Creek Sawmill saga. My dad's journal mentioned it as going on for about two years before the fire broke out. If you can find some info about the mass hysteria of 1811, that'll help. Oh, and any references regarding the Night Weaver will be much appreciated—that's a personal request by the way."

He nods before looking her up and down. "Have you done this before?"

"Staged a compromising scene?"

"I don't mean a simulated version," Greg says.

"You mean to ask if I've ever *been* in a compromising position?" she clarifies. Greg gives a tiny shrug. "I've fooled around, but nobody's ever walked in," Rachel says. "You?"

"My mom's walked in on a few of my make-out sessions in the past," he admits. Greg inhales deeply. "If we're going to do this, we're doing it right. We are, after all, both over-achievers, so there's no use in us doing this halfheartedly." He reaches over and tugs down the sleeves of her dress until her bra is almost fully exposed. "Take one arm out of your sleeve," he instructs. Rachel does as she's told, feeling her bravado trickle away. "Now, scoot down and lie back."

"Who says *scoot* anymore?"

"I do. Now scoot." He stands up, making room for Rachel to lie down. He fumbles with her hair as she keeps her dress from running up too high. "Put this knee up." Greg points to her knee closest to the back of the sofa. "Put this foot on the floor."

Rachel rolls her eyes but doesn't argue.

"You look like you're ready to be ravished." Greg unbuttons his jeans and shakes his head. "If Luke could see us now."

"Are you kidding me? This would've been Luke's idea, and I'm sure it wouldn't have been for the sake of finding missing children or fixing our moms. I recall your brother having a sick sense of humor when it came to his pranks."

Greg grins. "Actually, I think you may be right."

Rachel smiles up at him. "You ready?"

He clears his throat, walks closer, and carefully climbs onto the sofa. After a bit of repositioning, he lowers himself over her, and whispers, "This is so weird." He pushes one hand underneath her body, resting his palm against the small of her back.

She shifts beneath him to get comfortable, drapes one arm around his neck, and places her other hand against his chest. "Just think about the kids."

He frowns. "That's even weirder."

"Not like *that*, jeez," she says in a high-pitched whisper. "We've both acted in the school plays, so think of this as a performance for a smaller crowd. Stay in character and all will be well."

Rachel sees his Adam's apple bob as he looks down at her. "Who'd you fool around with before?" he asks.

"I don't kiss and tell," she says. "We should probably make this thing seem more authentic now, especially seeing as my mom hasn't texted yet. Do you have any rules I should adhere to?"

"No. You?"

"Nothing below the belt, please. I require, at least, dinner and a movie for that type of action."

Greg chuckles, one of those real, breathy chuckles he hardly ever uses anymore. "I forgot how funny you are, Rach."

The faint *clickety-clacks* of shoes against wooden floors drift into the apartment, cutting their conversation short. The footsteps don't appear in a hurry, but they definitely seem to be heading toward the apartment.

Rachel nods at Greg, ready to give her mother the shock of her life. She just hopes Mrs. Crenshaw's doing her part now and saving what clothes she can from being thrown out.

"Compartmentalize and kiss me like you mean it or none of

this will look real," Greg whispers. He leans down and presses his lips against hers.

Rachel parts her lips to deepen the kiss and pulls him close enough so there's almost no space between them. She closes her eyes, tuning out his roving hands and focuses on the next step of her plan, but the pleasant sensations resonating in her core and quickly spreading throughout her entire body keep interrupting her thoughts. She moves with him, rubbing up against him for that *genuine* look they're hoping to achieve. Her fingers travel up the back of his neck and push into his hair. Greg's mouth moves away from her lips for a millisecond, and she inadvertently sighs, before he returns to muffle the sound. She feels him smile and the rumble of laughter that he quashes reverberates against the hand she's pressing against his chest.

What she expects to hear is a shout of outrage, maybe an argument where hurtful insults are thrown around. What she expects is for their mothers to act like mothers and discipline them for their wayward behavior.

Mrs. Pearson, however, simply says in an apologetic tone, "Oh, dear. I forgot to knock again."

Greg pulls away in mock surprise, a worthy thespian if ever there was one, and turns to look at his mother standing in the doorway.

"Mom! Some privacy, please." His discreet sternness effectively conveys the fake humiliation and disbelief anyway.

Rachel shifts beneath him to look at Mrs. Pearson, who wears a dopey smile plastered across her face, staring through the two teenagers. Beside the washed-out woman—and yes, Mrs. Pearson does look bleaker and thinner and unlike her usual trophy-wife self—Rachel's mother stands with wide, almost glazy eyes, wearing a similar smile.

"I'm sorry for bothering you, but Mrs. Cleary just wanted to say she'll be home late tonight, Rachel. Isn't that right, Jenny?"

"It sure is, Iris." Rachel's mother laughs, sounding like some drugged-up TV game show hostess. "Honey, Mrs. Pearson was kind enough to invite you to stay over tonight. Isn't that nice?"

Greg glances down at Rachel and mouths, "What's going on here?" as if this is a math problem she has a better grasp on.

"What do we say, Rachel?" her mother asks, still smiling broadly at her.

"Thanks, Mrs. Pearson?" Rachel's unsure what else to say—she certainly doesn't know what more she can do to get a rise out of them. Her eyes dart between the two women in their identical dresses and wearing their matching smiles, looking like they couldn't be happier with their not-as-advertised Stepford lives.

"Now, you two have fun," Mrs. Pearson says a tad too cheerfully, shooing Rachel's mother out of the apartment's living room and shutting the door firmly behind them once they're outside.

Dumbstruck, Rachel stares at the space where their mothers had stood, their unseeing eyes already haunting her thoughts. This was not the intended outcome of her stunt, not by a longshot.

"What just happened?" Greg asks in a whisper. "My mom flipped when she walked in on me and Maggie Dawson a few months ago. It rained hellfire and brimstone for a week. Now, she's invited you over to stay the night?"

Rachel grimaces as she drags her gaze from the door and meets his eyes. "Maggie Dawson? *Really?*"

"She's a nice girl. Nicer than most," Greg says, shrugging.

She sniggers. "That's slightly offensive." Rachel looks back to the closed door, her humor evaporating. "It's like they've been brainwashed to see only what they want to see. I mean, your hand is clearly on my boob," she says, and glimpses down to where his hand is still cupping her breast through the white padded bra. "That reminds me, Greg. You can remove your hand now."

Chapter Nine
Mother Knows Best

Rachel's mother doesn't explode into anger when she returns home that night. Words like *slut* and *whore* aren't thrown around like they hold some magical power. There is no lecture about how bad sex before marriage is—the automated argument parents tend to use when it comes to these types of things. The unsubtle mention of how God punishes sinners isn't mixed into casual conversation as an indirect warning either. Rachel expected her mother to stomp up to her bedroom in a fit of rage, throw open the closet doors to chuck her remaining clothes and shoes into garbage bags, but nothing as absolute as that occurred. Instead, an uncaring and obstinate Rachel had to watch as her mother carefully unpacked the half-empty closet into a box marked *Goodwill* while chatting cheerily about her day.

The less Rachel seems to care about what's happening, the happier her mother becomes.

When the closet is empty and the box is removed from her room, Jenny returns with five dresses and their matching sensible shoes, all in Rachel's sizes. The smile her mother wears—seemingly proud if Rachel's eyes aren't deceiving her—is the creepiest part of the entire exchange, which says a lot. She looks at the dresses, identical to the ones her mother wears these days, and tries not to lose her cool at the shapeless, ugly garments. If she'd been forced to wear these potato sacks last year, she definitely wouldn't have lost her V-card to an undeserving Jules—*Jules. Just Jules*—while they were spending the Christmas break at her aunt's house in Bangor. Then again, clothes—or the lack thereof—hadn't really mattered at the time.

Rachel puts on a dress, which hangs to the middle of her calves and reaches to the top of her neck, and listens to her gushing mother. There isn't much more she can do.

Her mother loses steam eventually, but only after she's snapped a few pictures of Rachel in her horrible new attire. Jenny heads to her bedroom, because 'too much excitement isn't good before bedtime', leaving Rachel alone once more.

Rachel takes the four dresses out of her closet, hangers and all, and makes her way downstairs. She finds her phone where she'd left it behind a throw pillow and unlocks the screen. No new text messages, no new emails, only a few inconsequential WhatsApp updates—Greg apparently hadn't seen the need to follow through on her request due to their plan's failure. After quickly copying and pasting Greg's number into a new contact, she makes her way to Mrs. Crenshaw's house for a meeting—this time with a whole other objective in mind.

Mrs. Crenshaw used to work in one of Shadow Grove's now-defunct factories as a fashion designer, between the late 1970s and early 1990s. She still has a keen eye for fashion, is an impressive tailor, and understands how to work under pressure.

Operation Fashion Police can't wait until the morning.

Rachel lets herself into Mrs. Crenshaw's house, hearing the ancient TV crackling in the living room. "Mrs. Crenshaw?" she calls, not wanting to frighten the poor woman by arriving unannounced.

"What are you wearing?" Mrs. Crenshaw says in way of greeting, perched on her armchair when Rachel walks into the living room.

Dougal, who's lying on the sofa, twists around and laughs when he sees Rachel. "Och! Ye look … ye look … like a disgraced nun," he howls through the laughter.

Mrs. Crenshaw's hand moves to her mouth to muffle her snickers and giggles. "I'm sorry, dear, but he's not wrong."

Rachel sneers and dumps the dresses onto the back of the empty armchair. "After the day I've had, forgive me for not finding any of this funny," she says, crossing her arms.

Mrs. Crenshaw reaches over and pulls the top dress into her lap to inspect it. "My mother wouldn't have worn these travesties."

The disgust is a justified response. The fabric is heavy, has no ventilation, and feels terrible against a person's skin.

Mrs. Crenshaw turns to Rachel and says, "I take it you would like some alterations made?"

"If you could shorten it and give it an open back—" Rachel tugs at the stiff sleeves, which make her feel like she is in a straitjacket. "Maybe do something with these sleeves? I'll do the rest."

"What's the rest?"

"Bedazzling it to death comes to mind," Rachel says, turning her nose up at the ghastly dress. "What do you think?"

"I think you should leave it to me. Your mother's going to have a fit anyway; let's not overdo it with sparkles."

"I doubt it," Rachel mutters, walking around the armchair and plopping down. "Greg and I staged a scene for our moms to walk in on, and we went all out. His hands were everywhere. We were kissing like it's nobody's business. Now, guess what happened when they came across our steamy performance? Zero. Zilch." She exhales loudly, frustrated with her failure. "Mrs. Pearson went so far as to ask me to stay the night."

"Should I say something parental on the matter to make you feel better?" Mrs. Crenshaw asks.

Rachel puffs out her cheeks like a disgruntled child, mumbling, "It won't be the same."

"Well, I tried." Mrs. Crenshaw stands with a groan, clutching the dress. She grabs the rest of Rachel's new wardrobe and says, "Get comfortable, Rachel. This may take a while." The old woman shuffles into the dining room, mumbling about how nobody in their right mind wears Crimplene anymore and how forcing a child to wear that type of nonsense is cruel and unusual punishment.

"I love you, too, Mrs. Crenshaw," Rachel shouts after her.

"You'd better."

Dougal chuckles as he stretches out on the sofa, keeping his eyes glued to the grainy TV screen.

"How was your first day at the new job?" Rachel asks.

"Good, thanks," he says. "Nan said ye came over lookin' for me."

"Yes. I got a visit from our mutual friend last night," she says. Dougal perks up, the humor fading from his expression. "She calls herself the Night Weaver."

He sits upright, eyes wide. "Aye. And?"

"She has a sentient cloak with ghost faces staring up at her, worshiping her with their eyes. I suspect those are her victims. It's all super narcissistic."

"And?" he says, fishing for more information.

"She said if I wanted the kids back, I should go get them, so that's what I'm going to do," Rachel says. "Wanna help me save some children from an egotistical, blue-faced monster?"

"Aye, it'll be a good way to get my blood pumpin'," Dougal says, grinning.

"We'll have to work with Greg Pearson, though."

Dougal's smile vanishes and he groans as he lies back on the sofa. "I leave ye alone for one day and yer already makin' googly eyes at a hurdie. How'd ye get by before I came along, eh?"

"What does 'hurdie' mean?"

"Doesn't matter," Dougal says, smirking. "What matters is that I did some diggin' of my own today. Asked old Joe Farrah—" He clears his throat and says, "Joe Farrow, about the town a wee bit. He's a talkative man if he likes ye."

"Yes, and what did Joe tell you?"

"For starters, he told me not to go into some or other cave. He said folks tend to go in one way and come out another," Dougal answers. "Ye ken what cave he's talkin' about?"

"No. I just know about the Siren's Pit located on the Other Side. The pit's one of those verbal histories that gets around every now and then, revolving around yet another tragedy that befell Shadow Grove during its formative years. I told you about it, didn't I?" she asks.

"Aye, ye did."

"What did Joe say about the cave?"

Dougal shrugs, his eyes pinned on the TV, but slowly drooping as exhaustion seems to take him under. "Not much more than that, but he did mention folks have been actin' strange lately."

Mrs. Crenshaw's sewing machine comes to life in the dining room, hammering out a rhythmic *rat-tat-tat-tat.*

"Interesting," Rachel says, tapping her fingers against the armrest. "Did Joe mention any names?"

"No," Dougal says. "Do ye think it's connected?"

"At this point, Dougal, I think everything wrong with this town is connected. The kids going missing, the adults acting strange, the forest coming alive, you name it."

"Don't go lookin' for trouble without me," he says, beginning to drift off. "Yer a capable lass, but Nan'll castrate me if ye get hurt. The old witch isn't one to forgive or forget."

"Go to bed, Dougal," Rachel says, pushing herself to her feet. Dougal's eyes snap open and he blinks a few times. "Go to bed before you fall asleep on the sofa. Neither your grandmother nor I can carry you." She points to the staircase. "Move."

"Yer worse than Nan, ye know?" he mutters, getting up.

"Yes, I know." Rachel moves around the armchair to join Mrs. Crenshaw in the dining room. "Goodnight."

Dougal says goodnight in passing, dragging his feet as he heads upstairs to his bedroom. Meanwhile, Rachel steps into the brightly lit, outdated dining room where a six-seater dining table is surrounded by unmatched chairs. A white crocheted tablecloth is draped over one of the chairs, while the battered metal cookie bins—holding all of Mrs. Crenshaw's sewing supplies—stand on the scratched surface of the table. The sewing machine's needle never ends its work as Rachel takes a seat beside the old woman and pulls an open cookie bin closer.

"Where's that grandson of mine?"

"I sent him off to bed," Rachel says, poking through the various laces and ribbons stored in the bin. The sewing needle stops hammering and Mrs. Crenshaw pulls the dress away from the machine. She evaluates her handiwork before grabbing a pair of scissors to cut the thread. "You'd tell me if my theories about the kids were wrong, right? About there being more to this story than what meets the eye?"

"I would," Mrs. Crenshaw says with a needle resting between her lips.

"Why don't you help us?"

"I am helping, even if you think I'm not."

Rachel finds a roll of shocking pink ribbon and places it on the table. "This will brighten up those drabs."

"Sweetheart," Mrs. Crenshaw says with a sigh, setting the dress down on her lap.

"Okay, no pink ribbon then." Rachel returns the roll of ribbon to the cookie bin.

"The ribbon is fine, Rachel," the old woman says. "You've heard the saying about teaching a man to fish, so he'll be fed for a lifetime?"

"Yes."

"It's like that. If you and Dougal don't learn to spot the signs and handle this crap by yourselves, Shadow Grove is doomed," Mrs. Crenshaw says. "I'm not going to be around forever, you know?"

Rachel drops her gaze back to the cookie bin. She hates it when Mrs. Crenshaw brings up her mortality, hates the idea of coming over to the Fraser house one day and not seeing the witty busybody doing something borderline insane before she drags Rachel into the thick of things. Who else would willingly help Rachel undermine her mother by staying up the whole night only to redesign an entire wardrobe? Nobody in Shadow Grove, that's for sure. It's more than mischief tying Rachel and Mrs. Crenshaw together. It is friendship and family and years of teaching each other skills. Mrs. Crenshaw wouldn't know squat about how to operate a cell phone or a computer if Rachel hadn't shown her. Rachel, in turn, wouldn't have a clue about catering an entire Thanksgiving dinner if Mrs. Crenshaw hadn't taught her.

"Save your tears for my funeral, dear. I'm not dying anytime soon," Mrs. Crenshaw says, getting back to work. "I'm turning this gray dress into short-shorts and a crop top. Pick out some lace for it, maybe something with mini pompoms."

Rachel swallows her premature grief and says, "Ooh, it sounds hippie-chic. I like it already."

Mrs. Crenshaw grins and pins the dress off along the area she wishes to cut. A while later she says, "If something does happen to me before my intended time, I need you to look after Dougal. He's a good boy, even if he believes differently. Keep the border of the forest clear, don't let anyone pass by the sign, and make sure Dougal's other cousins don't enter this house ever. They'll steal anything of worth and then some."

"Are you leaving everything to Dougal?"

The old woman glances at Rachel. "Is there something you wanted?"

"No, no. I'm just curious. Sorry."

"Except for my late husband's remaining assets and a few other things, I explicitly mention in my last will and testament, Dougal will receive my entire estate. Don't let his cousins in here, Rachel. You scare the money-grubbing trailer trash off my property with my shotgun or I'm going to haunt you for the rest of your life."

With wide eyes, Rachel says, "Sheesh. That's your family,

Mrs. Crenshaw. Whatever happened to *flesh of my flesh* and *blood of my blood—*?"

Mrs. Crenshaw interrupts with an indignant snort. "In some cases, family is an overrated concept. My son, Matthew made a mess of his life when he left Shadow Grove. He got into drugs and spent most of his adult life in and out of prison. His wife isn't the sharpest tool in the shed, and their children are … Well, money-grubbing trailer trash and convicted felons is the only way I can describe them. I love them, don't get me wrong, but they would squander my estate."

"But if Dougal gets everything, won't they take him to court and try to get a slice of the pie?" Rachel asks.

"Oh, they're going to try. Thankfully, I have a good lawyer with clear instructions, a grandson with a warrior's heart, and you." Mrs. Crenshaw smiles at Rachel. "You're my secret weapon."

"I don't follow."

"You'll figure it out when that fateful day dawns," Mrs. Crenshaw says, finding her measuring tape. "Okay, stand up so I can see how short I need to make the crop top. We don't want to show the world Greg Pearson's toys."

Rachel barks an unexpected laugh.

For most of the night, they work together on redesigning the dresses into fun, fabulous, and wearable pieces that will hopefully irk her mother so much she will return to her former self. The gunmetal horror show becomes a sleeveless two-piece with colorful ribbons crisscrossing the bodice and a billowing mini skirt, thanks to repurposing an old petticoat gathering dust in one of Mrs. Crenshaw's unused bedroom closets. The khaki dress turns into a playsuit with an open back and deep pockets. The ochre-colored dress turns out to be the most difficult one to save, so they leave it for another time—*If I'm being honest, I doubt even the Lord Almighty can save this one.* The black dress is shortened, the sleeves are removed, the neckline is lowered, and voila. Rachel has a perfect little black dress. It takes them hours to fix those dresses up, of course.

Just after midnight, a red-eyed Rachel leaves with her updated clothing while Mrs. Crenshaw stands on the porch and watches her cross the dark, desolate road. Rachel sneaks inside her house, where the lights still illuminate the interior with their energy-saving yellow glow and waves goodnight to her elderly friend. Mrs. Crenshaw signals from afar for Rachel to lock the door, gesturing the motion in the air. Rachel nods, closes the door, and bolts it shut. She heads upstairs quietly, switching off lights as she goes, and turns toward her room when she reaches the second-story landing.

A flirtatious giggle comes from the other side of the house.

Rachel stops in her tracks and slowly turns to look toward her mother's bedroom. She waits for a minute, hears nothing else, and decides it must have been her imagination. Before she can turn and head for her soft bed, however, a low whisper comes, breathy and mysterious. Rachel frowns as she stares at the bedroom door, unsure if she should go check on her mom.

She inhales a lungful of air and walks to the main bedroom, the door only partially closed. Knowing this is an invasion of privacy, and certain she shouldn't intrude on her mother's personal life, Rachel still presses the palm of her free hand against the wood and pushes. Miraculously, there are no creaking hinges to indicate the intrusion.

The dark bedroom is illuminated by one of Rachel's old

nightlights, a bluish glow reflecting from a plastic butterfly against the wall's electric outlet. Her mother's back is turned to her where she sits on the bed, legs folded underneath her. Beside her mother, a shadowy silhouette sits closely. The broad-shouldered figure seems familiar enough to make Rachel's heart skip a beat and allow a sense of elation to creep up on her, but it simply can't be. She squeezes her eyes shut and regulates her hope, because there's no way what she's seeing is real. When she opens her eyes again, the figure is still there beside her mom.

Her mother throws her head back and laughs with abandon like she's just heard a joke.

Through her snorting, she says, "I remember."

Rachel is about to step into the room when the silhouette turns its head and she sees the outline of her father's face. The sudden onset of grief shatters her heart into a million pieces.

"Daddy?" she chokes on her barely audible whisper.

The shadowy figure bolts forward with unnatural agility, standing in front of Rachel, while two pinpricks of iridescent light shine brightly from where its eyes should be. The look is filled with malicious intent, weighed down with a *feeling* resonating in the same place her conscious resides.

In the back of her mind the little voice, one not belonging to her personal Jiminy Cricket, says loud and clear, *"You are undeserving of acting as a witness to this visitation. Leave."*

Those eyes start radiating blinding white, pulsating with what can only be described as a warning, while the rest of the figure remains an indefinable black. It opens its mouth and reveals needlelike teeth, illuminated by thousands of microscopic lights shining from within its unending throat.

Rachel stumbles back, understanding the warning without

ever hearing it expressed in words.

Leave now or your mother will suffer the consequences.

She backs up the way she came, eyes pinned to the main bedroom door until she reaches the staircase. Still clutching the clothes, she rushes downstairs and grabs her car keys from the glass bowl in the living room. Rachel makes her way to the front door in a few long strides, unbolts the locks, and runs across the road to seek sanctuary at the Fraser house.

Her knocks are loud, frantic, beats.

She yells, "Mrs. Crenshaw. Mrs. Crenshaw. Mrs. Crenshaw."

Inside, heavy footsteps run down the stairs, too heavy to belong to the wispy old woman, and the locks of the front door slide open. The door swings inward and Dougal nearly loses his balance as Rachel pushes her way inside.

Mrs. Crenshaw stands at the top of the stairs in her nightdress. "What is it?" she asks, a concerned edge to her question.

"I—" Rachel can't explain what she's seen without sounding like a complete basket case. She has no idea how she knows the creature in her mother's bedroom has somehow, some-freaking-way, convinced a highly intelligent woman that it's her deceased husband. She slowly formulates the words to make her account sound plausible, but nothing comes out of her mouth.

"Dougal, go check on—"

"*No!*" Rachel cuts Mrs. Crenshaw off and almost knocks Dougal over as she throws an arm out to stop him from leaving. "There's something in my house," she says slowly. "I think my mom invited it in, but I *know* if you go in there and disturb them while they're doing whatever it is they're doing, it'll turn on her."

Mrs. Crenshaw's brow furrows, while Dougal raises an

eyebrow.

"Bolt the door, Dougal," she says, coming down the stairs. "Rachel, the Sky Room is yours to use for as long as you want. The clothes I raided from your closet this afternoon are already in there, so go put on some pajamas and go to sleep." She moves toward the kitchen, the shuffle more of a slide-slide-step as she hurries.

"What if it comes in here?" Rachel asks.

"Nothing unwanted is coming into my house. Not tonight. Not ever. I promise," Mrs. Crenshaw says over her shoulder. "Now go to bed, both of you."

Chapter Ten
Fester

Rachel's unceremonious banishment doesn't deter her from sneaking back to the MacCleary house the following morning. Right after her mother leaves for work, she jogs across the road, glancing at the forest as she goes. It'd been eerily quiet since Sunday's hellish exploration. Quiet, yes, but the forest isn't asleep. The forest doesn't sleep anymore.

It has never slept, you silly girl.

She mentally shakes herself back to the present as she steps onto the lawn. The profound nihilistic gloom, which seems to cocoon the entire property in a decaying membrane, gives her pause. Rachel's body responds as all the telltale signals of fear kick into overdrive. Her hands become ice cold, her breathing becomes deeper and more rapid, and the increased heart rate causes her blood pressure to spike. She trembles, forcing her tightening leg muscles to loosen up as she moves up to the porch. The closer she gets to the front door, the heavier the weight of nothingness becomes. The void sticks to everything like warm clingfilm.

Cautious, Rachel opens the front door and is instantly consumed with a terrible thought. What if she somehow loses herself in the vacuum?

Everything in her immediate view appears unchanged, but at the same time everything looks wrong.

"Daddy, if you're tuning in, I'd seriously appreciate a break right now," she says out loud, gathering her courage.

Rachel steps inside the house while her heart beats frenetically. When the midnight monster with deadlight eyes doesn't jump out at her, she makes her way up to her bedroom to pack a few extra things for the *hopefully* temporary stay with Mrs. Crenshaw—toiletries, pillow, laptop, chargers, her notebook, and a box full of her dad's journals. She hauls her meager possessions to the staircase, sets them on the floor, and glances toward the main bedroom across the hallway.

The door seems to pulse with energy, inhaling and exhaling. This significant contrast to the utter lifelessness of the rest of the house doesn't do anything to quell Rachel's worries.

It's alive but not … living.

She wants to investigate the anomaly, but common sense—and an almost unhealthy obsession with horror movies—forces her to pick up her box and turn away from the temptation. Today isn't the day to be a hero. She is wholly unprepared for what lies beyond the door, still too raw from losing her mother to whatever promises or lies she's been fed, and there is unfortunately no back up if things go south. No. Today is one of those days where it's best to tuck tail and run.

Rachel peers over the box, careful not to miss a step and fall, makes her way downstairs, and exits through the open front door. She pulls it shut behind her, more from habit than decency, and begins her trek back to Mrs. Crenshaw's house. As soon as she sets foot off the MacCleary property, the veil of dread lifts. The air tastes sweeter, the world seems brighter, and the despair vanishes.

Glad to be free of the morbid poison, she looks back on impulse.

"Infestations can spread," she whispers, halting her advancement. Rachel turns around and examines the air around the physical walls and roof, searching for some type of indication that all is not well on the inside. Aside from the general feeling, she sees nothing abnormal. The infestation is there, though, festering like an untreated sore. "Diseases can spread." The thought had come out of nowhere and washed away most inconsequential things swimming around in her head until only those three words remain. For some reason, the epiphany is overwhelmingly important in this particular moment. Because this *thing* is a disease, a nasty one that cannot go untreated. "I've been looking at this all wrong."

She pauses as one puzzle piece slips into another, and the broader picture starts to reveal itself. She's nowhere near to rescuing the children from their otherworldly captor—Rachel has no idea where to start her search for the Night Weaver—but as she's suspected this entire time, everything's connected. She's just been so obsessed with the symptoms she hadn't diagnosed the cause. Rookie mistake.

Without wasting further time, she continues her walk to Mrs. Crenshaw's house, pondering the revelation. She drops the box at the bottom of the staircase and rummages around for her notebook. As she searches, Rachel recalls seeing something strange in one of her father's journals—a name and number written in the corner of a page. She'd thought it an unrelated discovery at the time, due to the journal belonging to a teenaged Liam Cleary and because it came across as him finding the nearest piece of paper to write someone's contact details down. But *everything is connected.*

"You look like a woman with a plan," Mrs. Crenshaw says from the dining room's doorway. Rachel blindly carries out the search for the notebook, rummaging around as Mrs. Crenshaw's lip curls upward. "Care to share?"

"Diseases can spread if they're left untreated," Rachel says. She finds her notebook and pen, and quickly scribbles the words down over two pages, underlining the sentence several times for emphasis.

"Not to my house, it won't." Mrs. Crenshaw grins. "I do appreciate the sentiment, though."

Rachel doesn't respond. She places her notebook on the floor and continues her hunt, searching for the journal where she'd seen that name. What is it again? Something starting with an 'M' … Melissa? No, not Melissa. It's something else. Rachel finds the correct journal at the bottom of the box, pulls it out, and pages through to where the overuse of thick black marker obscures most of the entry's contents. In the top corner, written in block letters, the name waits—Misty Robins.

"Mrs. Crenshaw, have you ever heard of a Misty Robins?"

Mrs. Crenshaw's papery skin becomes almost translucent as the blood drains from her face. "I haven't heard that name in years," she says. "Listen, Rachel." She takes a wary step closer, halts, and continues, "What you're dealing with isn't as bad as it seems; it's a drop of trouble in an ocean of nightmares. Believe me, there are much more terrible things out there. So, whatever you do, don't call Misty Robins unless the apocalypse is upon us. That's your 'get out of jail free' card, your H-Bomb if there's no hope to be found. Do you understand?"

"Yes, but who is she?"

Mrs. Crenshaw shakes her head. "Misty is a weapon of destruction, not a cure. Focus on curing the disease. You already have everything you need to figure it out. Just use your brains." The old woman turns around and walks away, effectively shutting down Rachel's Q&A session.

For most of the day, Rachel sits in the Sky Room and works through more of her father's journals. Surrounded by cornflower-blue walls and white cumulus cloud murals, she reads more about Shadow Grove's historical triumphs and failures. It's a tedious chore, with little reward—a gamble if nothing else—but Mrs. Crenshaw has never been insincere when giving direction or advice. Rachel pushes through and absorbs as much information as she can possibly squeeze into her brain.

There isn't anything pertaining to the Night Weaver in the journals. There are, however, other interesting tidbits of information—vague references—which may become important later.

Greg texts her around midday, asking if she wants to go over to Pearson Manor and look at some of the information he's retrieved from the town council's archive.

Around fifteen minutes later, Greg ushers her inside the manor for the second time in as many days. Pearson Manor harbors a familiar emptiness, though, which had descended over the house since her last visit. An otherworldly vacancy, not entirely of the inhabitants' making, overwhelms her in an instant. The distinct feeling of being watched, faint but there nonetheless, accompanies the hollowness of the large house.

"Do you feel it, too?" Greg cautiously broaches the subject.

"Oh, yeah."

It takes her longer to notice the bags under Greg's eyes and the hopelessness he seems to carry on his shoulders. There's a sense of trepidation in the air, fearfulness laced with panic. She's sure it wasn't there the day before, and she's almost certain Greg hadn't looked so exhausted either. As she follows him through the manor toward his apartment, she wonders how far Mrs. Pearson is into her personal decline. It can't be *too* long, otherwise word would've spread around town by now.

Keep telling yourself that, Rachel.

"I regret to say, there wasn't much to find in the archive," Greg says, gesturing for her to enter his apartment first. "There were some records pertaining to the Mass Hysteria of 1811, a few mentions of the missing Eerie Creek Sawmill child laborers, but that's about it."

"Did you find anything about the Night Weaver?" she asks quickly, almost breathless with anticipation.

Greg closes the door behind them, turns into the apartment's short corridor, and says, "Yes, but what do you want with old folk legends?"

"I'd like to cover my bases and make sure nobody's hidden anything crucial in stories, songs, or poems. People often overlook the importance of those records," she says, following him into the second bedroom. The utilitarian office space, decorated only with a wall of books on one side and an L-shaped desk in the opposite corner, waits. A large file is neatly placed in the center of the desk, which contains a stack of printouts that are already labeled and color-coded for efficient researching. Two chairs—one a swivel desk chair, the other a run-of-the-mill wooden chair—stand at the ready.

"Nice," she says, glancing to the blind-covered windows.

"I don't like visual distractions in my study," he explains.

"Hey, I don't like using colored pens in my revisions. I get it," she says, taking a seat on the wooden chair. Rachel opens her saddle bag and removes her notebook. She places it on the table and searches for her pen. "Let's get to it, then."

"What exactly are we doing with all of this?"

"It's vital for us to establish a timeline. We need to figure out exactly where things went wrong if we want to understand *how* everything connects." Rachel writes down the most obvious 'first event'—eight-year-old Dana Crosby's disappearance, right after Christmas break—but scratches it out immediately. "The children going missing are a symptom of the disease, *not* the cause," she whispers, staring at the black ballpoint pen in her hand. "What's the cause?"

"How far back do we need to go?" Greg asks, opening the file. "Does Ms. Heely's peach cobbler play a part in the greater scheme of things?"

Shadow Grove's strangeness had only become a priority at Ridge Crest High when Tamsin Lansdale, the former Editor-in-Chief of the *Ridge Crest Weekly*, walked in on Ms. Annie Heely, the cafeteria lady, spicing the peach cobbler with a generous amount of rat poison. This was the same peach cobbler the cafeteria served at lunch to hundreds of students every week. It must've been going on for a while too, considering how many kids had been admitted to the hospital for food poisoning, or who'd stayed home because of stomach cramps the day afterward.

It's probably just one of those stomach bugs doing the rounds again. Bulltwang Bill's excuse enters her thoughts, riling her up anew.

One would assume the school would immediately dismiss

Ms. Heely to avoid some sort of legal dispute with worried parents. At any other school, in any other town, the principal and school board would have tried to distance themselves from a homicidal maniac who likes to poison children. Not in Shadow Grove. In this town, people like Ms. Heely are given the benefit of the doubt, even with indisputable evidence from a reliable witness.

Tamsin Lansdale hadn't had any of it, not when her reputation and a scholarship to Princeton University were on the line, so she'd set out to do an exposé on Ms. Heely.

How Tamsin learned about Ms. Heely's sketchy past, nobody knows. She claims a reliable source had fed her the information to fill in the gaps in her research. Nevertheless, the *Ridge Crest Weekly* ran a fantastic, albeit disturbing, article on Ms. Heely's life within a month of the peach cobbler incident. Turns out, not only had Ms. Heely been widowed thrice, but her dearly departed husbands had succumbed rather suspiciously, according to the autopsy reports Tamsin somehow got her hands on. Throw in a couple of dead stepsons and a few dead tenants over the years, who'd all keeled over while living under her roof and eating her food, and the pattern became clear.

Ms. Heely is a serial killer, a real-life Arsenic Annie.

Tamsin couldn't definitively prove anything. The article did, however, expressly state that the bodies needed to be exhumed in order to verify poison had been used. That said, there was more than enough evidence to get a judge to sign off on the exhumations if the sheriff's department cared to do their duty to protect and serve the citizens of Shadow Grove.

They didn't.

Ridge Crest High, on the other hand, had no other option

but to terminate Ms. Heely, thanks to the possible implications if the article had spread across the town's borders. But no criminal charges were ever brought against her. The information in the article, according to Sheriff Carter, was said to be conjecture at best and slander at worst.

The students of Ridge Crest High survived Arsenic Annie, but they were forever changed.

No longer did they see the pretty illusion specifically designed to fool people into thinking Shadow Grove was an idyllic little town with a rich history and a lovely view. No longer did they believe they were safe simply because the adults said so. No longer were they going to stand by and do nothing.

Rachel shakes her head. "I don't think so. Do you remember Tamsin Lansdale's exposé in the *Ridge Crest Weekly*? If she's right, and I'm pretty sure she is, Arsenic Annie's been killing off her nearest and dearest for decades."

"What about the Henderson tragedy? Should we go that far?"

Rachel recalls how Vince Henderson went insane one night and shot and killed his entire family before he turned the rifle on himself.

It was a burglary gone wrong; an isolated incident. Or so Bulltwang Bill claims.

"Maybe?" Rachel grimaces. "At first glance, the Henderson tragedy doesn't seem to fit into the timeline itself but could it have somehow acted as a catalyst." She recalls seeing Mrs. White—Vince Henderson's younger sister—at Pearson Manor with her mother the day before and decides the event *could* maybe be considered important. "Let's put it in just to be safe." She writes down *The Henderson Tragedy—2012* in her notebook.

"When did the mom club start gathering?"

"About a year ago," Greg says, already copying the same words into his notebook. "Maybe we should make a list of all the members and see if there are any patterns there?"

"I was going to suggest it in a minute," Rachel says, smiling. "How would you feel about a visual brain map against your wall? I think it'll help us get a better perspective of the big picture."

"Don't push your luck," he mutters, head bowed and hand moving with precision as he compiles the list.

When Greg finishes, he slides his notebook across the table for Rachel to copy. She studies the names for a good long while, swallowing back the bile pushing up into her esophagus. She tries not to panic. Rachel knows each name on the list, and every one of those seventeen women's lives—and their families' lives, by extension—are in grave danger.

"What's wrong?" Greg asks.

"I didn't think there were so many."

Rachel studies the names again, wondering what common denominator binds them together. They aren't all moms, as Greg had inadvertently led her to believe. Carla Andrews is only twenty-three years old, the youngest member of the lot, while Mrs. Jenkins is the eldest member at sixty-eight years. Age clearly isn't a factor. There are also a couple of women who live on the Other Side, which means social status isn't an issue either. Some of the women have careers, whilst others are home executives. Some have families and some don't have anyone.

"What do they have in common?" she asks.

"Grief," Greg automatically responds, paging through the color-coded file. "From what I understand, they've all lost someone."

Rachel gapes at him, both astounded and impressed. "How'd you figure that out?"

Greg turns his attention to her, the muscle in his brow twitching. "They were all part of a grief support group. After Luke died, your mom practically dragged my mom to the church's basement twice a week so she could talk about her feelings," he says. "Didn't you know?"

"*No,*" she drags the word out. What other secrets has her mother kept from her? Rachel frowns, diverting her gaze to look at the members' names again. "My mom was really in a grief support group?"

"For years," he says, rubbing salt into her new wound.

She meets his gaze, glaring daggers.

Fully composed, he continues, "A few weeks after your dad died, your mom had a nervous breakdown in our living room. She was angry at everything and everyone, but mostly she was angry at God. Luke and I learned a lot of colorful words that day, words I won't repeat. My mom somehow got her to calm down. Then she decided to call your aunt in Bangor, because your mom seriously needed to get away from Shadow Grove for a while, and right after that she set you up to live with Mrs. Crenshaw. I think you stayed there—"

"For nearly three months, I remember," Rachel says. "Mrs. Crenshaw told me my mom had to go look after my aunt, not the other way around. Why didn't *you* tell me?"

"Luke said I shouldn't, so I didn't." He shrugs. "You'd just lost your dad, Rach. The last thing either of us wanted was for you to feel like you'd lost your mom, too."

Rachel's eyes sting with tears as volatile emotions clog her throat. She inhales through her nose, picks at her thumb's cuticle again, and pushes the chaotic feelings away. What's the point of talking to people, of forging friendships and cultivating relationships, when everyone's always keeping secrets? She knows how death works, has witnessed it firsthand. She's been on both sides of the fence when it comes to the guy with the scythe. A hollow, euphemistic platitude, combined with guilt-ridden gratefulness hidden behind polite tears, is unavoidable when a traumatic event affects others. After all, social norm dictates a certain type of behavior in such circumstances, even if the general consensus screams: "Thank God it didn't happen to us." The receivers of these half-hearted, albeit well-meaning sentiments are typically expected to mourn with a semblance of dignity, to accept and move on because the world keeps turning.

Death has become a sanitized ritual; grief has an allotted timeframe.

Rachel is old enough to know all of this, so why do people continue to hide essential truths from her? She's not some dainty flower that wilts at a sharp look. She isn't sad—oh, she's far from sad—but there's a modicum of unhappiness coating her developing fury.

"I need to read what you found on the Night Weaver," she says.

Greg fumbles with the file, and hands her a thin packet of printouts. He doesn't say anything, hardly breathes beside her. She would've loved if he'd provoked her then if only to get rid of some of her anger, but Greg chooses his battles with infuriating proficiency.

She scans through the copies made of a timeworn, untitled text, where barely-decipherable handwriting covers nine pages, followed by a typed poem called, "On a Cave Called Black

Annis's Bower" by John Heyrick. A few reasonably accurate depictions of the Night Weaver follow, produced by unknown artists, seeing as nobody thought to sign their work.

Rachel goes back to the first page of narrow, cursive script. The words curl together and flow into one another as if the author had gone out of his way to torment the reader—or to dissuade them entirely. At first only words like *tainted, banished,* and *alone* stand out, promising a tantalizing tale with surreptitious undertones. Rachel hopes for a complete 'How To' guide on getting rid of the Night Weaver. She's not jaded enough to believe a simple story could hold all the answers, but it would've made for a nice change of pace. Rachel sighs, gets comfortable on the hard chair, and reads the document from the beginning. It's a slow process because the words sometimes seem to swim on the paper, but after some frustrating restarts, her eyes adjust to the handwriting.

> *The Night Weaver feeds on pain of the highest order; the grief of a mother, the sorrow of a widow, the distress of a child. It answers their call when the night feels darkest, when the despair has weakened them to such a degree that they've become tainted with misery and will do anything for just another moment with their lost loved ones.*

Misogynistic subtext aside, the passage gives Rachel the creeps. So, what? Mourning the dead will summon the Night Weaver? How unsympathetic. People across the world, for however long humans have existed, mourn their dead. Some cultures even celebrate the dead. They don't have a Night Weaver to contend with, do they? Rachel reads on:

> *The Night Weaver is a master manipulator, an adept liar, a demon banished from Orthega, the home of the fair folk. Her dwelling, often a cave of some kind, is no more than a lair of evil where she fattens her sacrifices for slaughter, and consorts with her unintended worshipers. She sends her Darklings to those she owes a debt, disguised as the ones they've lost. Alone, she can destroy a village, but with a large enough following the Night Weaver can destroy the world.*

She'd hoped her theory about the missing children being symptomatic of something far worse would be wrong, but this revelation—hard evidence, as it stands—confirms the adults as having been part of some sort of wrongdoing. Had her mother snatched an innocent kid off the street? Rachel's heart aches as she realizes it could very well be the case. Her mother, who'd raised her to know right from wrong, may have actually kidnapped another woman's child as an offering to the Night Weaver. For what? Midnight meetings with a monster whose shape somewhat resembles her father? Surely Jenny Cleary isn't gullible enough to believe the Night Weaver can bring people back from the dead.

"Oh, this *can* get so much worse," Rachel says, grimacing. She has no idea who her mom is anymore.

"Huh?"

"Don't mind me," she says offhand.

> *She possesses a great and horrible power, an ethereal artifact forged by Death's own hands when the Seven Worlds were still veiled in darkness. Beware her cloak, for it is as conscious as you and I.*

The next few pages go on to describe how the Night Weaver seduces her followers, how she torments her prisoners, and how easily she can corrupt a person into doing her bidding. It's dark and frightening, but Rachel pushes through, hoping the author is one of those "every cloud has a silver lining" people. There needs to be some way to put an end to the Night Weaver's reign of terror.

Beside her, Greg stands up and stretches his back.

"Coffee?" he asks.

"Please."

She watches him walk out of the room and returns to the document she's been clutching for the better part of an hour. Finally, she gets to the good part. A way to, at least, subdue the creature from Orthega.

> *It is a commonly known fact that the fair folk have a natural aversion to pure substances, be it salt or iron. Silver is often considered another way to deter these creatures, although some races are more prone to the side-effects than others. None who've had the misfortune of dealing with the Night Weaver has ever found a true method to put her down permanently. There are certain*

temporary ways, tested by either Fraser or MacCleary descendants, to trap her.

Greg sets a mug down on the desk in front of her and takes his seat. “Found anything interesting in there?”

“I’m getting to the good part now,” she says. “Thanks for the coffee.” Rachel shifts around on the chair to get comfortable again, reading as she takes sips of her coffee. As she nears the end of the document, the final sentence—written in large, properly spaced, block letters—catches her eye:

LIGHT WILL ALWAYS DEFEAT DARKNESS

If only.

Chapter Eleven
Suffer The Little Children

A plethora of questions run amok in Rachel's mind as she stares at the historical documents. The symptoms of being under the Night Weaver's influence, like the so-called mom club, eat away at her. The black letters against the crisp white pages are meaningless symbols, redundant information. She flips the page dutifully when it seems like an appropriate amount of time has passed.

If she says something and it turns out her theory is correct, Shadow Grove will be forever changed. Whatever trust there is between the townsfolk will disintegrate and suspicion will grow into an amorphous, hateful beast that devours people from the inside out. There's a good chance she'll be ostracized if she opens her mouth and reveals who's behind the kidnappings. The community may condemn her, may very well hold her responsible for ruining families in an entirely different way. Rachel's own mother will be torn away from her, doomed to spend a justifiable amount of time behind bars for her crimes—crimes Rachel prays her mother won't remember committing.

If she says nothing, the possibility of more kids going missing is indubitable. Innocent, unsuspecting children will be fed to the Night Weaver so selfish adults can reminisce about the good old days with monsters parading around as their loved ones.

Either way, how will she ever be able to live with herself?

More importantly: if she decides to tell someone about Shadow Grove's matriarchs' sinister hobby, to whom should she speak? Sheriff Carter isn't going to do jack about anything, and the deputies aren't exactly the sort who'll go against their superiors. The current mayor is a sniveling coward with more money than brains, while the town council is too keen on making sure people believe their illusion. The other aspect she needs to consider is how much she should reveal *if* she reveals anything. Nobody will accept a story about some blue-faced bogeywoman influencing the adults and stalking the quaint New England town's children. Nobody will believe the mom club being under the influence of some supernatural force. What can she do?

"We need a map of the town," Greg says, sounding none too pleased about it.

Rachel drags her gaze away from the papers she holds. "Why?"

"Because I suspect our moms have something to do with the missing children and if we incorporate both lists onto a map it'll be easier to see if I'm right." He pushes his hand through his hair and slumps back into his chair. She's rendered speechless at how fast he'd come to the same conclusion without taking into consideration the more fantastical part of the story. "I just can't figure out *why* they'd kidnap the kids in the first place or where they'd hide them."

"Have you thought about going into law enforcement after high school?" she asks.

Greg frowns. "No. Why? Were you thinking along the same lines?"

Rachel shrugs. "I'm not cop material—"

"I meant about our mothers being involved with the kidnappings," Greg interrupts.

"Yes ..."

"Damn it, Rach. How long have you been sitting on that piece of info?" He pushes himself out of his swivel chair, walks toward the door. He turns on his heel and paces back. "How can you expect me to trust you if I'm not shown the same courtesy?"

Rachel shifts in her chair to catch his eyes. "I haven't known long, and the only reason I haven't told you is because I've been preoccupied with listing the pros and cons of going public with this knowledge."

"It's our duty as decent human beings—"

"Get off it already," she snaps, standing. "Think about what'll happen if we go to Sheriff Carter and tell him our moms have been partaking in some good ol' kiddy snatching around town. *If* that moron even believes our insane-sounding story, what do you think will happen to them?"

He blanches. The internal conflict she's been struggling with is now a shared burden, one with dire consequences no matter what they do from here on out.

Rachel inhales deeply to calm herself, and says gently, "Exactly, so cut me some slack."

"You obviously know more than you're telling me. So, what's happening in Shadow Grove?" he asks, dead serious.

She bites her bottom lip and shakes her head, eyelids falling shut from the unspeakable truth. As she stands there, considering whether to tell him or not, hands are placed on her shoulders. The clean soapy scent drifts closer. Rachel senses the solidity of his body nearing, and she opens her eyes to look up at him. "You really don't want to know."

"I *need* to know, Rachel." Greg stares at her until the point seems to drive home. He releases her. "You need to tell me everything from the beginning, otherwise we're going to work against each other and neither of us will get anything done."

"You'll think I've gone crazy."

He leans back against the desk, crosses his arms, and says, "You're the most logical person I know."

Rachel tilts her head to the side and raises both eyebrows in bemusement.

"Well, it's true."

She relents with a heavy sigh. "We'll both need some fresh air for this."

Greg nods and leads her out through the apartment's separate entrance, which is situated on the side of the main house. They walk together into the back garden at a leisurely pace, where green lawns and expertly designed gardens are interspersed with stone pathways. A sparkling blue pool, inviting on this sweltering midday, stands to one side of the yard. The pool house—better described as an entertainment lounge—is shut up tightly, though. Usually, if there's some activity at Pearson Manor, the French windows are thrown open to allow guests entry to the built-in bar, billiards table, and dartboard. On those eventful days, the outdoor furniture is carried out, too—beautiful rattan loungers and recliners, and large white umbrellas set into circular cement blocks—so guests can laze away in luxury.

This used to be a hostess' dream home, a lively house where parties were the talk of the town. Not so much anymore.

Rachel tells him what she's learned from her father's journals, about what she and Dougal saw on Griswold Road after they left the Roberts' farm on Friday night, about Orthega, and the late-night visit from the Night Weaver. She doesn't skip over anything, though she hesitates when it comes to telling Greg about the creature who'd taken her father's form. The implications of there being a Luke imposter in his house are too horrible to imagine. Greg doesn't interrupt her once. He doesn't scoff or look disbelieving, but Rachel can see him formulating questions she probably won't be able to answer.

As they head back toward the apartment's door, she concludes her retelling of events with a disheartened, "That's *everything* I know."

Greg remains quiet for a long time afterward, pensive expression fixed in place. "It's a lot to take in at first," he says, not betraying whether he believes in her fantastic recounting of the past few days. "Are you up for a field trip? There's someone I think you should meet."

Mrs. Crenshaw's voice enters her mind, urging her to keep the umbrella close. She glances up, where a few straggling, fluffy clouds drift across the forget-me-not blue sky. There isn't going to be rain today, but it won't hurt to have it on hand, Rachel decides. Rather safe than sorry, right?

"Sure, let me just go get something out of my car," she says.

"I'll meet you out front in five."

Rachel hurries around the side of the house, to her car, and pushes the key fob to unlock the doors. On the backseat, her umbrella lies enveloped in a winter coat she's been promising herself to take out for months now. She grabs the umbrella by its wooden handle and slams the door shut. She presses the key fob and listens to the satisfying beep, which signals the locks falling into place. Rachel leans against the exterior of her Hyundai, waiting for Greg to arrive. She inspects the silver-coated clasp keeping the indigo waterproof fabric tied up neatly against the wooden staff.

If Greg doesn't think I'm weird yet, my hauling around an umbrella on a sunny day will certainly convince him otherwise.

The New Range Rover Sport—a sleek, white monstrosity with a gorgeous interior that makes Rachel's Hyundai i10 look like an insignificant bug in comparison—drives out of the garage and follows the driveway to where she's standing. Greg rolls to a stop and she opens the passenger door.

"Didn't want to take the Mercedes out today, huh?" She climbs inside the Range Rover and fumbles with the seatbelt.

"I only take the Merc out when I'm going on a date," Greg answers, smirking. Rachel laughs, setting down the umbrella in the slight gap between the seat and the door. "What's with the umbrella?" He puts the Range Rover into drive. "Are you trying to make an ironic fashion statement of some kind?"

She sits back against the comfortable passenger seat, the new car scent still filling the interior, and keeps her gaze pinned on the windshield. "Do I look like the type of girl who deals in subliminal messages?" Rachel spies his subtle shrug. "No, the umbrella is not ironic."

"Okay," Greg says, sounding unconvinced.

"Oh, shush. You have your quirks and I have mine. Let's leave it at that."

He grins. "I don't have any quirks."

"You're pretty particular when it comes to your study," Rachel says. "I bet you ten dollars if I opened one of your desk's drawers, all your stationery will be perfectly aligned and sorted by color."

"You'd be out of ten dollars if I'd taken that bet seriously," Greg says as he turns the vehicle into Eerie Street. The absence of noise on this side of town is not unfamiliar but the lack of life in the prominent suburban neighborhood is somewhat disconcerting. Not a single dog barks. No children play on the lawns. There isn't a single friendly face outside. "I'm neat, not obsessive compulsive."

"Not even a little?" Rachel could swear his nervous habits include excessive handwashing and constant organizing.

He shakes his head, still smiling. "Don't get me wrong, I like certain things done a specific way, but it's not OCD."

"Everyone has some idiosyncrasies. It's what makes us human," Rachel says. "Anyway, who're we going to see?"

Greg keeps his gaze fixed on the road ahead. "A friend."

"Ooh, look at you being all mysterious." She laughs, watching the expensive houses roll by. Those pretty façades hide so many terrible secrets. "Have I met this friend of yours?"

"I doubt it," he mutters as his humor recedes. "People like him don't usually socialize with people like you."

"People like me?" she asks, surprised. "What type of person am I?"

"You know." Greg shrugs, but doesn't elaborate.

"No, I don't know. Enlighten me."

Greg doesn't reply. He turns onto Main Road and drives past the bustling historical sector, where kids cling to their mothers' skirts and teenagers cast suspicious glances at whoever passes. There's a cloud of mistrust blanketing the small establishments and their customers, masked by fake smiles and the curt exchange of pleasantries. The gloominess which has taken over portions of the town doesn't seem to stretch farther yet, but the atmosphere has changed all over Shadow Grove.

The Range Rover crawls to a stop as they hit some early afternoon traffic.

"Where does this enigmatic friend of yours live?" Rachel asks, staring out of the passenger window.

"You'll see," Greg says as the car moves forward again.

Rachel shifts her attention back to her companion, eyes narrowing.

The corners of his lip twitch upward again. "You hate not being in control, don't you?"

She doesn't respond, because Greg is not wrong. As a self-confessed control freak, few things in life irk her as much as trusting others. Rachel turns back to face the road, deflating as her anxiety rises to the surface. Since Luke's death, she and Greg haven't always had an amicable relationship. He has found ways to make her life extremely difficult, but those instances were never malevolent in nature. Nevertheless, Rachel works at her thumb's cuticle again, her nail quickly reopening the jagged wound.

Greg steers the car down to the center of town, past the roundabout park, and toward the Other Side.

As they enter the industrial sector, the traffic systematically dries up to a trickle. Soon, the Range Rover passes by the large junkyard and the sun-bleached sign comes up for PINE HILL TRAILER PARK. She doesn't hold any prejudices against Other-Siders, but the area isn't exactly known as a wholesome neighborhood. Drugs circulate through Shadow Grove thanks to some undesirable figures that have made their homes here. Due to numerous socioeconomic circumstances, even a small town like Shadow Grove has a lively, booming sex industry. On top of that, there is some gang activity to contend with. Of course, according to the sheriff's department and the town council, even factual evidence of these criminal activities is considered no more than rumor and hearsay.

"Where are we going?" Rachel asks. Her apprehension increases the deeper they travel into the Other Side.

Greg grins again but chooses not to answer her question.

"Seriously, Greg, where are we going?"

"Sheesh, give me a moment to revel in your distress."

"Stop screwing around."

"Relax, we're here," he says, turning into the oversized, desolate parking lot of Shadow Grove's tallest building.

The asphalt is scarred with deep potholes. A myriad of massive construction debris, left behind decades earlier by a disgruntled construction crew, litters the area. In the distance, Rachel sees a burned-out vehicle turned on its side—charred, dented, and rusty wherever it was not touched by the long-ago fire. There, situated at one end of the parking lot, Ashfall Heights stands in all its putrefying glory. The nine-story structure has an H-shape layout and is constructed of concrete and hollow clay tile. There are no exterior details to draw the eye. It's simply an ugly building, unadorned and wholly malapropos in relation to the rest of Shadow Grove's architectural stylings.

Greg parks the Range Rover and releases his seatbelt. "It's not as bad as it looks."

"Not as bad as it looks? Greg, even the Pine Hill meth-heads give Ashfall Heights a wide berth," Rachel says as he opens his door and climbs out of the car. She quickly unclicks her seatbelt, grabs her umbrella in case she needs a weapon, and gets out of the Range Rover. "Since when does the heir apparent hang out with people from Ashfall Heights?" she asks, walking around the car.

"It's a great parkour site," he says.

"Now you're doing parkour?" Rachel brushes her hand through her hair in frustration. "Who are you?"

Greg shakes his head as he walks toward the building's entrance. Rachel catches up with him and studies the indecipherable, faded graffiti that covers the foyer walls. She grips her umbrella tightly, ready to strike back if something looks even moderately threatening. He leads her into the unimpressive elevator and presses the uppermost circular button—unmarked after years of use.

"I don't like this." Her whisper is a scream in the hollow space, even as the elevator's gears churn sickly overhead.

Maybe the cables are fraying?

The elevator gears squeal, and the cart starts its precarious jerking. She grabs onto Greg's arm with her free hand and digs her nails into his skin. He says something, but his words are incomprehensible, and she can't focus on reading his lips to get an idea of what he's talking about. Dizzy with fear, Rachel holds her breath and waits for them to plunge to their deaths. Warmth covers her hand as Greg comforts her—or attempts to release her hold, she can't be sure. But she can't break free from the crippling dread overwhelming her every sense.

Instead of a gruesome ending, however, a loud ping sounds, and the doors creak open.

"You're brave enough to explore the forest, but Ashfall Heights scares you?" Greg asks, prying her fingers off his wrist. He gently nudges her out of the elevator and onto solid ground. "Rach, you need to get your priorities in order."

She releases the breath she'd been holding during the ride

up. "Give me a sec."

Greg steps away to evaluate the crescent-shaped marks she had left on his wrist.

She composes herself, pushes away the crippling anxiety, and asks, "Did I hurt you?"

"I'm fine. You?"

She gives him a curt nod as she mentally shakes off the residual fear before following him into the hallway.

A middle-aged woman exits one of the first apartments, her pendulous breasts applauding her as she waddles toward Rachel and Greg with a garbage bag in one hand and a lit cigarette in the other. Her thin lips pucker around the filter, lungs wheezing as she sucks greedily on the cancer stick, until the ember burns red hot. She closes her turquoise-colored eyelids for a beat. Ash falls from the tip, spilling across her white tank top. The threadbare fabric outlines those slap-slap-slapping breasts and saucer-sized nipples, which leaves little to the imagination. She exhales the noxious smoke and offers the world a yellow-toothed smile.

As they pass one another, Rachel chances a glance at the woman's pancake butt and chicken legs—riddled with cellulite and age and stuffed into a two-sizes-too-small cropped denim. Flab drapes over the woman's waistband, pushed up by the too-tight shorts, and pokes out wherever her top doesn't cover.

Rachel suppresses her disgust as best as possible but feels her facial muscles pull into a grimace regardless.

So much for not being prejudiced, huh? The sarcastic thought pops into her head and she silently chastises herself for judging someone based on their looks rather than their personality.

The door at 9-D opens and allows the distinctive smell of offal to escape the apartment along with bits of a heated discussion in an unknown language. She collides with the wave of boiling animal entrails, and gags. The odor moves sluggishly through the hallway, agile enough, though, to infiltrate every corner of the building and thick enough to overpower the senses. Her stomach churns and her lunch pushes up her throat. The door closes again, muffling the foreign voices on the other side, but the stench lingers.

They hasten down the hall, ignoring the barking Pomeranians at the locked security gate at 9-E and the incessant screams of a colicky infant at 9-F, and turn the corner.

Discolored eggshell walls and faded red doors line their path. Tacky red and white linoleum flooring—stained unrecognizably in places or degraded enough to reveal the raw concrete beneath—scuffs up Rachel's shoes. Stale urine, which had seeped into the very bones of the building, infuses with the nauseating stench following them through the hall.

A flash of cotton candy pink tulle rushes out of 9-I and skids to a stop in front of them. Rachel halts a few paces away from the little girl, who couldn't be older than six years old, and studies the suspicious numbness in her eyes. The mini-ballerina's lips curl into a sadistic smile, devoid of any natural emotions, and those haunted eyes glimmer with amusement. She clasps her hands behind her back and sways from one side to the other. The knee-length tutu swishes its dry whisper into the otherwise silent hallway.

"Hello," Rachel says, getting over her initial startle.

"Rach," Greg whispers, his hand snaking around her waist.

The girl's mouth grows wider, revealing a gap where a milk tooth had fallen out to make room for her permanent teeth. Those rosy cheeks twitch with the effort of holding the plastered-on smile in place. She tilts her head, rolls her eyes up to meet Rachel's gaze, and stops swaying.

"Let's go," Greg says louder now.

Rachel decides to heed his warning and go on her merry way before things could get any weirder, but the little girl bunny-hops into their path to block off their escape. Greg pulls Rachel closer and makes a second attempt to escape the attention of the creepy ballerina, which is quickly foiled as the girl slides into their way again. The muscles in Rachel's forehead pull into a frown. The girl releases her hands from behind her back and her arms swing limply in their sockets. Rachel looks at the open door of 9-I. Pots and pans clang in the kitchen, the sound drifting out in muted staccato. Somewhere inside the apartment, the TV plays sing-a-longs, and a girlish *la-la-la* tries to keep up with the tune.

The girl in the tutu raises one of those limp arms and points an index finger at Rachel.

"They'll never find your body," she says in a little-girl singsong voice.

Then, the little girl's amusement is replaced with abject horror, and the creepy smile vanishes as her jaw drops open. A shrill scream tears out of her, the pitch without intonation. Her eyes bulge, bloodshot veins apparent within the whites.

Terror keeps Rachel fixed in place, while Greg pulls her behind him.

"Gina Newman!" An adult's shout comes out of the apartment, sounding more annoyed than concerned.

The attractive thirty-something-year-old runs out of the apartment, brows knitted together in the typical no-nonsense look most children seem to inspire in their parents. She kneels beside the girl—the resemblance between the mother and daughter is uncanny—and brushes her fingers through the girl's wheat-colored hair. The scream ends abruptly. The girl giggles, twists out of her mother's arms, and skips back to the apartment as though nothing had happened.

The woman looks up. "Her no-good father allowed her to watch horror movies over the weekend," she explains, which doesn't make the situation any better. "This is the third time in as many days that Gina has freaked out a neighbor." She gets back onto her feet. "You've got to excuse her," she says. "I'm trying my best to raise my girls right, but it's hard." The woman wipes her hands against one another, casting a nervous glance over her shoulder to the open door. Inside, the telltale sounds of an argument between siblings replaces the happy sing-a-longs. "I've got to go. Sorry again."

She marches back to her apartment and slams the door shut. A whiny, albeit muted, "Mommy!" filters through the keyhole, accompanied by a child's howl of frustration.

"Congratulations, you've succeeded in traumatizing me," Rachel says, wiggling out of Greg's grip.

"That was nothing by Ashfall standards," Greg says. "Come on, we're burning daylight."

Rachel pulls a face at him when his back is to her but follows closely.

They pass the remaining apartments without incident, heading for 9-M. A faded red door is outfitted with multiple brass bolts, and black apartment numbers hang on rusty nails in a crooked line against the wall.

Greg knocks on the door twice and pushes one hand into his jeans pocket.

On the other side, keys jangle as bolt after bolt is unlocked, then a mighty kick to the bottom of the water-damaged doorframe resounds through the hallway. The door swings open, hinges squealing in agony. Out steps a guy, who can't be much older than Rachel or Greg, with tattoos covering the entirety of his left arm. The ink moves beyond his muscular bicep and beneath the short sleeve of his tightfitting black T-shirt. His shoulder-length black hair hangs haphazardly across his face, obscuring high cheekbones and luscious lips. Something about him, however, gives Rachel the impression that he's much older than he appears.

The guy's attention snaps to her as if he's read her mind, and she feels her cheeks warming with embarrassment. His eyes are multicolored spiraling galaxies, where flecks of gold swirl unabated. They seem to bore into her soul while he stares at her, picking apart the threads of time to study her beginning and end, and evaluate pieces of her she doesn't know exist.

"You brought a friend along," the guy says, regarding Rachel from the doorway. "She doesn't look like the typical parkour enthusiast." His gaze dips to the umbrella in her hand and the smug charm dissipates as he studies her again. "Oh, no. No, no, no." He shakes his head and glimpses at Greg. "You brought a MacCleary to my house?"

"Are you going to let us in?" Greg asks as he moves his foot over to block the door from closing.

"Are you insane?" he asks angrily. His beauty becomes dangerous, his allure turns deadly. "She's a MacCleary."

"Come now, she's only a teenaged girl," Greg counters, waving it off as if she's a harmless child. "Every drug dealer in the county is going to come after you if they hear how Orion Blackwood is afraid of a girl with an umbrella."

The guy flashes an animalistic sneer at Greg. Tendons bulge in his neck as he bares his sharp, elongated canines that look deadly enough to rip throats out solely for the enjoyment of it. Greg simply stares back at Orion, clearly untroubled by the display.

A tense heartbeat passes before Orion gives in and opens the door wide enough for them to enter.

"I didn't pick you to be a narc, Pearson," he growls.

Greg shrugs and walks through the doorway. Rachel is not as keen to enter the stranger's apartment, but she quickly follows Greg inside, clutching her umbrella with all her might.

A large, clean kitchen is situated on her right, while an entryway closet stands to her left. There isn't anything particularly spectacular about the décor. A few pieces of essential furniture fill the space, a couple of crappy posters hang against the walls, and mismatched curtains cover the windows. It doesn't smell like offal or smoke inside; doesn't smell like neglect or dirt. That helps.

Behind her, the door closes and the locks slide into place. She looks over her shoulder only to find the stranger glaring back at her.

They'll never find your body.

A shiver runs across her skin.

The hot guy passes Rachel and makes his way deeper into the apartment. He tosses his keys and cellphone onto the scratched coffee table and finds the TV remote. The news anchor pops onto the screen, wearing a tailored dress and a serious expression that spells doom, and although her mouth moves, words don't fill the awkward silence.

"I'll be right with you," Orion says, heading down the

narrow corridor.

He disappears into the farthest bedroom.

Rachel grabs Greg's arm and hisses, "You brought me to meet a drug dealer?"

"Orion is not a dealer. He's a manufacturer of designer—"

"That's not any better," her high whisper cuts him off. "Are you using?"

Greg studies her like a few new appendages have sprouted from her neck. "Literally everyone at Ridge Crest High is using. Even the principal is on one of Orion's products."

Rachel releases Greg's arm, eyes widening in horror. "You're joking, right?"

"My merchandise is one hundred percent natural," Orion's voice intrudes on their private conversation.

Rachel pivots, prudent in keeping the dangerous man in her line of sight at all times.

"It's what gives me an edge over the other manufacturers." He gestures for her to take a seat. "Sit, please."

"I'd rather stand." She basically spits the words.

"Suit yourself." He walks around her and picks up a wooden box from the coffee table before he takes a seat on a leather La-Z-Boy recliner.

Greg sits on the sofa, looking too comfortable for Rachel's liking.

"I take it this isn't a social visit or a business deal, so what can I do you for?"

"Remember that cave we found a few weeks ago, near the creek?"

"I do," Orion says. "What about it?"

"You said you know where it leads."

Orion closes the box. "Yes, but if I remember correctly, I told you not to go in there."

"Where does it go?" Greg wears a grave expression. When Orion doesn't answer immediately, he continues, "Look, I wouldn't ask if it wasn't important, and this is quickly becoming a life and death situation. Tell us about the cave."

Orion considers Greg for a second longer before he turns his attention to Rachel. He appraises her from afar like she's a gourmet meal and he's a starving man. He laps up every inch of her, making her feel self-conscious and confident at the same time.

Rachel returns the look, though her bravado ebbs when the girl's warning repeats itself again in a whisper.

They'll never find your body.

"Did you really come all the way to Ashfall just to hear about a forgotten cave, MacCleary?" Orion says.

"Lose the 'Mac' if you want to make an impact next time," Rachel says, swinging her umbrella to and fro. "Also, I have no idea why Greg dragged me here."

"Where does the cave go, and what lives in it?" Greg pushes.

A cheeky smile crosses Orion's otherworldly face as he stares at Rachel. His eyes, those swirling galaxies that make Rachel go weak in the knees, glint with danger. "Do *you* want to know?" he asks Rachel, ignoring Greg completely.

Rachel shrugs, nonchalant. "Sure, why not?"

"The cave doesn't go anywhere. It's just a cave," Orion says, his voice barely a whisper. "What are you doing searching for forgotten caves, *Rachel Cleary?*"

They'll never find your body. They'll never find your body. They'll never find your body …

"What are you?" Rachel asks in the same tone he used, horrified that he knows her name without her or Greg mentioning it.

Orion pushes his black hair out of his face to reveal an unnaturally pointed ear, and says softly, menacingly, "I'm what the MacCleary and Fraser families are supposed to keep out of Shadow Grove."

Chapter Twelve
Extinguishing The Stars

Faster than her synapses can transmit the message of danger through her brain, Orion vanishes into thin air from his seat across the room and reappears directly in front of her. Rachel slams with her back into the wall and loses her grip on the umbrella, which clatters to the linoleum floor. He's so close she can feel his body heat radiating off him and smell the earthy scent that clings to his skin.

She looks at a blank-faced Greg, who's still staring at the recliner, before she turns her gaze on Orion.

"What did you do to him?" she hisses, her voice steady, stern.

"If I were you, I'd be more worried about myself," Orion says, amusement flickering in his eyes. "Your family is remarkably bad at keeping Fae contained in our realm. All it took me to get into Shadow Grove was a bribe and some sweet talking. Of course, everyone was preoccupied with Adolf Hitler at the time.

"I hear the Fraser family is much more difficult to persuade, though. In fact, ever since Nancy Crenshaw's taken over her father's responsibilities to keep the Fae out of Shadow Grove, there are rumors that only a single Halfling has crossed into the Human Realm, and it took a MacCleary to convince Nancy to open the border."

"Misty Robins," Rachel blurts out the name without meaning to, surprising them both.

He presses one hand against the wall beside Rachel's head and leans forward. "That's who you let out of Orthega? Oh, your family truly is an inadequate bunch."

Rachel stares at him. "At least my family doesn't manufacture and sell drugs to high school students."

Orion grins viciously as he places his other hand against the wall, effectively trapping Rachel in place. "You're right, they don't. They just allow a Halfling with extinction level abilities to enter the Human Realm. Damn it!" He slams his fist into the wall beside her head.

Rachel flinches, squeezes her eyes shut, but doesn't permit herself to show any other sign of fear. Spider web cracks reach out to either side of the impact zone. Plaster crumbles and rains down over her.

"Where is she?" Orion asks, all pretense of him having the upper hand gone. "Where?" he says louder, his voice angrier now.

Rachel opens her eyes and slowly turns back to face him, defiant. "Even if I knew, I wouldn't tell you."

He regards her, studies her face intently. "Of course you won't, because she made a deal with your family."

Orion steps away from the wall and pushes his fingers through his hair. Just as she's about to try and make a run for it, his voice enters her mind with a callous: "*Sorry in advance, but this is the least painful option I can offer you.*"

Without warning, faster than she can comprehend, Orion spins and pins her back against the wall.

His lips suddenly crash into hers, and Rachel struggles

against him by slamming her palms up against his torso with as much force as she can muster, pushing him away in the hope of breaking free. Her outrage is muffled by his mouth, turning her hateful curses into weak, helpless sounds. His one hand moves to caress her cheek, his fingertips softly tracing their way from her temple to her chin. She bends her knee, ready to lift it straight up into his groin and battle off the unsolicited advance, but he simply blocks her by stepping closer.

Something changes then. She feels her fight draining away, her anger fizzles out. It's as if her entire being is thawing, like her every atom is melting into him. She closes her eyes and savors the way his lips mold perfectly to hers. Rachel steps closer to his solid, warm body as his hands snake around her waist. Orion gently parts her lips with his tongue, begging for entry. She gives into his request, deepening the kiss, which grows more sensuous. Fire seems to run through her veins, sparks fly wherever their bodies touch. Her heart races and her mind quietens as her hands lock around his neck.

"Forgive me." Orion's whisper intrudes into her thoughts as his tongue slips a tiny, circular object into her mouth. She barely has a chance to register the bitter coating of the pill before she automatically swallows it down.

Rachel's eyes shoot open again only to find him looking back at her.

"Don't fight it. I'll be with you the entire time."

Orion's face blurs at the edges, slowly dissipates. His hands are still wrapped around her waist, even if he's nowhere in sight. She averts her attention to Greg, who's still in his catatonic state, staring at the recliner, before the apartment vanishes. Her breath hitches as the world as she knows it is replaced by an opulent chamber, bedecked in ivory and gold. She stares into a gilded frame, but the reflection isn't hers. Instead, she sees Orion, an older, cleaner version of him—possibly in his early twenties, if she has to put a number to him—with shorter hair and clothed in the finest brocaded silk money can buy.

It's the crown on his head that steals the show.

"I'm still here, don't worry," Orion says into her mind. *"You're in one of my memories."*

"Your highness," an unfamiliar voice says. Rachel—no, not Rachel, rather the older Orion—turns around to face one of his father's advisors. How she knows this is beyond her comprehension. The old man with hunched shoulders bows his balding head in respect, and says, "We've received word that a handful of maximum-security prisoners have escaped the Leif."

"Send one of our search teams to contain—"

"Your highness, I regret to say there's more," the advisor interrupts Orion. "According to witness accounts, Lady Robins is involved."

"You must be mistaken," Orion says. "Misty has been at court since she was twelve years old and has never set foot anywhere near Leif Penitentiary."

"Yes, your highness, but Lady Robins killed two of the guards protecting the Royal Vaults and kept the third alive to deliver a message to his majesty." The advisor pauses and clamps his hands together as if saying a prayer before he breaks the wax seal and unrolls a piece of parchment. He hands it over to Orion.

> *This is merely the beginning of the end for the House of Nebulius.*

King Auberon's ignorance and Queen Aerglo's prejudices against Halflings and Humans have paved the way for Prince Nova's cruelty. For years I was his toy, and everyone turned a blind eye to my suffering. I have endured unspeakable humiliations at his hand, simply because I was deemed lesser.

My vengeance starts when the Miser rises.

Misty Robins, Lady of House Goud.

Orion looks up at the advisor. "What did she take from the vault?"

"A few powerful artifacts," the advisor answers loud enough to be heard over the rushing footsteps making their way down the hallway.

"Be frank, man!"

"She cleaned out the restricted section."

Orion crumples the note and rushes toward the open door. "Send word to my battalion to ready themselves for war. I need to confer with the king and my brother before I can join them on the battlefield," he shouts over his shoulder.

"Yes, your highness."

Static clouds Rachel's vision for a few moments as the memory changes and she looks out on a dark, open field, surrounded by men and women in heavy armor. They wield swords and hold shields; some are armed with bows or axes. A cavalry stands at the ready, and the riders survey the sky as they keep their horses in line.

Something horrible is coming, she—no, Orion—can feel it.

"Why are you . . . ? Rachel, go back to the palace."

The older Orion, the one Rachel's currently embodying, sees a fast-moving dot grow larger in the sky, heading right for the troops. Behind him, a general shouts for the archers to ready themselves. Ahead, a woman with a silver braid twirls her broadsword in her hand a couple of times, making it appear weightless. She's a beautiful female with catlike eyes and skin the color of the Kalahari Desert. The woman stops twirling her sword.

"King Auberon should've put this Black Annis down when he had the chance. What type of monster cannibalizes her sisters' children?" The woman's voice is melodic, too sweet for the battlefield, but nothing about her says she's inadequate for the task that lies ahead.

"Don't underestimate her," Orion warns. "I saw what the Night Weaver did to the Halfling village on our Southern border . . . I would never wish what she did on my worst enemy."

"You don't want to be here, Rachel. Go back to the previous memory."

How had she changed the Fae channel in the first place?

The woman sneers, her nose crinkling as if she's smelled something particularly bad. "They're the reason we're in this mess in the first place. Halflings don't deserve our compassion."

"You sound like my brother."

"Your brother has his faults, Orion, but he always puts his people first. As the Holy Prophet says: 'Check your appetite when it comes to breeding with Humans, for the spawn of such unions will destroy—"

"Quoting scripture on the battlefield is inappropriate,

Arjean."

The silver-headed woman sighs, turns her attention back to the battleground, and says, "Without faith, our defeat is certain."

Rachel recognizes the Night Weaver's unnerving cackles long before she sees the blue-faced crone through Orion's eyes.

"She's wearing the Akrah Cloak?" Arjean asks Orion over her shoulder. "How'd the Night Weaver get her hands on it?"

"Misty," Orion answers as he unsheathes his blade. The broadsword sports mother of pearl inlays on the gilded hilt. It's heavy, flashy, and not his weapon of choice.

The Akrah grows longer until the tattered hem drags across the grassy field like it's the royal cathedral train of a demonic bride's wedding dress. One of those fabric tendrils fires forward and grabs an archer around his waist. The fabric wraps tightly around the man's body and lifts him off the ground. He kicks and screams, loses grip on his bow, while arrows rain down from the quiver on his back. When he's eye-level with the Night Weaver, the cloak unwraps itself.

Orion and Rachel watch in horror as the archer falls through the air, his terrified scream echoing through the dense, dark night, before ending abruptly with a sickening splat.

The Night Weaver turns her attention to Orion, wearing a smile of death. Her needlelike teeth gleam in the moonlight as she mocks a curtsy in midair. "You honor me with your presence, Prince Orion. Now, prepare to die."

She screeches with delight as the Akrah picks up several of the archers and lifts them off the ground. One after the other they fly through the air, catapulted to their demise. The remaining archers send arrows flying her way. Some find their target, but the arrows simply rebound and harmlessly fall to the ground as the cloak protects its wearer.

All around the army, creatures made of shadows materialize, taking humanoid forms as they rush into the fray. The confusion is interspersed with shouts of: "We're surrounded!" The battalion is charged from all sides and chaos ensues as the soldiers disperse while they fight against the Night Weaver's vicious attacks. The Akrah Cloak batters its opponents, while an army of solid shadows finishes the job.

Orion wields the sword with precision, slicing away tendrils of fabric shooting his way, while the generals scream their orders, or his men yell for mercy.

"They'll never find your body," The Night Weaver shouts at Orion. "They'll *never* find your—"

Before Rachel can hear the rest of the Night Weaver's manic threat, static fills her vision again and she's back at the palace, staring up at a golden throne where a painfully beautiful white-haired man sits. Behind him, stained glass windows depict the wise kings of old, warrior queens who sacrificed their lives for the Fae kingdoms and prophecies that are yet to come to pass. Dressed in purple velvet robes and wearing a crown fit for a king, he is utterly breathtaking.

There's a glimmer in the man's eyes, one that doesn't befit someone of his station. It's unsettling, profoundly evil.

"You're not supposed to be here. How are you doing this?" Orion asks, stricken with panic.

"You banished the Night Weaver to the Human Realm without attempting to reclaim the Akrah Cloak, one of the House of Nebulius' most treasured artifacts. What do you have to say for yourself?" the man says in a matter-of-fact voice.

"My attempts would not only have put the battalion in

jeopardy but the whole of Orthega. By banishing the Night Weaver to the Human Realm, her magic is limited. The Akrah's power is restricted now," Orion answers. "I … I cannot wield the Akrah Cloak even if I wanted."

"You disappoint me, brother," the man says. "How difficult can it truly be to contain these criminals? Are you inadequate to lead my army?"

Rachel's view dips to the marble tiled floor, and she notices Orion's hand ball into a fist by his side.

"The Akrah feeds on darkness and *I* do not possess the amount of darkness required to change the cloak's allegiance back to the House of Nebulius. Perhaps if you were on the battlefield, instead of frolicking in a brothel, we might've succeeded in your impossible task." Orion's tone is one of belligerence, which earns a gasp from somewhere in the throne room. He doesn't look up, much to Rachel's frustration, but the tense atmosphere congeals like blood.

"You forget yourself, Orion. I'm your king, and I won't have my brother disrespecting me in my own kingdom. Do you understand?"

"Yes, my *king*."

"Now, let's see how horribly you've failed at your job." He claps his hands, a feral grin in place. "Silencio, how many escapees has Prince Orion recaptured?"

"Two out of twenty-five, your majesty," a husky voice answers.

The king tuts as he shakes his head. "How many of those twenty-five escapees has Prince Orion banished to the Human Realm, Silencio?"

"Twelve, your majesty."

"How many of the artifacts that were stolen have been retrieved by my brother, who acts as a general to my men?" the king asks.

"None, your majesty."

"Thank you, Silencio."

The king stands and walks down the gilded steps, unnecessarily dragging the process out. Orion averts his gaze back to study the marble floor as several nerve-wracking beats pass before two polished black shoes come into view.

"Brother," the king says, stretching out his hand so Orion could see his offer. Orion takes his hand and allows the king to help him to his feet. "Are you deliberately trying to sabotage my rule?"

"No—"

The slap is hard, unexpected, but most of all, humiliating. Orion doesn't retaliate, but there's an instant where red spots fill the image as rage blossoms into existence. He slowly returns his gaze to the king, who seems giddy with power. The giddiness decreases as the king inspects Orion's eyes, looking closer.

"Well, well, well," he says. A terrible smirk forms on his unforgettable face. "Aren't you a pretty thing?" The king grabs Orion by the chin and forces him to look directly into his quicksilver eyes. "Orion has the best taste in women, but I never thought he'd find a human with Fae-like beauty. My, my, isn't he a lucky one?"

"Get out of there, Rachel. Get out, now!"

The king's hands move to rest on Orion's temples. "Let's see where you are, pretty thing. Let's see where my brother is hiding you." Those eyes bore into Orion's, and Rachel shivers as she looks back. "Do you think I should make him watch while I break you in for my harem, pretty thing?"

Blackness promptly fills her vision.

Nothingness follows.

Then the real-world crashes back into place around her, faster than when she left it in the first place. Instead of looking through Orion's eyes, she once again stares into them. Instincts take over as her anger floods back. She shoves him away from her.

"You bastard," she growls, pulling her arm back, and—with as much power as she can muster—slams her fist into his jaw. She stumbles back into the couch and presses her hands to her knees to brace herself while she catches her breath. "Is there something mentally wrong with you? Guys can't just go around kissing girls without their permission. Not to mention the fact that you slipped me a pill while you had your tongue down my throat! What's wrong with you?"

Orion flexes his jaw. "It was either me sticking my tongue down your throat, as you so eloquently put it, or hiding the pill in some food and tricking you into eating it. I doubt you would've enjoyed being treated like a dog on antibiotics." He rubs his jaw again. "Besides, if you'd listened and gone back when I told—"

"Yes, because I'm such a pro at whatever the hell that was." Rachel huffs as she rights herself, flipping her hair over her shoulder. "I'm not going to involve myself in your family squabble." She picks up her umbrella and glances at Greg, who's as immobilized as when she'd gone into Orion's mind. She gestures toward Greg and looks at Orion, unable to string together the proper words to convey her indignation.

"He's perfectly fine," Orion says, waving his hand as if Greg's of no consequence. "You, however, are not. Nova's seen you—"

"Blah, blah, blah, I *don't* care," she interrupts him again. "Now you listen closely, Faerie Boy. I'm going to take Greg and we're going to leave this infernal place, and if you come anywhere near either of us again, I'll tell Mrs. Crenshaw where you've been holing up so she can personally take care of you. Do I make myself clear?"

Orion lifts an eyebrow. "Faerie boy? Do you have any idea how offensive that is to a Fae male?"

She uses her right hand and gestures to her face, making circular motions in the air. "See this? This is how it looks when someone stops giving a crap about being PC. Now, fix Greg."

"Do you take me for a total idiot?" Orion crosses his arms. "The moment I let you leave, you're just going to run off and tell Nancy Crenshaw where I am."

"You're at the bottom of my list of concerns," she snaps back. "Because you decided to 'banish' the Night Weaver to Shadow Grove instead of handling her in your world, I now have to deal with her demented taste for children. Thank you."

"Yet another reason why I can't let you leave. You're just going to get yourself killed and you're probably going to drag Greg down with you, because you, dear Rachel, don't understand the severity of the situation."

"Don't presume to know me," she says through gritted teeth. "I'm cleaning up *your* mess."

Orion continues as though Rachel hasn't spoken, "The Night Weaver's powers are considerably subdued in the Human Realm, but she still has the Akrah Cloak in her possession. If an army of Fae—each soldier possessing the strength of five humans, some enjoying added abilities that your species cannot even begin to understand—can't put her down, what chance do you think you have against her?"

"I repeat, don't presume to know me." She pushes past Orion, deliberately bumping into his shoulder as she makes her way to her catatonic acquaintance. Rachel haunches down and snaps her fingers in front of Greg's face. The blank stare, nothing short of creepy, doesn't dissipate. "Greg? Greg, we need to leave." Rachel snaps her fingers again. When nothing changes, she grabs him by the shoulder and gently shakes him.

"He can't hear or see you," Orion says. "Greg thinks we're having a productive conversation."

"Fine. If you want to play, let's play," Rachel mumbles, standing to fish her cell phone out of her denim skirt's pocket. Before she can even swipe the screen, her phone disappears. She looks across the room, to where Orion stands and sees her lifeline in his holding. "How did you—? Give it back."

"You can have it back as soon as you start acting like an adult. Sit down and listen." The firmness in his voice is the same tone a parent would employ when speaking to a defiant child.

Rachel grits her teeth—despising being ordered around by some arrogant, privileged guy who doesn't even belong in this world. She halfheartedly takes a seat beside Greg and sets her umbrella across her lap, gripping it with both hands.

"Thank you," he says, pocketing her phone as he crosses the living room. He sits on the recliner. "Hand me your umbrella."

Rachel narrows her eyes at him. "Why?"

"Your umbrella is actually an artifact, which protects its owner from Fae influence. I gifted it to a MacCleary in order to pay for my passage into Shadow Grove," he says, holding out his hand. "If you want, I can refashion it into something different for you, something practical. Umbrellas aren't exactly unnoticeable accessories in this day and age, but a necklace is often ignored. It's also harder to lose a priceless object if it's around your neck."

"It can change shape?" Rachel holds up the umbrella to study it, unsure if she believes him. It's a nice umbrella—unique, but it's just an umbrella.

Orion smiles as he says, "Not by itself, it can't." He wiggles his fingers at her. Rachel moves her gaze to his face but doesn't give him anything more than a dirty look. "If I wanted to hurt you, I would have done it already. Unlike my brother, I don't take pleasure from hurting people."

"You promise you'll give it back?"

"I promise." He crosses his heart.

Rachel reluctantly relinquishes her hold over the umbrella and watches as Orion crumples it into his hands like it's made of tinfoil. "Only a Nebulius can mold the Ronamy Stone into new shapes." He grins. "In the old days, the Ronamy Stone was often used as a sort of magic DNA tester, especially if there were rumors circling a kid."

"Nebulius is the house you're born into?"

"Yes. Blackwood is a pseudonym I use in the Human Realm. My real name is Orion Nebulius, Prince of Amaris."

Orion stretches the object, as though it's made of putty now. She watches as he first pulls and pushes the matter, kneading it roughly with his fingertips, before rolling it around between his palms. Transfixed, she stares until a strange blue glow emanates from the unearthly substance that's both a liquid and a solid. The light changes colors the longer Orion works, first to pink and then to green, brightening the gloomy atmosphere in the apartment. He cups his hands together after a while and a bright golden light seeps through the spaces between his fingers. When he opens his hands again, an umbrella pendant—made of smooth stone, almost reminiscent of his eyes—sits at the center of a golden chain.

"How's this?" he asks, picking up the chain with his index finger and thumb to reveal the transformed artifact.

She reaches out to inspect the pendant. When nothing feels *off* about the necklace, she says, "It's lovely."

"Nova won't be able to get into your head if you always keep it on your person," he says. "Got it?"

She nods, unclasps the necklace, and quickly fixes it around her neck. The pendant lies heavily against her chest, but it feels as if it should've been there all along instead of being hauled around in her hand.

"What happened to your father?" she asks, pulling her fingers through her hair as she allows her brunette locks to cascade over her shoulders.

"Misty happened," he says. "She gave one of the escaped prisoners another stolen artifact, the Travolis Ring, which granted him entry into the King's Chambers. My father was disemboweled before the King's Guard could open the doors to investigate his cry for help."

Orion's candor on the matter is disconcerting, but his eyes tell a story of unhealed pain that continues to chip away parts of him. She finally recognizes he carries the same sadness she's lugged around for the past eight years, ever since her father was taken by pancreatic cancer. Granted, Liam Cleary went quietly in comparison to disembowelment. Rachel can't even bring herself to offer him a sympathetic platitude upon hearing of his loss. After all, what do you say to someone whose nearest and dearest was disemboweled?

"Don't worry. That particular prisoner was recaptured and executed," he continues. "Nova made sure of it."

"Okay," she whispers. "Do you honestly think Misty Robins let those prisoners out?"

He smirks and shrugs. "That's the million-dollar question, isn't it?" Orion pauses, allowing the words to sink in, before he clears his throat and shifts in his seat. "You can't go after the Night Weaver, Rachel. Leave her alone. After a while, she'll grow bored and go into hibernation again. It's better that way."

"Better for whom?" Rachel sits forward in her seat, keeping her spine ramrod straight and her shoulders pushed back. "Right now, my mother, Greg's mother, and fifteen other women are being controlled by the Night Weaver. There could be more people we aren't aware of. If my suspicions are correct, these brainwashed victims are the ones responsible for kidnapping innocent children in order to hand over to the Night Weaver, who in turn sends over a shadow creature—"

"We call them Darklings."

"—that vaguely resembles their dead loved ones. This type of stuff destroys more than a few people, Orion. It can destroy the entire town."

Orion's expression changes to disbelief. "Someone would've said something if the Night Weaver's influence was half as bad as you claim it to be."

"Ask Greg if you don't believe me."

His lips pull into a tight, thin line. Orion is about to talk when Rachel's cell phone's ringtone sounds, muffled by the denim fabric of his jeans. He pulls her phone from his pocket and looks at the screen, before holding it her way.

"If you want my help, I suggest you don't get me into any unnecessary trouble."

Rachel reaches for the cell phone. "I won't," she says.

He pulls the phone back before she can touch the sleek, plastic protective cover.

"I mean it. If you go into the Night Weaver's lair, guns blazing, the only people you'll hurt are those under her control. She'll make them suffer, drive them mad, and then you'll be the only one to blame."

"I get it. May I have my phone now, please?"

He hands her the cell phone. "Put it on speaker."

She obliges him and answers the call from an unknown number with a casual, "Hello."

Chapter Thirteen
Despairing Light, Prevalent Night

Hollowness fills the apartment's living room as the phone changes hands, or the speaker is brushed up against fabric. Footsteps echo. A distinctive dragging follows, paired with labored breathing—fearful, jagged inhalations and exhalations. The background noise is full of distant whispers: urgent, yet unclear commands.

This isn't a typical telemarketing or phishing call unless those scumbags have gotten creative. Rachel doubts this is the case.

"Hello?" she repeats, holding her cell phone between herself and Orion.

There's a sudden scrambling like shoes trying and failing to find purchase on a gravelly terrain. Judging from the dull, albeit solid, sounds that follow and the *oomphs* or *ughs* matching the rhythm to those hits, someone is clearly being beaten up.

"Damn it, Dougal, stop struggling," an unfamiliar male voice comes through loudly.

Rachel covers her mouth in time to muffle a whimper, while her other hand constricts around the phone. A mantra of some kind starts. Indistinct praising comes from multiple voices. She waits, trying to figure out the words, hoping Dougal is all right.

Her anxiety levels rise.

"Sheriff." The weakness in Dougal's voice is frightening. "Sheriff, this isn't right. Ye can't do this. My Nan—" His protests are cut short with a definite slap, which comes over the call loud and clear.

"Shut your mouth, boy. You're in the presence of a goddess."

Sycophantic chants start anew as numerous voices—the Night Weaver's acolytes, no doubt—praise their newfound false idol.

"Yer all gonna be in big trouble for bringin' me to the forest, especially once Nan realizes I'm late for dinner." Somehow Dougal makes those innocent words sound like a vicious threat. More than that, though, he just kind of gave Rachel his location. The forest isn't small, but it does narrow things down. "Ye don't want to get on Nancy Crenshaw's bad side, do ye?"

The chanting doesn't end, but there is a miniscule falsetto during their recitation when Mrs. Crenshaw's name is mentioned.

Dougal's breathy laughter interrupts them once more, before he says, "Aye, I thought so. Yer fake goddess won't save ye from Nancy Crenshaw's wrath, not wh—"

The call ends with a *beep-beep-beep*, possibly due to Dougal's signal weakening. The hairs on Rachel's neck stand on end. What now? What can she do to help him? Stunned, she can't do more than stare at her cell phone.

They'll never find your body.

Orion stands from the recliner and walks toward the corridor—giving Rachel the chance she needs to inform Mrs. Crenshaw of Dougal's precarious situation. If this insubordination makes her a bad captive, so be it. Dougal saved her life. It's only good manners to return the favor. She pulls the phone closer to her body, swipes across the smooth surface with her thumb to unlock the screen, and then dials Mrs. Crenshaw's number.

"I was just about to call you," the old woman answers. "Will you kindly buy some milk on your way home?"

"Th-they've taken Dougal," Rachel says, her voice quivering.

A prolonged silence settles between them before Mrs. Crenshaw says in a calm voice, "He's too old, isn't he? Except ..." Her sentence drifts off. "There's an unofficial curfew in place if I'm not mistaken. The Pearson boy put it in place, no?"

"Yes, Mrs. Crenshaw."

She sighs. "Ah, so the wicked bitch has fallen on desperate times. I should've known she would broaden her net and go for the older kids next."

Rachel frowns. Mrs. Crenshaw's cool, collected response is not the way Rachel would've reacted to the news. Most people will blow a gasket if their child or grandchild is kidnapped. Add in the prospects of them becoming someone's lunch and you might as well call the men in white for an extended stay at Casa del Hawthorne Memorial.

"As my father liked to say, best to kick them while they're down," she says. "Dear, do me a favor and meet me at home in, oh, let's say twenty minutes? I might need a hand getting my grandson back."

"Err ... okay."

"Good girl. See you soon."

The call ends, leaving Rachel speechless.

"Greg." Orion's voice startles her back to her present predicament. Rachel turns to face him and follows his gaze just to see Greg come out of his stupor. "Go home, take a long bath, and forget all about coming here today. In fact, Rachel and you just hung out for a while today at your place. You never brought her here."

"Okay, Orion," Greg says, obediently standing. Rachel stands, too, watching him move away as though he's in a trance. "Check you on the flip side, bro." They bump fists as Orion opens the front door for him.

"My car—"

"Go straight home now," Orion interrupts Rachel by speaking directly to Greg.

"You got it," Greg answers.

Orion watches Greg leave, closes the door and slides the bolts into place, before turning to look at Rachel. "If I'd known how bad things have gotten, I would've dealt with her sooner." He takes a step forward and cocks his head until his neck clicks. He repeats the action for the other side. Orion loosens his shoulders by moving them in circular motions, looking like he's warming up for a heavyweight boxing match.

"What are you doing?"

"It's been a while since I've gone into a real battle," he admits, stretching his arms next. "I'll just be a minute."

She blinks a few times. "How—? Did you eavesdrop on my conversation?"

Orion points to one of his ears and says, "It's kinda impossible not to eavesdrop when you're a Fae."

"Well, okay, but I thought you wanted to steer clear of Mrs. Crenshaw?" Rachel says.

"What type of person would I be if I allowed a teenaged girl and an old lady to go after the Night Weaver alone?" He bends down to reach for the floor, touching his toes. "It's my fault she's here in the first place."

"You're an odd duck, Faerie Boy."

He looks up at her, a frown marring his forehead. "This time you didn't spit venom when you used *that* term. Progress, I suppose." Orion slowly rights himself. "I'm going to remove my glamor now. Don't have a fit."

The younger, scruffier Orion vanishes an instant later, and in his place stands the older, strapping Orion, the one she'd seen in his memories. He doesn't look nearly as regal without his crown or lavish garb, but he's not at all unappealing to the eye. The word *delectable* comes to mind.

"All right," he says, clapping as he looks around the apartment. "Let's go—Wait." Orion cuts himself off and lifts an index finger, glancing at the wooden box on the coffee table. "No, I think we're good. Come on."

"Are you sure?" she asks, heading toward him. "Do you need to use the bathroom before we go?"

"So, you do have a sense of humor. Color me surprised." He stretches his arms out, blocking Rachel's way to the front door.

She stops in her tracks, out of his reach. "What are you doing?"

"Beating traffic," Orion says. He waits for a few seconds, before he says, "If I need to explain my every move, we're never going to have time to save your friend. Come over here and see for yourself what I mean."

Rachel grimaces as she steps closer and his arms wrap around her. "Mark this as one of my life's regrets," she grumbles.

"The best regrets are often worth it," he says, pulling her closer. Orion grins, looking far too triumphant for her liking.

"Get it over with, already."

Rachel closes her eyes, holds her breath, and waits for this 'beating traffic' thing to happen. At first, there's only a slight pressure surrounding her, and a faint headache thrashes behind her eyes. The density of the air increases, pushing into her from all sides until her breath is forced out of her lungs. Her stomach does a somersault. Head pounding, she latches onto Orion—gripping his shirt for everything she's worth—and hides her face in his chest. The world tilts for a fraction of a second and then rights itself once more. The immense force that had made her feel like she would implode fades away.

"You can let go now. We're here," Orion says.

Rachel opens her eyes to see the bright afternoon sunlight reflect off the windows of the Fraser house. She unfurls her hands from Orion's shirt, gulping air and swallowing down bile as she takes an uncertain step away.

"You good?"

She leans back against a tree and gives him a thumbs up. Her arms and hands tremble, while her legs wobble. It's a minor problem in comparison to what Dougal is probably facing.

Orion walks over and stands beside her, looking in the direction of the forest. "I'm impressed with how well you're handling these revelations. Some MacCleary and Fraser descendants went through their entire lives without ever laying eyes on a Fae. You, however, have been subjected to some intense mindbenders in a relatively short time. Do I need to be worried about your mental wellbeing?"

"It's a bit late to worry about how your actions have affected my mind," Rachel says, hooking a stray strand of hair behind her ear. She hears Mrs. Crenshaw long before she sees her.

"Truthfully, though, I tend to dissociate completely or compartmentalize stuff until I find an opportunity to work through them. When I can take stock of my victories and failures at my own pace, the outcome is better."

"Post-event rumination," he says in a thoughtful voice, as if he can relate.

Rachel nods and turns to regard her seemingly normal home, which still feels as damning as when she'd left it this morning. "If you want to stay off Mrs. Crenshaw's hit list, I suggest you don't tell her what she can and cannot do. She also despises arrogant people, so stay humble and don't tell her you make drugs for a living."

He responds with a nasal sound to convey his displeasure. "My merchandise cannot be compared to modern drugs. What I produce are Fae elixirs and potions, packaged in a convenient pill form, yes, but they're not harmful in any way."

"Right. Keep telling yourself that."

Rachel sees the old woman exiting the house, dressed in a pair of slacks and a button-up shirt. She glances at Orion first, curiosity flickering in her piercing blue eyes, and turns her attention to Rachel.

"You told me you were going to Pearson Manor," Mrs. Crenshaw says, grabbing her cane from the porch's railing. Slowly, she makes her way down the steps. "Next time send me a text if your plans change. I don't want to hear someone found your body in a ditch somewhere. Are we understood?"

"Yes, ma'am," Rachel says, walking closer.

"I'm not getting any younger. Come on, both of you," Mrs. Crenshaw continues in her no-nonsense tone, heading for the forest's entrance.

Not wanting to annoy her any further, Rachel quickly follows. Orion straggles behind, seemingly wary to get too close to Nancy Crenshaw.

The old woman casts a glare his way. "Do I want to know how you got into Shadow Grove?"

"I've been here since before you were a twinkle in your parents' eyes," he answers, his voice no longer holding the same self-confidence as earlier.

Revenge truly is sweet. Who knew?

Mrs. Crenshaw harrumphs.

There's an edge to the silence between them, a tension that could curdle milk. Rachel looks between Mrs. Crenshaw and then to Orion, wondering who'd say the wrong thing first. Her money is on Orion, but Mrs. Crenshaw's an unpredictable firecracker by nature. It could go either way.

Hoping to diffuse the situation by keeping them focused on the more pressing matter, Rachel asks, "How are we going to get Dougal back?"

Mrs. Crenshaw catches Rachel's eye, before averting her gaze back to the road as they near the ACCESS PROHIBITED sign. "The Night Weaver hibernates for long periods of time, only awakening to feed. Sometimes centuries pass without her coming out of her slumber. As a result, she hasn't assimilated well into our society and knows next to nothing about technology," she explains without giving away any details of the plan she's concocted.

"That's not really an answer, Mrs. Crenshaw. How do we stop her once and for all?"

Mrs. Crenshaw pulls her shoulders up. "If there were instructions available on how to euthanize the Night Weaver, I would've done it years ago," she says. "Maybe you should ask your friend if he knows how to kill her."

Rachel crosses her arms. "Yeah, I already tried. Orion doesn't have a clue on how to do it either."

"Correction," he says. "I know how to destroy the Night Weaver, but we'll need an army and an Intra-Canter or two."

"Intra-Canter?" Rachel asks.

"Intra-Canters are best described as mind-walkers or internal-influencers. Some can possess you. Others can kill you from the inside without laying a hand on you physically. The most feared Intra-Canters, however, are able to enter your mind and wreak havoc."

"Like your brother?"

"Mhmmm."

"So, if he's an Intra-Canter, what are you supposed to be?" Rachel continues, dropping her arms to her sides as Mrs. Crenshaw comes to a stop in front of the forest entrance.

"I'm considered an accomplished Omni-Opus," Orion says. "An Omni-Opus can easily do a bit of everything but specializes in one or two schools of magic. I specialize in five."

"Enough chitchat," Mrs. Crenshaw says. "We need to focus." She steps through the unseen barrier and shudders. "After all these years, I still hate going into the forest," she mutters, moving onward.

Rachel goes through the invisible barrier next, shivering as the electricity-that's-not-electricity runs through her body. She takes a second to gather herself before rushing after Mrs. Crenshaw. Orion takes up the rear of the traversing trio, staying close but keeping quiet.

"Mrs. Crenshaw, are you sure this is wise?" Rachel asks,

ducking beneath a low branch as she catches up to the old woman, who moves through the uneven terrain without much difficulty.

"It's never wise to go after Fae," Mrs. Crenshaw says.

"You know what I mean."

Mrs. Crenshaw shoots a penetrating glare her way, a not-so-subtle suggestion to drop the subject. Rachel raises her hands in surrender. She studies the woody landscape, wondering how far they are from the path she and Dougal had taken when they had first entered the forest a couple of days ago. Everything looks the same in here.

"Do you know where we're going?" Rachel asks.

"Yes," Mrs. Crenshaw says, blowing out air through her nose. "Honestly, Rachel, what is it with this interrogation?"

She shrugs. "I'm curious. How did these followers—"

"Acolytes," Orion offers.

"All right. How did the Night Weaver's *acolytes* slip past us and get into the forest? There's always someone at home, keeping an eye out. I didn't even see any cars near the entrance."

"There are other ways to get in and out, I'm sure," Mrs. Crenshaw mutters.

"I found some tracks over here," Orion says from somewhere farther to their left. "Also, there seems to have been a substantial scuffle."

"Dougal's a big boy and too smart for his own good sometimes," Mrs. Crenshaw explains, walking off to study the tracks. "He wouldn't have gone quietly. Here." She points to a specific area in the dirt with her cane. "This is what we follow."

Orion joins Mrs. Crenshaw. He scopes the area before he waves his hand across the ground. The sound of pebbles and rocks rolling against each other, sweeping the forest floor clean, makes Rachel stare in awe. Beneath a thin layer of dirt and foliage, a brick path leads deeper into the woods.

Mrs. Crenshaw walks down the path revealed by Orion's magic trick, cane tapping every now and then when she needs to put her full weight on it. "You unnecessarily wasted magic, but it's a kind gesture," she says over her shoulder.

"That's Mrs. Crenshaw's way of saying thank you," Rachel explains as she passes Orion, patting him on his shoulder. "Good job with the brown-nosing."

"I was not—" Orion sighs. "You're an incredibly difficult person to please."

She follows her elderly neighbor, sensing the Fae on her heels, and smiles. "In my experience, complicated people are more interesting."

"Rachel, you do realize your Fae friend is possibly old enough to have had a dinosaur as a pet, right?"

"I'm not *that* old," Orion argues.

"Either way, you two should stop flirting," Mrs. Crenshaw says.

"I wasn't flirting." Rachel purses her lips together. Behind her, Orion chuckles quietly. "What's the plan to get Dougal back, anyway?"

"Confuse, scatter, rescue. Simple," Mrs. Crenshaw says softly over her shoulder. "Now hush or you'll give away our position."

About fifteen minutes later, they come across an area where large trees seem to have been woven together to create a tunnel through the forest. Dead branches are braided into an archway at the entrance. A copious amount of petrified tree roots hang across the unassuming entrance and massive weeds grow unabated along the front. Mrs. Crenshaw uses her cane to whack the nuisances aside as she enters the gaping mouth of the tunnel, while Rachel bats away roots to follow her inside.

A flashlight beam suddenly cuts through the darkness, brightening the area.

The interior consists of gigantic dead trees that create arches, which are emphasized by shadows that recede into pitch-black darkness. Soot and smoke, redolent of ancient fires, and with a sense of stygian gloom, stain the walls. The pitter-patter of rodents changes the place from semi-eerie to über-creepy.

How many ghosts lurk in this underground labyrinth? Better yet, who built this place to begin with?

When Rachel glances behind her, she finds Orion's silhouette standing there. A soft, golden glow emanates from his hand, bright enough to act as a flashlight, but not a manmade object.

"Fae light," he explains, releasing the ball of light. It floats forward, toward Rachel. Suspended in the air, hovering at eye level, the ball only moves when she does. She reaches out to poke the sphere of light and the surface ripples with a variety of golden shades—from antique gold to bright yellow gold. The ball bobs up and down, seemingly gleeful from the contact before it spins in place.

"Thank you," she says as he creates a second ball of light for himself.

Mrs. Crenshaw sweeps the area with her flashlight again and a rat scurries away, dashing into a pile of garbage lining the walkway. "Do you believe in ghosts, Rachel?"

"These days, I don't oppose the existence of anything. Why?"

"No reason," Mrs. Crenshaw says in a solemn tone.

They walk through the ink-black tunnel, which branches off in different directions. Now and then, when the lighting is just right, Rachel can just make out immense groined vaults running parallel to their current route. She can hear the turbulent waters of a forgotten river echoing through the dank subterranean landscape as Mrs. Crenshaw leads them into lesser-traveled tunnels. Foreboding darkness overpowers both the flashlight and the Fae lights, swallowing the feeble halos of brightness after only a few feet. How she knows where she's going is anyone's guess. Nevertheless, this place, hidden within the forest, would be the perfect breeding ground for all kinds of evil. Vermin flourish here, too, considering how many beady eyes lurk amongst the many scattered alcoves and grates, which accounts for at least some of the smells wafting through the air.

Tap-tap-tap. The hollow sound comes from somewhere close. Rachel jerks in surprise. Orion walks up to her, holds his hand out to the side, to where she could've sworn the sound originated from, and his Fae light rushes forward to brighten the area. The Fae light isn't a match for the utter darkness.

Tap-tap-tap.

"What is that?" Rachel whispers.

"Knockers," Orion whispers back.

"Knockers?" She raises an eyebrow.

"Knockers are displaced when mines close down, so they have no other option than to move to long-forgotten underground ruins. New York's underground mazes are filled with knockers," he explains and shrugs. "They're mostly harmless, but we'd better get a move on lest we get on their nerves."

Rachel nods and gives Mrs. Crenshaw a swift once-over. She looks paler than usual, drained of energy. "Are you okay, Mrs. Crenshaw?"

"I'm geriatric, not an invalid. Relax."

"Don't be stubborn. If you're tired—"

"Rachel, we're not having this conversation now," Mrs. Crenshaw hisses. "You two are lagging. Move it or leave."

Tap-tap-tap.

The sound grows louder, closer, more insistent.

Rachel looks over to where the arched vaults are, into the nothingness they had left behind.

"That knocker is trying to get our attention for some reason." Rachel points in the sound's general direction and her Fae light moves over the area, stopping only when it hovers above the creature that's been following them. The knocker is a two-foot tall teenager, dressed in a pair of tiny jeans, a plaid shirt, and a small hard hat that probably serves as protection from cave-ins. A utility kit is strapped around his waist, but the place where his hammer should've been is empty. The hammer—small but remarkably modern—is held firmly in his hand, resting against the brick wall.

She smiles, opens her mouth to greet the little guy, but Mrs. Crenshaw stops her by placing a firm hand on her shoulder.

The old woman leans closer and says, "Don't. Knockers are classified as a subspecies of Fae. Most of the creatures in that taxonomic ranking are vicious."

Rachel closes her mouth but keeps her gaze fixed on the knocker. He taps his hammer against the wall a few more times, his expression turning grave as he regards her for a while longer, before he dashes off in the opposite direction. The darkness swallows him whole.

As soon as he's gone, Mrs. Crenshaw visibly relaxes beside her. "Knockers, pixies, and some other garden variety faeries cross over into Shadow Grove unchecked. Their magic keeps the border up and the troublemakers out. It's a symbiotic relationship."

Rachel snaps her fingers and her Fae light returns.

"How are you doing that?" Orion asks Rachel.

"What?"

"The Fae light—"

A gravelly titter interrupts him, coming from beyond the trickle of light shining ahead of Mrs. Crenshaw's flashlight beam. Rachel glances at Orion as stone-cold calmness drains out of his face and an almost worried expression takes its place. A second, shriller giggle joins the first. Behind them, a third voice cackles along. Rachel, Mrs. Crenshaw, and Orion begin to search for the owners of those voices, their lights weakening with every passing second. They find nothing, just an all-consuming darkness.

The flashlight flickers in Mrs. Crenshaw's hand.

"I can't see jack," she mumbles, tapping the bezel against her palm. The flashlight goes out. "Damn it."

"We seem to have wandered into a Darkling nest," Orion says.

The Fae lights both lose their buoyancy, sinking toward the ground. Darkness swoops in. As the glowing balls touch down, their lights fade out.

The laughter grows hysterical.

Chapter Fourteen
Dark And Twisted

Mrs. Crenshaw's panicky breathlessness is emphasized by the way her dainty feet shuffle hesitantly across the gritty floor. There's an uncharacteristic worry in her voice as she says, "Make yourself useful and create more of those glowing ball thingies."

Rachel fears for her elderly neighbor's wellbeing. What if Mrs. Crenshaw has a heart attack? What if she falls and breaks her hip in this incredible darkness? There are too many variables working against the old woman, regardless of her fierce stubbornness, to allow her to come along further.

"They'll just feed on the light," Orion responds in a calm, collected tone of voice.

Something slimy and cold touches Rachel's ankle. She jumps away, heart pounding as she discerns a silhouette of whatever's in the darkness. "Orion, can you get Mrs. Crenshaw out of here safely?" she quickly asks, suppressing a shiver of revulsion.

"Don't you dare, Rachel Cleary," Mrs. Crenshaw growls her warning.

"Yes," he says, ignoring the old woman's protest. "Will you be okay for a few seconds by yourself?"

Before she can answer him, something elongated smacks

across her ankle, curls around her calf, and crawls up her leg. She's half-certain it's a tentacle with suckers kissing her skin.

"Y-yup, but come back fast." Every part of Rachel's skin creeps with increasing disgust as this unseen entity moves higher up her leg, making slurping noises as it goes. Slime runs down her leg and collects on the brim of her sneaker, a thick mucus discharge of some kind that smells like rot. It could be an alien snake, maybe a weird octopus' arm—maybe something completely different.

Mrs. Crenshaw shouts, "Unhand me. Let go o—"

Silence falls.

It's almost as if every Darkling has taken a collective breath, anxiously anticipating Orion's return. The tendril around her leg creeps higher. She reaches down and tugs at the tentacle. It rebels by constricting tighter, squeezing hard enough to make her snatch back her hand. Rachel suppresses an urge to touch it again and somehow force herself free from its nauseating undertakings, to pull the ghastly tentacle off and to stomp on it until the *thing*—because it can't be called anything other than a *thing*—shrivels up and dies.

She balls both her hands into fists and inhales deeply through her mouth, the putrid stench somehow tasting even worse than it smells. She gags, covers the lower half of her face with the back of her hand, and clears her mind of all thoughts involving the sordid thing now crawling up her thigh.

"Rachel?" Orion's voice rebounds from the vaulted ceilings and the laughter surrounding them begins anew.

Something bumps into her knee, almost making her lose her footing. She blindly kicks out with her free foot and connects with something solid, which crunches sickly beneath her sneaker.

This time she can't stop herself from cringing.

"Over here."

In the distance, she hears a distinct punch. Flesh meets flesh. A nearby crash echoes. The laughter fades as a battle wages in the darkness.

"Hold on," Orion calls out. "I'll be right with you."

"I literally can't go anywhere," she says, the tendril already moving up to her hips, wrapping her in a tight, slick embrace. The slime drips down, covering her lower body in goo.

"Problems?"

"Nothing serious, I hope," Rachel says. "Tell me something interesting while I wait?"

His laughter is unlike the Darklings' tittering and giggling and cackling. There's warmth there, a pleasant geniality. It's infectious enough to make her smile without having any reason to do so.

An enormous crack reverberates through the tunnel and dust—she truly hopes it's only dust—rains down. This darkness is more than an obstacle. It plays with your head; makes you imagine the worst. It's psychological warfare at its finest.

A few more forceful impacts sound, violent and remorseless. "What do you want to know?" he asks, hardly sounding winded.

"I don't know. What does Nebulius mean?"

She hears bones crunch and sickening squelches coming from somewhere closer. A terrified screech, both angry and afraid, sounds. It's cut short by another loud crunch.

"Nebulius means heavenly bodies," he says.

"Okay. Let's try something more difficult. Misty's note mentioned something about her vengeance starting when the Miser rises. What's all that about?"

Hands land on her shoulders. "Orion," she yells, heart thumping like crazy. If she could see anything at all, her reaction might've been less frantic, but the blinding darkness is so comprehensive she can't help herself.

"It's me," he says gently, not without humor. "To answer your question, the Miser is what we call the members of the Dark Court. Aurial are members of the Light Court. Now, what's the problem?"

Rachel moves her hands over his arms and up his shoulders. They travel to his neck, over his chiseled chin, touching high cheekbones, before coming to a rest on either side of his face. After making sure it really is Orion, she says, "There's something wrapped around me and it's moving up my waist."

"I don't see anything."

"Thank you for stating the obvious, Faerie Boy. I can't see anything either, but it's there. I feel it."

"Show me," he says, covering her hands with his, and allowing Rachel to guide them to her waist, to where the constricting tentacle now sits, unmoving. "Here?" Orion asks when she stops.

"Yes. What is it?"

"It's a type of Darkling. A rare one," he says, fingers pushing into the space between her body and the creature.

She feels his hands grip the width of the tentacle, sliding down slowly until he reaches the point where her navel is before he gently tugs at it. The Darkling responds by squeezing and curling tighter around her body, trapping Orion's hand in the space between. He tries a second time, slowly loosening the creature's grip, but the entity's reaction is the same. It clamps fast, strangling her waist.

Rachel gasps and reaches for his forearms, digging her fingernails into his wrists as she desperately sucks oxygen into her lungs. "Stop." It feels like her insides are being liquefied by the pressure the Darkling exudes, squeezing her like she's a ripe, juicy orange. "Please, stop."

More and more voices surround them, laughing at their expense, drowning out all other sounds.

Orion leans closer and says in Rachel's ear, "Trust me, Clarré."

Using both hands, he pulls harder at the Darkling, bending it slowly. The crisp sound, reminiscent of breaking a fresh carrot, quietens the taunting laughter. The creature around her waist battles back by sucking harder at her exposed skin, constricting even more. She's ready to start screaming from the pain when a golden light—similar to the Fae lights he'd created earlier—envelops his hands and brightens the gloom. The tentacle glows reddish-brown under his touch, illuminating the cracks where he bent it.

"Almost there ..."

The shrieking begins, grisly dying sounds echoing through miles and miles of tunnels. An indescribable cacophony, the uproar of outrage, joins in as the remaining Darklings scream along with their burning brother, almost as if its pain is their pain.

Rachel watches the reddish-brown turn white-hot, the coloring and cracks spreading across its serpentine body. She doesn't burn along with the Darkling, but its deadlight eyes dim as its surface sizzles and floats away like burning tissue paper drifting on a breeze. An unpleasant odor, unlike anything she's ever smelled, fills the space. It's something between decay and sulfur and assaults her nostrils. Her gag reflexes are stimulated again, causing her to dry heave.

"Don't vomit on me," Orion urges over the ruckus.

She offers him a queasy smile as she holds her breath, waiting for him to finish burning the infernal entity off her body. Just as Rachel feels herself becoming faint from a lack of air, she can move freely again. Not wanting to get any of the residual smoke into her lungs, she clasps her hand over her mouth again and breathes in shallow breaths.

His warm hand finds hers in the darkness. The rough exterior of his palm, riddled with callouses and peppered with scars, presses against hers, before she laces her fingers with his. With her thumb, she traces one of those linear marks running up the side of his index finger, crisscrossed with other thicker welts. At first, she wants to ask if he'd lost a fight with a blender, but when her fingertips graze against the back of his hand where more raised scars mar his skin, she decides not to make jokes.

He leads her through the darkness, carefully navigating the area in near-blindness.

"I feel like I should take you on a date after this is over," Orion says.

"You wish."

Chuckling, he says, "Harsh, Clarré. Harsh."

"What's with you calling me Clarré all of a sudden?"

"It's your new nickname since you insist on calling me Faerie Boy." He halts his advancement and Rachel stops by his side. A soft droning, a repetitive sentence spoken with the fervor of zealots, comes from nearby. "Here's the plan: I'm going to go in and keep the Night Weaver busy while you sneak in afterward and save the kids."

"Solid plan, but there's a problem."

"Which is?"

"I can't even see my hand in front of my face," Rachel says. The golden glow forms in his hand, swirling and churning and growing brighter as it shapes itself into a sphere. "That helps."

"Keep it in your hand, otherwise it'll die out faster," he says, placing the ball of light into her cupped palm. "Now, close your hand into an open fist."

Rachel obliges and the sphere becomes smaller, shining through her skin and bones. She unfurls her fingers again and the sphere grows bigger.

"There we go. Are you ready?"

"One last thing before we walk towards certain death ..." Rachel releases his hand and moves it up to his neck. She pulls him down to her level and presses her lips against his with the same intensity as when he'd kissed her earlier.

Orion snakes one hand around her waist and rests it against the small of her back.

Her heart both races in excitement and pounds hard with desire. Before the kiss can turn into anything else, Rachel pulls away from him. She moves her hand down his shoulder and pats him gently on his chest. "There's nothing quite like kissing a guy your mother won't approve of to help get the adrenaline pumping. Don't get yourself killed, okay?"

"I'll try my best." Orion's voice is husky, seductive.

"You'd better because I might need you in the future when I have the urge to be rebellious again." Rachel pushes herself onto the tips of her toes and brushes her lips against his a final time before stepping away. "Lead the way."

Orion walks ahead of her, toward the voices repeating a one-sentence mantra in a language Rachel can't understand. The tunnel opens into a large chamber with a high ceiling. In the center, a meager flame burns inside a metal trashcan, making more smoke than light. Rachel spots the mom club and a few men she's seen around town, all standing in front of a distorted, elevated throne. Sheriff Carter stands at the front, his blubbery figure recognizable even from this distance.

The Night Weaver perches on her throne, basking in the adoration of her devotees. She has a raven-like quality about her, seemingly resting on a gravestone, ready to caw at the first passerby so she can steal their soul. She's in her element here; a queen of death in her court of rot.

"Where are they?" Rachel whispers. "Where are the kids?"

He points to the farthest wall—no, it's not a wall. The hollowed-out tree grows alongside others, which are so densely packed together they form a realistic-looking wall. Inside the hollowing, however, something bulges outward, like a black tumor ready to explode. Rachel gazes across the wall of trees and finds others with similar black lumps, malignantly spreading to every part of the chamber. An oily sheen coats those devilish sores, gleaming in the faint firelight as shadows dance across the macabre wall decorations.

The shadows flicker in and out of existence, humanoid, yet monstrous in shape, creating a grim atmosphere.

"Do you see those trees covered with the black membranes?" he whispers back.

"Yes," Rachel says.

"She keeps the children in stasis for years, feeding off their fear, then she moves on to their souls, before eventually eating the empty shells they've left behind," Orion explains. He remains quiet for a while, evaluating the chamber, and says, "Do me a favor? Run if it looks like I'm losing. Call for the knockers and they'll guide you to the entrance."

"Okay," she says. "You won't lose, though?"

Orion grimaces and shrugs. "It's best if I have a Plan B in place. Cockiness gets people killed, you know."

Rachel rolls her eyes. "Go annoy her, Faerie Boy, so I can do my part."

He winks and casually strolls out of the tunnel to enter the chamber. Orion studies his nails, acting like he doesn't have a care in the world, and heads past the flaming trashcan. He sidesteps a pile of debris littered across the floor and pushes through the congregation of adults with a courteous 'pardon me' or 'excuse me', interrupting their adulation. The chanting stops and a confused mumbling starts up as the Night Weaver's acolytes stare at the disruptive newcomer.

Rachel spots her mother in the crowd, wearing a blank expression, and she wonders—for the umpteenth time—whether there's anything left of the woman who'd given birth to her.

Orion sets his hand on the raised dais, tilts his head, and says, "I love what you've done with the place."

The Night Weaver's cloak lifts her off the throne, angles her upright in the air and the tattered hem spreads out every which way. From afar, she looks like a demonic peacock ruffling its feathers as a predator comes into its line of sight. Her acolytes scatter out of the way of danger, whether they're compelled to do so or because their instincts override her influence. Rachel can't be sure, but she uses the opportunity of disorder to dim her Fae light and sneak inside the chamber.

"You dare to enter my domain uninvited?" the Night Weaver

asks.

"Inertia has rendered you soft." Orion barks a laugh. "The Night Weaver *I* know wouldn't have partaken in idle chitchat. Is it possible that one of Orthega's most feared criminals, the infamous Night Weaver who fills the nightmares of Faelings across the Realm, has lost her—what's the word—pizzazz?"

Rachel reaches the nearest hollow tree with its distended tumor, located in a corner on the farthest wall from the throne. The membrane consists of slimy black ribbons covering the hollowing, which feels semi-hardened, but is still full-on gross. She imagines the children inside undergoing a pupation period, transforming into beautiful butterflies instead of withering away as the Night Weaver drains them of everything they are. Imagining good things is all she can do to prevent the fear from getting the better of her.

She places her hand against the oily substance, which squelches through the gaps between her fingers and squirts onto the back of her hand. She meets resistance with her palm. The gross-factor involved in penetrating the squishy, thick membrane underneath those icky ribbons is the stuff of nightmares. She pushes her arm elbow-deep until she feels something solid on the other side and stretches her fingers to trace the object—a familiar chin, tight-lipped mouth, and an improperly-healed nasal fracture on the bridge of the nose.

Dougal.

She slips her hand back through the hole, grabs the edge of the membrane, and tears one-handedly at the thick, slimy covering entrapping her friend. The gooey, palm-sized pieces fall away easily enough, and soon Dougal's entire face is uncovered. Using her sludge-covered hand, she grabs him by his shoulder and shakes him. Rachel whispers his name loudly, hoping he'll wake from his unnatural sleep. She glances behind her, sees Orion and the Night Weaver still catching up, while the acolytes' attention is fixed solely on them.

"Dougal," she hisses again, shaking him harder. "Wake up."

Nothing happens.

Hoping he won't be angry, she raises her hand and slaps him hard across the cheek, leaving a black, sticky handprint against his pale skin. His eyes shoot open and his jaw goes slack as he readies to yell. Not wanting to take chances, she covers his mouth with the same sticky hand, muffling his enraged words.

"Shush," she says, looking over her shoulder again. "She'll hear." Dougal nods in understanding, and Rachel slowly removes her hand. "Can you get out by yourself?"

"Aye," Dougal whispers back, already tearing through the remaining membrane. "Go. I'll help get the weans out."

Rachel moves on to the neighboring hollow tree a few steps away. She repeats the process of sticking her hand through the membrane but saves time by immediately tearing a large piece of the gooey substance off. She drops it to the ground, leaving a big enough hole to ease a small child out. Eight-year-old Dana Crosby sits there, her eyes shut tightly and her face ashen, too big to fit through the hole Rachel's created. The poor girl looks like she could use a good meal and a long bath, but otherwise, she's physically sound. Mentally and emotionally, it's a whole other story, Rachel's sure.

If any of these kids remember what they've been through, the local therapists are going to make a lot of bank soon.

Rachel struggles for what seems like forever to rip open the tough membrane of Dana's prison cell in the hollow tree.

Eventually, as she becomes so desperate to release the girl, her own comfort no longer matters. She bites at the membrane, tearing it apart with her teeth. Thick, inky liquid runs from her mouth and drips down her chin and onto the front of her shirt, staining the fabric. She spits out the oily fluid and wipes her face with her already ruined shirt. The Fae light in her left-hand acts nervously, pulsing faster—on what she decides to call its 'low setting'—the longer she struggles.

Dougal, now free, takes over the task of helping Dana out.

Rachel moves on to the next protruding growth against the wall, then the next, and the one afterward. Meanwhile, she keeps a wary eye on Orion, who's insulting the Night Weaver to keep her interest from wandering off to what's happening in the shadows. Somehow, someway, he knows exactly which of the crone's buttons to press, because more than once it seems like she must hold herself back from attacking him. Behind Rachel, Dougal wakes the kids one after the other, then leads them into the tunnels two-by-two and returns for the rest. He's efficient and able to keep the children calm and quiet during their great escape.

As Rachel nears the last couple of hollow trees, located behind the asymmetrical throne of trash, something crunches underfoot. Well-hidden by the dais, she opens her hand slightly for the Fae light to grow brighter, lifts her foot, and looks at the ivory fragments beneath the sole of her shoe. She bends down to study the odd garbage, wearing a grimace.

A little voice inside her head, the one that always warns her when things aren't kosher, tells her to look up. Rachel's gaze moves across the gritty stone floor, across to the back of the dais.

More of the ivory fragments litter the ground, surrounding a pile of blanched bones. Thousands of different types of bones—

femurs and vertebrae and phalanges and ribs—belonging to countless victims, lie there in a heap. At the top, a tiny, cracked skull with hollow eye sockets stares back at her.

Her heart skips a beat.

The harrowing imagery takes a moment to process, and she tucks away the information for later evaluation. She stands up ever so slowly, her legs wobbling as she gathers her courage, and drags herself to the next cocoon.

The child's skull is seared into her memory.

Such a tragic, indescribable end to an unlived life.

"Prince, you try my patience with your lies." The Night Weaver's menacing voice indicates she's had enough of the cajoling.

Rachel agrees; it's time Orion put an end to her existence.

She goes about opening the last cocoons with cold, systematic movements, struggling to keep the visual of the skull tucked away in one of her mind's many compartments. If she starts wondering who the kid was before the Night Weaver sank her claws into some unsuspecting adult, she'd not be able to function. She won't be able to help get the living kids to safety.

Rachel shuts her eyes and inhales deeply, clearing away anything in her mind that could put her out of commission. Later, when this is over, she'll allow herself to have a good, long cry over the lives lost, thanks to the Night Weaver's insatiable hunger and horrendous brutality.

She opens her eyes and punches a big enough hole in the second-to-last membranous cell. Becky Goldstein sits inside, an expression of dread prominent on her sleeping face.

Don't think about it, Rachel. Don't think about the things they've had to endure. Just get them out.

On the other side of the throne, out of Rachel's line of vision, she hears a whip-like strike, like a wet towel slapping through the air. A whoosh is followed by a crash against the throne, which rattles unsteadily on its elevated pedestal.

"Misty Robins used you like she used the rest of the Miser," Orion shouts as a second crack cleaves the air. "She promised you freedom and power when she released you from Leif, didn't she? Instead, you were nothing more than a victim to further her treasonous agenda."

"Misty gave me the vengeance I craved," the Night Weaver screams back.

"What vengeance?" Orion laughs as a golden light brightens the gloom. "Your *sisters* turned you over to King Auberon, claiming you were preying on Black Annis younglings."

"*Lies.*" Another deafening crack sounds. "I never touched Black Annis younglings."

"Your own kin accused you of raiding the nests, feeding for months off those precious and rare younglings before—" Orion's words are cut off as something clatters to the ground. "You're no match for a Prince of Amaris."

"We need to hurry," Dougal says upon returning to Rachel's side, breathless.

"Is it bad?" she asks, still working on the last membranous covering.

"The adults left. They ran right past the weans without lookin' back," he says, easily pulling Becky out of the hollow tree and into his arms. "The other Fae is toyin' with the Black Annis, but I don't know how long she'll fall for his games." Dougal cradles Becky in his arms, gently waking her up with soothing words.

"Is he okay?" Rachel asks, peering around the throne to catch a glimpse of Orion.

"Rach, there isn't time to worry about what's goin' on somewhere else," Dougal says. "Get the last wean."

Rachel shakes her head as if she can shake her worries away, but it's impossible. She returns her attention to the otherworldly womb-like prison and peels away a large piece of the membrane to reveal the little boy held captive inside. The boy can't be older than four, small enough for Rachel to lift out of the tree with one hand and swing onto her hip. His head rests against her shoulder. She doesn't bother waking him, there's no time and he doesn't need more fuel for his nightmares anyway. Still, as Dougal convinces his sleepy charge to get up, hold his hand, and rush through the shadows, she can't help feeling if she follows, she'll be abandoning Orion.

"Dougal," she hisses before he can get out of earshot.

He turns around. "Aye?"

Rachel walks closer. "Take the boy," she says.

He takes the child without question, saying, "This is fair folk business, Rachel. We've no right gettin' involved."

"Your grandmother is waiting outside," Rachel says, ignoring his statement. "Do you have your phone?"

"Aye."

She looks at Becky, the oldest child to be found in the Night Weaver's lair and takes her cell phone out of her skirt pocket. She quickly unlocks the screen with one hand, bends her knees to get to Becky's level, and looks the twelve-year-old straight in the eyes.

"You know where to find the flashlight app, right?" she asks.

"Y-yes," Becky whispers.

In the background, there's a crash followed by a groan. The

Night Weaver cackles with glee.

Rachel straightens as Orion gets back on his feet, his galaxy eyes almost black with rage.

"Becky, you're going to have to be brave and help Dougal get the littler kids out," Rachel says softly, handing her phone over. "Can you do that?"

"I … I don't …" Becky looks up at Dougal with wide, fearful eyes, clutching Rachel's phone tightly. She inhales deeply, nods, and says, "I'll try."

"Atta girl," Dougal says.

Rachel gives Dougal a halfhearted smile. "Whatever you do, don't come back for me."

"Rach—"

"Don't, please," she interrupts him. "I'm going to try my hardest to get out of this alive, but if I don't …" Rachel inhales deeply, hating the possibility of how this could turn out for her. She forces a smile, and continues, "Make sure the kids get home safely. Tell your grandmother she's my favorite person in the world. Also, if it looks like my mom isn't dealing well with the aftermath, get in touch with my aunt in Bangor."

"Och, Nan's gonna kill me."

"Run now, grumble later," she says, glancing over a pile of rubble to see Orion holding a glowing sword, forged of Fae light. He swings it expertly at the cloak as the fabric reaches out to him, testing his defenses.

When she turns back, Dougal has already left with the remaining children.

Her gaze drops to the ball of light dancing in her hand. It grows larger and brighter as her fingers unfurl while she mentally readies herself to risk her life for a stranger from a strange land.

Chapter Fifteen
Stardust

Rachel's life plan has always been pretty straightforward. Graduate high school with honors, get accepted into a college with a great pre-veterinarian program, go to veterinarian school, find a well-paying job in the city, pay off her student loans, buy a house, fall in love, get married, have a few kids, grow old. *Then* she can happily die without any regrets. It was a safe plan; more than enough for a girl who couldn't care less about fame or fortune. She knows people would've criticized her decisions in the end. They might've said she was wasting her intelligence by sticking around near this godforsaken town to tend to the needs of farm animals instead of being *more.* Those were her dreams, though, and she liked the idea of what her future could've been. She worked hard toward achieving her goals, and she's sure it would've been a good life to live.

As she climbs onto the pedestal and looks at Orion, who's grown weary after having to outmaneuver the Night Weaver's cloak, she realizes a good, easy life wouldn't have sufficed in the long run. At some point, in ten or twenty years' time, she probably would've grown bored with the monotony of a prescribed existence. Dying young, however horrible the idea might sound, doesn't scare Rachel anymore. She helped save seven kids from a heinous end, after all. Seven lives ... How many people can say they've done that?

She makes her way in front of the throne just as the Akrah cloak wraps one of its tendrils around Orion's neck. It lifts him off the floor slowly, until he looks into the Night Weaver's face.

They've run out of time.

"Any last words, *Prince*?" the Night Weaver spits his title like it's a curse.

Rachel opens her hand wide, allowing the Fae light to grow as large as it can, before she yells, "Hey!"

Startled, the Night Weaver spins through the air to look at Rachel. The Akrah cloak drops Orion unceremoniously onto a pile of dead leaves and branches at the same time, as if it's also been shocked by her arrival.

Rachel grins at the Night Weaver, the Fae light pulsing brighter and brighter.

"Eat some sunshine, you miserable old hag." She pulls her arm back as far as possible and using all her strength, pitches the Fae light straight into the Night Weaver's face.

The Fae light dims before it hits home. It bursts into sparks in her face and rains down the Night Weaver's front. An uncontrolled scream of anger and frustration rings through the chamber before the Akrah cloak suddenly flings itself forward and wraps around Rachel's waist. Inky vines shoot from the earth and grab hold of Rachel's ankles and wrists, wrapping around her tightly.

Rachel is forced to spread out as the vines become taut, pulling her every which way. It's uncomfortable at first, and she suspects it will become painful soon, but the pulling stops before they reach that far.

The Night Weaver shoots forward and halts just in time for her acrid breath to hit Rachel's face. Her scream ends, her black eyes staring at Rachel. The Night Weaver's gaze drops to the umbrella pendant around her neck.

"Want to hear something really funny?" Rachel says, daring to flash her captor a mischievous smile. The Night Weaver looks back into Rachel's eyes, the black somehow becoming even blacker. "You still haven't noticed that I've freed all the children."

The Night Weaver pulls away and looks at the trees where her destroyed, empty cells are located. She lets loose another scream, this time one of anguish. Rachel watches as her hands go to her face, and she drags her iron claws down. Deep gashes appear and black blood seeps from the wounds. She inspects every hollowing from afar, the endless scream becoming more tormented.

A sword made entirely of Fae light slices through the vines binding Rachel's right arm and leg, while the Night Weaver is still distracted by the empty cells. Rachel's left arm and leg are released, leaving only the Akrah cloak around her waist.

With graceful footwork, Orion is in front of her, the blazing light searing the Akrah's tendril in one clean swipe. The sword disappears and he grabs her around the waist with both hands, pulling her close. He grunts, his expression twisting in agony, as the pressure builds around them. A sharp pain resonates in her right shoulder, an ice cold flame that burns as it moves through her skin and digs into her flesh. His hold weakens around her waist and Rachel instinctively grips him tighter, holding him up as the world evaporates around them.

In the blink of an eye, the chamber is replaced with bright fluorescent lighting. Gravity takes its revenge on their physics-defying tactics and they crash to the floor. Orion rolls over, breathing hard, while Rachel sits upright by his side.

"Crap," she says, seeing the blossoming pool of blood seeping onto the concrete floor. She shifts over and pulls up his shirt, spies the edge of an angry, gushing wound in his shoulder. "We need to get you to a hospital."

He coughs his laugh. "I'll be all right, Clarré. Just get me some stardust," he says, pointing off to the side.

Rachel follows his index finger and sees potted plants—weird plants with strange colors and unfamiliar flowers and leaves—surrounding them. He'd brought her to an indoor greenhouse, where the exotic plants grow lush and healthy, even in the semi-confined space. She gets to her feet, still dazed after the unnatural form of travel, ignoring the persistent sting in her side, and heads toward the unusual plant.

"Which one is it?"

He struggles for oxygen as he says, "The one with broad, silver-edged leaves."

Rachel finds one large potted plant, too big to move, growing in the center of the table. Not knowing what else to do, she reaches over and grabs a handful of leaves, strips them off the stalk, and rushes back to his side.

"These?" she asks, holding them up for him to see.

Orion nods, eyelids drooping, while he uses one hand to rip off his shirt. A large wound mars the skin on his shoulder, bleeding profusely with each movement he makes. "Crush them in your hand and sprinkle it over the wound," he says weakly.

Rachel does as she's told. The leaves crush easily in her fist, turning into silver dust, which trickles out of her grip. He gasps as the stardust touches the deep, circular wound, which—from the look of it—has gone straight through his body. Orion squeezes his eyes shut and his Adam's apple bobs. Another gasp, then he bucks beneath her.

"I bet you've never heard the story about the magical dress," Rachel says, continuing to sprinkle the stardust. She hopes it'll soon staunch the wound. Her gaze travels across his paling face. An empathic stinging shoots through her shoulder as she witnesses the anguish he has to endure. Her stomach twists into knots. "Once upon a time, a young man took his daughter out to the village in search of a perfect gift for his beautiful wife. The young man, like many young men, thought that if he wanted to show his devotion, he would have to shower his bride with as many expensive jewels as he could afford. They traveled the market, his daughter bouncing up and down as she tried to help her father find something special for her mother. 'A diamond bracelet? Perhaps an emerald ring? What about some pearl earrings?' the merchants asked, showing off their most beautiful items. 'No,' the daughter responded every time she saw their merchandise."

Orion bucks again, groaning in pain.

"The young man became disheartened as the daylight faded. 'Why didn't you like any of the jewels? They're expensive and beautiful and will last a lifetime,' he said to his daughter. The girl thought about it for a while, before she responded, 'Pretty as they may be, they don't seem half as special.' The young man didn't understand, so he asked her to explain. 'Well, Daddy, how can you call a sapphire special if there are hundreds of other glittering gems surrounding it?' The young man hadn't known how to answer her, but he seemed to understand. After all, it's difficult to find something special when everything looks the same," Rachel says, brushing the last of the stardust off her palm. "So, the young man took his daughter's hand and was ready to make the journey home, when suddenly the girl spotted something glistening in the blushing light. 'Daddy, Daddy,' she shouted, pointing at a headless mannequin. 'That's it! That's the special gift.' The young man and his daughter quickly walked up to the shop and took a closer look at the dress." She folds her legs underneath her, takes Orion's hand, and watches as his body continues to fight against the near-fatal wound. "The dress was something out of a fairytale," Rachel continues. "Made from the finest lilac silk, with a hint of gold thread woven into the brocade bodice, something about the dress just felt incredibly unique. As they stepped inside the shop, the slight breeze that entered along with them made the skirts of the dress flutter. It sounded like butterfly wings softly beating. Both the young man and his daughter thought the dress was the most … magical thing … they'd ever s—"

Rachel stops and peers more closely at the wound as the fascinating healing process begins. Muscle and flesh weave together in front of her eyes. She glances back at the potted plants, her logic immediately turning to nano-technology as the reason for the quick healing.

Orion squeezes her hand again, gently this time, as if urging her to go on.

"The young man bought the dress, and he and his daughter left the market," she says, feeling silly for telling him this story now. Rachel clears her throat. "The next day, the young man gifted the dress to his wife, hoping she wouldn't be disappointed that he hadn't bought her jewels. 'Oh, oh, this is absolutely beautiful,' the wife said. She inspected the fine silk and the intricate brocade bodice, her eyes glistening with tears. 'This is the most perfect gift I've ever received, my love,' she continued." Rachel pauses, still keeping a watchful eye on the wound. "What made the dress magical, however, wasn't the fabric or the craftsmanship put into making it. It's what happened not too long thereafter that gave the magical dress its power. For, you see, the young man died unexpectedly, leaving a grieving widow and daughter behind. They felt their loss in every quiet moment. One day, for no reason, the grieving mother put on the dress for the first time since his death and twirled around in front of the mirror. 'Remember how your father and I danced together the first time I wore this dress?' she asked her daughter. 'I remember,' the daughter said." Rachel inhales deeply. "Whenever the wife put on the dress, memories flooded back. Memories of a husband who loved her so much, he would've given her the stars if he could, but instead, he gave her a dress."

"What's the moral of the story?" Orion asks through his labored breathing, clearly about to pass out.

"The stars may be everlasting, but the most precious things are fleeting and fragile and one of a kind."

His breathing steadies and his body relaxes beside her.

Rachel releases Orion's hand and stands. She looks around the indoor greenhouse, where the strange plants are lined up underneath an intricate misting system, and sees a banister poking out above the second to last row. Rachel makes her way to it. She doesn't recognize any of the plants as she walks through the greenhouse, although there is one flower which looks like it could be a rose-daisy hybrid.

Rachel reaches the ornamental wrought iron railings, where curlicues intertwine to create a continuous pattern. Linoleum covers each step down, a tasteful green design—reminiscent of

1940s flooring trends—hidden under a thin layer of dust. The walls are a lighter shade of green, almost a balmy mint.

She hesitates at the top of the stairwell, wondering if leaving Orion is a wise choice, but her feet seem to make the decision for her. Rachel descends the stairs, too hungry, too tired, and far too dirty to be afraid of something jumping her anymore.

What I wouldn't do for a shower, BLT sandwich, and a comfortable bed right now. In that order.

She crosses the landing and continues downward. As she nears the end of the stairwell, golden letters spell out: FLOOR 9—engraved into the matte black display sign. A gilt arrow points toward the sea-green door ahead. She reaches for the brass doorknob, turns it, pushes the door open, and steps into Orion's apartment—through the closet door.

"Of course, he lives in a TARDIS," she says, shaking her head. "Why wouldn't he?"

After some exploring, and some 'accidentally on purpose' snooping, Rachel learns the apartment is a humble, homey space. The bathroom has definitely been remodeled and modernized—a glass shower, a corner porcelain bathtub, and gleaming Italian faucets are the eye-candy focal points against the light-gray walls. The entire room beckons her to indulge a little, to clean off the grit and grime she's covered in. The second bedroom is barely big enough for the single bed and built-in cupboard space, but it's neat and would do fine if an unexpected guest came around. The main bedroom is more basic, though. Fitted with a queen-sized bed with a standard headboard, and indigo-colored bedding and curtains adding some color to the plain white walls, it seems almost military in style. Then there's the built-in wardrobe, where all his clothes are neatly stacked into various piles.

She closes the wardrobe door and walks to his bed, where she grabs a pillow. Rachel makes a detour into the kitchen and finds a glass on the drying rack, which she fills with water before she heads back to the staircase in the closet.

Orion is still asleep on the hard concrete, the wound already half-closed. She kneels by his side, and as she lifts his head to place the pillow underneath, his eyelids flutter open.

"I can't carry you down without hurting you, so you're going to have to be happy with a pillow," she says, avoiding his gaze.

He gives her an easy, crooked smile.

"Do you want some water?"

"Please," he croaks.

She cradles his head and brings the glass closer to his lips. Orion drinks deeply. Water runs down the sides of his mouth, dribbling onto his chin and wetting his chest. At least he doesn't choke. She lays his head down on the pillow.

Rachel picks up the glass and gets to her feet when Orion tries to sit up. "I'm not leaving," she says, thinking that's the problem.

"You're bleeding," Orion says, wearing a mask of pain as he continues to try and push himself upright.

"Lie down," she says, averting her gaze to study her top. Scarlet droplets stain her shirt, exactly where she'd felt the searing cold pain when they had left the Night Weaver's lair. Rachel pushes down the sleeve of her shirt to evaluate the wound. "It's superficial," she says.

"You're a bad liar, Clarré," he mumbles.

"I'm not lying, look," Rachel says as she takes a step closer and shows him her graze. "See? Whatever stabbed right through you barely broke my skin."

"I don't have the energy to argue right now," Orion says, lying down. "Just put some stardust on it anyway."

She steps over him, back to where she'd found the stardust plant earlier, and takes a handful of leaves. "Don't get used to me complying with your requests. I'm only doing this because you saved my life and I suppose I owe you." Rachel crushes the leaves in her fist and pushes her sleeve down again. "Do I have to sprinkle the stardust, or can I just slap it on there and call it a day?"

"Why would you want to do that?"

"Well?"

"It'll work, but you'll lose out on—" Orion is cut off by the sudden slap of her hand against the wound, her sharp intake of breath through her teeth.

"Motherf—"she bites back her curse just in time.

"You do realize there's more to healing than this impersonal nonsense you humans insist on calling medicine, right?"

Rachel needs to lean against the table for support as the debilitating pain spreads through her body via her bloodstream. The actual injury hadn't even felt this bad, had been a mere prick in comparison. She slowly moves back to Orion, gripping the tables along the way to keep herself from plummeting to the concrete floor. Rachel falls to her knees beside him, rolls over, and lies on her back. If she didn't have her dignity to think about, the chances are good she might writhe in agony.

Orion pushes his arm underneath her head to make her more comfortable on the floor, chuckling softly, and pulls her closer. "It helps when there's someone telling you stories to keep your mind off the pain," he says. "Shall I tell you about Orthega?"

"Dougal and I visited Telfore over the weekend. Great place, fine folks," she says, digging her nails into her palms as a spasm threatens to make her cry out. Could it have only been two days ago when arrows had been flying toward them and they'd had to escape through the sewers?

"I'm not sure if you're sarcastic by nature or if it's the stardust talking."

"A bit of both," she whispers. Her eyelids become heavy as her body relaxes. "My car is still at Pearson …" Rachel falls asleep before she can finish her sentence.

Chapter Sixteen
Will-O'-The-Wisp

"I strongly advise you to stay indoors until dawn," Orion says, blocking the front door.

She crosses her arms. Three hours have passed since their escape from the Night Weaver's lair. Two and a half of those hours she's spent sleeping while her superficial wound knits itself shut. Mrs. Crenshaw must be worried sick by now, probably thinking Rachel has met her end at the Night Weaver's metallic claws. Not to mention, Rachel needs to check in on her mother.

Had the kids gotten out all right? Was Dougal safe?

"I need to get back home," she says. "My mom—"

"Your mom doesn't know who she is anymore. She'll summon the Night Weaver as soon as she lays eyes on you." Orion blinks slowly, his thick, dark eyelashes brushing the top of his high cheekbones. "Call Nancy, tell her you're all right and that you'll see her in the morning. I doubt she's an unreasonable woman who'll insist on you going out when a psychotic Black Annis is hunting for you."

"With what phone? I handed mine over to Becky so she could use it as a flashlight."

Orion throws his head back and stares at the ceiling, mumbling something incoherent under his breath. When he looks back to her, he pushes his hand into his pocket and produces a cell phone.

"Honestly, Clarré, you make it sound as if I'm a technotard," he says, handing it to her. "I even have a Facebook profile, in case you were wondering."

"Ew."

He frowns. "What ew?"

"That's so five years ago."

Rachel dials Mrs. Crenshaw's number and makes her way to the living room. It rings a few times before Dougal answers the phone with a weary greeting. She goes right into telling him that she's alive, unhurt, and in a safe place—*I'm waiting out the Night Weaver until dawn.* She then asks him if all the kids got out of the Night Weaver's lair in one piece and learns they have all been taken to the hospital to get checked out. The Sheriff's Department had, apparently, already notified their parents of their whereabouts.

"Everyone's accounted for, except a girl called Astraea Hayward," Dougal says. "We didn't miss one, eh?"

Rachel replays the events in the lair in her mind, and says, "No, I'm certain we got all of the cocoons."

"Then where is she?"

Good question.

The conversation moves on to her asking him if his grandmother's all right. As it happens, Mrs. Crenshaw isn't worried about Rachel—*If that Fae knows what's good for him, he'll keep ye from harm, because Nan will make him suffer.* Rachel doesn't doubt it. When she turns the topic to her mother, Dougal hesitates. Nobody's seen Jenny Cleary or any of the other adults involved in the Night Weaver's disturbing cult since they scattered.

"Could they be in the forest?" Dougal offers.

"No. From what I understand, the Night Weaver, or any other powerful Fae for that matter, can't cross the boundary without our families' approval. I wouldn't be surprised if they're still in the tunnel," she says, sighing.

"Are ye tellin' me we're glorified border patrol officers?"

"When you put it that way, it sounds rather awful." Rachel sighs. "We'll work everything out in the morning. Until then, stay inside."

"Ye don't have to tell me twice," he says. "Night, Rach."

"Goodnight, Dougal."

She ends the call, sets the phone down on the coffee table, and sits back. Rachel balls her hand into a fist and props it under her chin, scowling at the coffee table as she thinks about her mother. How will she get her out from under the Night Weaver's control? Unlike some mothers and daughters, who are total BFFs, Rachel and Jenny have never been especially close. Perhaps it's because they're such different people—Jenny isn't the most responsible person in the world, never has been. She's a wild-child, a social butterfly through and through. Rachel, however, likes structure and to-do lists and usually enjoys being alone. Their personalities often clash because Rachel won't ever be the popular cheerleader her mom wants her to be. Still, as different as they are, Rachel loves her mom deeply.

"Right, so I'm ordering pizza," Orion says, picking up his cell phone as he passes. "Or would you prefer something else?"

"Pizza is fine," she mutters. Rachel shakes her head. "Wait. They deliver to this … place?" She wanted to say *hellhole* but decided not to offend her host.

"Ashfall Heights isn't half as bad as people think," he says, scrolling through his contact list. "Apart from a few bad apples, most people tend to keep to themselves. And since I got rid of the previous tenant in 4-D, it's actually been relatively nice living here again."

Rachel grimaces. "I'll bite. What did 4-D do to deserve your special attention?"

"You don't want to know," Orion says, lifting the cell phone to his ear.

She waits until he finishes placing the order—a pepperoni pizza with a thick crust and extra cheese—before she says, "I'm curious now. What did the previous tenant in 4-D do?"

Orion sets the phone down on his armrest. "You've had a difficult day and I don't want to add to your nightmares." He stands from the recliner and makes his way past her again. "Why don't you go have a bubble bath while we wait for the pizza?"

"And wear what exactly?"

"That's up to you. You've already snooped around in my wardrobe, so take your pick of whatever," he says, shrugging. "I'll go find you an extra toothbrush."

"How—?"

"Most Fae have keen senses, Clarré, best to remember that in the future." Orion disappears down the corridor. Rachel quickly stands and goes after him. He gestures to the second bedroom, saying, "You're welcome to the spare bedroom, of course."

"Of course," she repeats to his retreating back.

Orion glances over his shoulder, eyebrow rising. "Well, if you'd prefer to share my bed, I won't deny you the pleasure."

Rachel feels her cheeks flush. "The spare bedroom is fine, thank you."

"Thought so, but my door is always open." He sniggers as he enters the main bedroom and heads to his nightstand. The drawer rolls open. He rummages around inside before pulling out an unopened toothbrush. "Clothes are in there, as you know," he says, gesturing to the wardrobe as he sets the toothbrush on the bed. "What else?"

"Do you have a hairbrush or comb?"

"There's one in the medicine cabinet," Orion says. "Oh, and extra towels beneath the bathroom sink."

"Thank you."

Orion begins to make his way out of the bedroom again.

"Hey," she says, and he whirls around. Orion places his hand against the doorframe, waiting. Rachel holds her elbows, and asks, "Do you have any idea if there's a way to free my mom from the Night Weaver's control?"

"I'm not sure," he says, releasing a disheartening sigh. "But I'm already working on it."

Rachel gives him a small nod. "I can't lose her."

"You won't. Go relax for a while, okay? I'll call you when the pizza gets here." He smiles reassuringly, slaps the doorframe as he turns around, and walks away.

As soon as he's gone, Rachel opens his wardrobe doors and reaches for a white T-shirt at the top of the stack and a pair of shorts on the bottom shelf. She picks up the toothbrush and heads toward the bathroom. Opting for a shower instead of a bath, simply because it's easier for her to wash her hair, she stands beneath the waterfall of hot water with her eyes closed for a good five minutes, allowing her troubles to wash away—if only for a while.

Orion wasn't wrong about it being a difficult day. With all

that's been happening, she's hardly had an opportunity to deal with all the life-changing revelations. Everything she knows about the world is wrong. Well, not wrong per se, just different to what she was taught to believe. No, not even different. Transcendent.

The children's faces flash in her memory, those innocent boys and girls who would've been lost if things hadn't worked out the way they had. The little cracked skull, perched upon a morbid pile of child-sized bones, reappears in her mind's eye, startling her back to reality.

Rachel puts more haste into her movements as she scrubs the dirt and dried inky residue and blood off her skin. A few minutes later, she's out of the shower and carefully pulling the comb through her wet, tangled hair, trying not to fall back into her thoughts where the skull stares back with its empty, beseeching sockets. She gets dressed in one of Orion's T-shirts, which reaches to just above her knees, while the shorts she'd chosen from his shelf are far too big around her waist and keep falling down.

"Pizza's here," Orion announces from the other side of the door.

"Screw it," she mutters, tired of struggling with the shorts. "Be right out," she calls back.

Rachel's reasoning is: if he wants to look, he's going to look regardless of what she's wearing. She walks with confidence out of the bathroom, wearing nothing other than the T-shirt. The pizza guy's eyes bulge as she passes by the front door, ogling her over Orion's shoulder. The Fae glances in her direction, before turning to face the delivery guy again.

"If you want to keep your tip, now's a good time to leave," Orion says tersely as he grabs the box from the pizza guy's hands and slams the door.

"So, I've been wondering, are the people from Telfore humans?" she asks, walking into the living room. "And if so, are they considered extra-dimensional beings?"

Orion gives her a once over before averting his gaze again as he sets the pizza on the coffee table. He walks over to the La-Z-Boy and sits. "There are humans in every realm, and physiologically they're the same in every way."

"Yes, but will they be considered extra-dimensional beings if they travel here?" Rachel takes a seat on the sofa, inhaling the mouthwatering smell of pepperoni filling the apartment. Her stomach rumbles in delight. She picks up one of the slices of pizza and takes a bite, savoring the meaty-cheesy goodness.

"That's the type of question you need to ask a physics professor," he says, reaching for a slice of his own. "Telfore is an island, approximately the same size as Madagascar, but it's a kingdom filled with bigots, racists, and zealots. Even the other human kingdoms in Orthega steer clear of them." Orion takes a bite of his pizza.

"How many humans are there in Orthega?"

His expression turns thoughtful as he swallows. "When I left there were about eighty thousand humans in Amaris alone, according to the census. With Nova in charge, though, the number could be significantly lower."

She doesn't respond, afraid of saying something about the white-haired man she'd seen in his memories—the one who'd seen *her*—and unintentionally rubbing him the wrong way.

"I have some questions for you," Orion says.

"Shoot."

"Why are you able to move through my memories so easily and why can you manipulate Fae light?"

"The memory thing was completely out of my control. It felt like channel surfing without a remote. As for the Fae light ..." Rachel pulls up her shoulders.

Orion opens his palm and forms a new Fae light. It bounces off his hand and rolls slowly through the air toward her. She smiles as she takes another bite of her pizza, regarding the beautiful sphere.

"I suppose all Fae can make Fae light?"

"Yes. A Fae light is like an extension of our souls. Every Fae's light differs, be it in shape, color, or power. Some of them even have personality, if the Fae wills it to have one," he explains. "Tendrils of darkness are, for example, how the Night Weaver's Fae lights look."

She reaches out to touch the Fae light again. Ripples move across the surface beneath her touch. Rachel uses her free hand to take the sphere out of the air, holds it in her palm, before she blows it away like a kiss. The Fae light travels across the living room and ricochets back to her.

"What else can you do?" she asks as Orion reaches for a second slice of pizza. "You did say you were proficient in five types of magic."

He changes back into the scruffy version of himself in a blink. "Glamor comes easily to me." Orion changes back to his original self. "Healing is another one of my talents, though I tend to rely on elemental magic rather than spirit magic. Then there's my glisser ability, which is what I call 'beating traffic'. In layman's terms, glissering is ... well, it's difficult to explain. It's almost like folding space and time and just jumping to where I want to be. Granted, I have my limits. I can't, for example, travel back in time. Nobody can. But if I envision a place I want to be, and it's within a ten mile radius, I can get there through glissering in no time whatsoever. It's not a common talent to have, but it's not the rarest gift either."

Rachel responds with a mumbled affirmative as she works on her second slice, still playing with the Fae light, which rebounds from the walls and ceiling, hurtling back to her.

"The other two schools of magic are particularly well-suited for life in the military. Free Form is an incantation-based magic we employ as an offensive tactic on the battlefield, while Abjuration is defensive magic."

"You can use influence, too, right?"

"Yes."

"So how come I can still see your glamor?" she asks.

"Glamor and influence are two wholly different schools of magic. Influence is an internal type of magic, whereas glamor is external. The Ronamy Stone only protects you from influence, which is basically mind control. Glamor, on the other hand, is illusion. It's the manipulation of light waves and electromagnetic frequencies." He shrugs.

"It's quantum physics?" Rachel asks.

"Pretty much, yes," Orion says. "Like I told you earlier, I'm an Omni-Opus. In order to be a full-fledged Intra-Canter, you must be able to do all types of Influencing, which I can't."

Rachel finishes her pizza, uses a paper napkin to wipe her hands and mouth, before she says, "Okay, so what kind of Influencing can you do?"

"I can speak in your mind when you're not wearing your necklace. Where is it?"

She hears his voice loud and clear in her head. "I must've forgotten to put it on again after my shower."

"You shouldn't take it off, Clarré."

Rachel blushes as she pushes to her feet. "Fine, I'll go get it now—" The apartment disappears around her, and instead she stands in a magnificent field of wildflowers. She looks around, surprised in the sudden change of landscape.

"Without your necklace, I can make you see things." Orion's voice whispers in her head.

A soft rose scent surrounds her, accompanied by a myriad of other floral fragrances. She can hear the song of birds, an unseen flock chirping happily in the distance. For the briefest moment, Rachel is sure she can taste frozen berries—a taste of spring.

"I can make you smell, hear, and taste things."

She feels a soft pressure against her lips as a ghost hand rests against the small of her back. Orion materializes in front of her, kissing her gently in the field of wildflowers. Rachel breathes in the alluring smells, reveling in the sounds and tastes featured in this enchanting hallucination as she kisses the ghostlike figure back.

Slowly the field disintegrates, and the ghostlike version of Orion vanishes, while the apartment reappears around her.

"I can also make you feel things," Orion says from the other side of the room, a half-eaten slice of pizza in his hand. "Don't take off your necklace or the next time it may not be so pleasant."

"But why aren't you considered an Intra-Canter then?" she asks.

"The most important thing about being an Intra-Canter is being able to influence people into doing things they don't want to do. I can entice your senses, speak in your mind, make you believe what I want you to believe, but I can't force my will on you," he explains.

"You made Greg leave," Rachel says.

"Yes, but it's because I made him believe he came alone, and he'd overstayed his welcome. I didn't exactly force him to do anything," Orion says.

"The Night Weaver is an Intra-Canter, isn't she?"

He shakes his head. "No, manipulating people isn't magical. She's an elemental practitioner who specializes in Shadow Magic."

Rachel remembers what she'd read about the Night Weaver earlier in Greg's office, the ancient document which ends with a glimmer of hope. She makes her way to the corridor. "Light will always defeat darkness," she repeats the line.

"That's an old Aurial saying," he says. "Where'd you hear it?"

Rachel turns around to find him setting his uneaten pizza back into the box on the coffee table and picking up a paper napkin from the pile. "I read it in some old text Greg pulled for me from the town council's archives."

"Interesting," he says, but doesn't elaborate.

Rachel lets the matter go, figuring an old Fae saying won't be of any use to them in another showdown with the Night Weaver.

Chapter Seventeen
Night Everlasting

Dawn doesn't come.

When Rachel opens her eyes the following morning, the room is still shrouded in the same type of darkness one finds in the wee hours, yet it feels like she's slept the whole day away. Her muscles are grateful for the much-needed rest, but she would've preferred to have been in her own bed, surrounded by her belongings, knowing her mother is safe and normal.

She rolls out of the single bed, sleepily pulls the sheets tight over the mattress, and yawns repeatedly as she straightens the covers and fluffs the pillows. Rachel pushes her fingers through her tousled hair and makes her way to the door. A whiff of coffee enters the bedroom through the cracks between the door and doorframe, growing stronger as she turns the doorknob. The artificial lighting in the corridor assaults her eyes, blurs her vision. She rubs at her eyes as she makes her way through the apartment, following the smell of coffee into the kitchen.

"Morning," she mumbles. Orion is already dressed in what seems to be his usual getup of jeans and a T-shirt, leaning against the counter, mug in hand.

"Sleep well?" he asks.

Rachel grumbles something unintelligible, complaining

about the pillow being too high and the bed too soft, while Orion pulls a second mug off the shelf and fills it to the brim.

"Not a morning person, I take it?" he says, offering the mug to her.

"I am usually." Rachel looks at the black, bitter coffee in the large white mug, and decides it'll be for the best to drink it without extra added sugar or milk, especially if she wants a proper jumpstart this morning. "What's the time?"

"Around nine," Orion says, taking another sip of his coffee.

Rachel frowns. "But it's still dark out."

"Yup." He pops the 'p'. "It's likely the Night Weaver's pissed off beyond our comprehension. On a more positive note, the phenomenon seems to be limited to Shadow Grove."

"Wonderful," she mutters. Rachel blows on the steaming coffee, watching Orion. "Do you have any good news to share?"

He pulls her car keys out of his pocket and places them on the surface of the counter. "I took it upon myself to retrieve your car from Pearson Manor, and I hope you don't mind but I ran a few errands on the way back ..." Orion grimaces as he sets his empty mug in the sink.

"I'm still too tired to mind much of anything," she says. "Back up. Why does it sound like there's a *but* missing in that sentence? What happened?"

"While I was at Pearson Manor, Greg informed me his mother didn't go home last night."

She squeezes her eyes shut and fills in the rest. "In other words, my mom hasn't gone home either." Rachel uses her free hand to rub her brow before she opens her eyes again and takes a sip of the freshly brewed bitter, black coffee. "Great."

What do I do? How do I fix this?

Going back to the cave isn't an option, not in this unnatural darkness. The Night Weaver will have the upper hand in her lair, and there's no telling how big her army of Darklings has grown after the intrusion she suffered the previous day. Besides, it's highly probable the town is cast in perpetual night due to the Night Weaver's search efforts outside of the cave. Perhaps her followers are out and about too, helping to look for Rachel and Orion, maybe even scavenging the area in search of new children to gift to their mistress.

"It all comes down to the Akrah cloak," she whispers.

"What about it?" Orion asks.

"It's her biggest strength and her greatest weakness," Rachel explains. "Our best chance of getting rid of the Night Weaver is to convince a piece of fabric to change its allegiance. How do we go about doing that?"

"It's sentient. You address the Akrah as you would address a living, breathing being," he says.

Rachel ponders before she asks, "How would it respond?"

"It speaks through its owner. Where are you going with this?"

"Never mind where I'm going with this," she says. "Tell me, how does the Akrah work—can it live without a host or is it parasitic? What makes it tick?"

Orion crosses his arms. "It's a magical cloak, Clarré. Its only purpose is to feed on darkness and to convert it into energy, which is why we had it in the royal vaults for centuries. It's an auxiliary power source for its wearer."

She narrows her eyes at him. "But it's sentient?"

"Yes."

Rachel throws out the remnants of her coffee into the sink,

places the mug beside his, and clucks her tongue. "No wonder the cloak changed its allegiance. You lot treated it like an object instead of respecting its needs."

"It *is* an object," Orion says.

She doesn't argue, but if Rachel's learned anything over the past few days it's that nothing is as it seems.

Entire universes exist outside the one she inhabits, so it figures that a magical cloak could be subjected to having a hissy fit if mistreated. If scientists and philosophers' theories on artificial intelligence are correct, then obviously it's plausible for non-organic algorithms to eventually find a way to replicate and surpass everything that organic algorithms can do. Ergo, emotions—whether biological or non-biological—can evolve.

She grabs her keys from the counter and heads back to the spare bedroom, formulating yet another plan to beat the Night Weaver at her own game.

"You want to do what?" Orion asks as he gets into the passenger side of her car.

"I want to offer the Akrah a new position," she repeats, turning the key in the ignition. "The only reason it's with the Night Weaver in the first place is because she actually gives it some respect. Seatbelt, please."

As he pulls the seatbelt across his body, she turns her car's headlights on and reverses out of the parking space. There aren't any other cars around, aside from the burned vehicle on the opposite side of Ashfall Heights' parking lot, so she drives across the faded lines marking the spaces in order to avoid the litter and rubble.

The town is blanketed in darkness.

Here and there Rachel sees lights twinkling dimly in windows as people go about their daily routines, seemingly unworried about how their nighttime hours extend far into the daylight's territory. Oncoming headlights of other cars float along the streets like ghostly orbs. In the nooks and crannies along the various buildings, beneath the trees, shadows appear to come alive. They breathe, inhaling and exhaling, shrouding the town and its people like a menacing blanket.

"This doesn't look *normal,*" Rachel whispers as if she's afraid they'll be overheard by the townsfolk. "It doesn't *feel* right." She reaches for the pendant around her neck, just to make sure this isn't some illusion created by Fae Influence. The pendant is solid in her hand, smooth and warm to the touch.

When they reach Eerie Street, she's certain the darkness is gradually intensifying. The silence surrounding the area also doesn't come across as natural. By the time they get to the Eerie Creek Bridge, which is usually alive with a multitude of sounds—water rushing across rocks and wildlife going about their business—the stillness is terrifying.

There is no moon to penetrate the gloom. No pinpricks of stars to brighten the devastatingly black heavens. It's like looking through obsidian-colored glasses.

"This isn't right," she says as they turn onto Griswold Road.

Orion doesn't break his silence. He just peers out of the windshield with the same calculating gaze Rachel ordinarily uses when she comes across a particularly difficult problem. She slacks off when the headlights no longer illuminate the road ahead of the car.

"Can you see anything out there?" she asks, clutching the steering wheel with both hands until her knuckles ache. She considers pulling over, but then what? She can't walk all the way home in this void.

"Somewhat," he says. "The road is clear."

"Okay, well, there's a curve somewhere up ahead and I can't—" She stops herself from saying more as she realizes her panicky tone isn't going to help either of them get over this hurdle. Rachel steps on the brake, pulls over to the side of the road, and loosens the seatbelt. "You drive."

"Wait. What?" Orion protests as she unlocks her door.

"Take over for me," she says, opening her door. "You already drove my car once before, so you might as well drive it again."

The scowl he wears is a testament to his bemusement. "Honestly, why don't we just glisser?" he mutters.

"Obviously we *can*, but what happens to my car when we do? We can't leave it out here and hope for the best."

He leans over to the driver's seat and looks up at her. "It's Shadow Grove, not Detroit. What's the worst that could possibly happen?"

"Said the drug manufacturer to the under-aged high school girl," she says, crossing her arms.

"I'm getting tired of your judgmental tone," he says, opening the passenger door. "Humans literally can't overdose from using my products. What I manufacture is medicine, which reduces pain or helps battle disease or heightens the senses. Granted, my sensory enhancing products seem to be the most popular sellers, but it's not my fault humans haven't figured out how to have mind-blowing sexual experiences without resorting to medication for assistance," Orion continues. "Are you coming?"

Rachel leans inside and switches off the engine, pulls the key from the ignition, and closes the door. "I assume what you slipped me yesterday wasn't any of the aforementioned products, so what was it?" she asks, pressing the key fob to lock the car.

"Goldmint," he says as he walks around the front of the vehicle. "Humans generally relax when they've consumed goldmint."

"I wasn't relaxed." Rachel walks into his arms.

"I'm aware," he says. The telltale signals of them traveling through time and space begin anew. Pressure, headache, air whooshing out of her lungs, dizziness, and then *bam*! In the blink of an eye they are approximately a mile from where they had been. Not that Rachel can see a thing.

"This way." Orion takes her by the hand and leads her up a few steps before she hears knocking. "Nancy?" he calls out.

"Is Rachel with you?" Mrs. Crenshaw calls back.

"I'm here," Rachel says.

"Then come in already," Mrs. Crenshaw responds. Orion opens the door and weak candlelight spills onto the porch. "Close the door behind you."

Rachel releases his hand and enters the Fraser house, with Orion hot on her heels. She sees Mrs. Crenshaw sitting on her favorite armchair, shotgun leaning against the armrest. Dougal is on the sofa, his face bruised and swollen from the beating he'd taken the previous day.

"A shotgun isn't going to kill a shadow," Rachel says. The weapon somehow still manages to glisten in the candlelight.

"Aye, I told Nan the same thing," Dougal says, waving his hand through the air as if suggesting it's useless to reason with his grandmother. "Does she listen? No."

Mrs. Crenshaw doesn't so much as look up from her lap, where she fumbles with the shotgun shells in a discolored box. "Sit," she instructs.

Rachel inches around the other armchair and crosses the living room to take a seat beside Dougal.

"You, too, Fae."

"My name's Orion—"

"I'm damn well sure who you are, Prince of Amaris. Sit and listen," Mrs. Crenshaw says in her 'don't mess with me' voice.

"I wouldn't cross her if I were ye," Dougal says.

Orion rolls his eyes as he takes a seat in the armchair beside Mrs. Crenshaw.

For a long, uncomfortable minute, the four of them sit together in silence. Suddenly an electric crackling comes from outside, rattling the windows within their panes, rocking the very foundation of the house.

"She's trying to break down the border?" Orion asks with wide eyes, moving toward the window to peer through the curtains.

"They've been going at it since last night," Mrs. Crenshaw says.

"They?" Rachel asks.

"The shadowlings, darklings, midnight minions, whatever you want to call them," she explains, shrugging. "Some of her friends are on the other side, waiting to get in, I guess. I reinforced the border to keep her trapped in Shadow Grove when I saw her sneaking out yesterday, so I don't have to go into that blasted forest again to end her miserable existence."

"How's it staying up against her onslaught?" Orion asks, glancing at Mrs. Crenshaw.

She looks at Orion. "My basement acts as a haven to the pixies, faeries, and knockers when dire times are upon us. As a result, they make sure the border remains up regardless of the situation and strengthen it when I ask them nicely. I think they may be tired after the beating the Night Weaver's been giving it, though." Her gaze moves to Dougal, then Rachel. "Why don't you two go downstairs with some refreshments for our guests?"

Neither of the teenagers moves.

"Don't look at me like I've gone mad. Go." Mrs. Crenshaw waves them off.

"Refreshments such as …?" Rachel asks

"Milk," Orion mumbles. "They also enjoy honey, cookies, sweetmeats, and cheese. Give them whatever gifts you can, and they'll be grateful."

Dougal gives Orion the side-eye as he stands, saying something in his mother tongue, a cutting remark no doubt. Orion turns in his spot, flashes Dougal a smile and responds in fluent Gaelic, as if he's lived in Scotland his entire life. Even in the flickering candlelight, Dougal's blanching at the exchange is obvious.

When Orion finishes, Rachel stands, too. "Can you make me a Fae light, please?" she asks, possibly off-topic to whatever transpired between the two males. He directs his attention to her, opens his palm, and forms a golden sphere. It bounces up and down a couple of times in his hand before gliding through the air to hover beside her head. "Thank you."

"Be careful of the pixies. They have a tendency to bite," Orion says as he turns back to face the window.

"Good to know."

Rachel makes her way through the dining room and toward

the kitchen, following Dougal out of the living room.

"When did the power go out?" she asks, opening the fridge as Dougal lights another candle, which stands on the kitchen counter. She's curious about what they said in Gaelic but decides not to ask.

"Sometime last night," Dougal says. "Ye shouldn't be friends with the fair folk, Rach. They're tricky bastards at the best of times." He opens the pantry and rummages around inside for the cookie jar.

"I'm more than capable of looking after myself," she says, pulling a jug of milk out of the fridge.

"I am sure ye are," he mutters.

"What did you two talk about just now?" Rachel places the bottle of milk on the kitchen table before going to find saucers in the cupboard above the kettle. Stacks and stacks of saucers, all differently shaped and decorated, sit on one shelf. She pulls one stack down and balances it in her hand.

"It doesn't matter."

Another crackle wracks the world, shaking the house and its contents. Glasses and china tinkle as they quiver, while kitchen utensils turn to noisy, chunky chimes when slammed together on the hooks beside the stove. Rachel shoots her hand out to the basement door to stabilize herself, praying the roof doesn't collapse and the walls don't crumble.

"She'll bury us in this house," Dougal says angrily, as if he's read Rachel's thoughts.

Rachel pulls the basement door open and directs the Fae light down the stairs with a slight hand gesture. The glowing ball bounces forward, illuminating each step enough for her and Dougal to descend without incident. The last thing they need is to miss a step, break their necks, and make the Night Weaver's life easier. The basement is empty, though, quiet aside from a tiny whisper which is quickly shut up when she reaches the bottom of the stairs.

"Don't mind us," Rachel says, not knowing how else to greet the creatures who're nowhere to be seen. She unstacks the saucers and sets them on the floor beside each other. The Fae light bobs deeper into the basement, taking its light with it. "Come back here," she mumbles.

"Who're ye talkin' to?" Dougal asks, breaking the chocolate chip cookies into quarters before he places the pieces into one saucer.

"The Fae light," she says, righting herself. Rachel looks to where the Fae light hovers. "I'm not going to repeat myself."

"Och! Ye sound just like Nan sometimes."

The Fae light reluctantly returns to her side, losing a bit of its bounce. "Don't wander off when I need you." She reaches out to it and tickles the bottom, creating tiny ripples on the surface.

"It's a ball of light, a will-o'-the-wisp," Dougal says. "Ye treat it like a pet."

Rachel bends and unscrews the milk bottle. "I treat it with respect. I mean, there's literally magic in our backyards and you don't seem in the least bit impressed. You can't even begin to understand how dull this town was before all this."

"I come from a small town, too, Rach."

"Then what is it with your aversion to these great and wonderful things, these ethereal creatures we have the privilege of encountering simply because we're descendants of the original Fraser and MacCleary settlers?"

Dougal shakes his head. "It's a long story for a different time.

Finish up. I need to go check on Nan."

"Your grandmother is no pushover either, especially when she's in her current mood," Rachel says, carefully filling the first saucer with milk before moving on to the next.

Tap-tap-tap.

She looks up to see the knocker she'd encountered in the cave the previous day, the teenager wearing a little hardhat and utility belt. "Problems?" she asks. The knocker nods. "In the basement?"

He waves her over.

Rachel rights herself and pushes the five-gallon bottle into Dougal's arms, still looking at the knocker. "Finish up," she says as she walks over to the corner.

The teenaged knocker disappears between some boxes and emerges from behind them. Rachel peers closer to see an even tinier knocker, lying on his side, clearly unconscious. "He got hurt?" she asks.

The older knocker nods, and then points at the Fae light bobbing in the center of the basement, which keeps the gloom from overwhelming them.

She glances over her shoulder, returns her attention to the hurt knocker. "Oh, so that's why the light was over here." Rachel snaps her finger and the Fae light hurtles closer. "Now what?"

The teenaged knocker hooks his hammer into the utility belt around his waist, cups his hands together as he steps closer to his fallen kin, and then parts his palms over him—suggesting the light should fall over the hurt knocker.

"Wash him in the light?"

The knocker nods, smiling broadly.

"All right, I'll try. Otherwise, I'll call Orion to come help you."

Rachel moves a few of the boxes away to get closer to the fallen knocker and reaches for the ball of light. She cups her hands as she's been instructed to do, holding the sphere in both palms, and bends down.

"Here goes nothing," she whispers, letting the Fae light wash over the tiny knocker. The ball melts as she releases it, covering the entirety of the little body on the dirty floor. His ashen skin glows with life once more, tiny fingers curl into a small fist as the Fae light heals whatever ailments the poor guy's been stricken with.

"It's working, right?" she asks the teenaged knocker.

He nods again, blinking away tears. The Fae light pulls out of the knocker's body and regroups in the air above him, slowly re-forming into a sphere.

"We can leave once yer done playin' with the wee folk," Dougal says behind her.

"Did you see what I did?" Rachel asks, awestruck by the magic *she* had been able to do with only the Fae light at her disposal. Stardust be damned, this is her new favorite thing about Fae.

"Aye," he says. "Very pretty. Now, grab yer toy and come on."

Rachel sighs, watching the older knocker hug the little one before she guides the Fae light back to her side. She turns in place and follows Dougal out of the basement.

The earth suddenly trembles, almost knocking Rachel off her feet. A pronounced and terrible rumbling accompanies the shaking. Boxes topple over and a ladder clatters to the floor. Out of the corner of her eye, she spots a variety of creatures erupting from their hiding places, searching for safer areas to wait out the latest attack on the border. Dougal loses his footing and grabs onto the banister to stop his fall. Dust rains down while crashes resonate from the first floor. Rachel grabs onto Dougal's arm as another unexpected quake takes her by surprise.

Panicky whispers, high-pitched squeals, and nervous titters surround them as they make their way up the basement stairs on uncertain legs.

"We need to stop her," Dougal shouts to be heard over the commotion, pushing Rachel up the stairs ahead of him.

He's not wrong. The only reason anybody—human, Fae, or otherwise—would go to such extreme lengths is if there's something worthwhile on the other side. Rachel decides then and there she'd rather not find out what the Night Weaver so desperately wants to reach inside the forest.

As she stumbles back into the kitchen, the world still shaking beneath her, a fist smashes through the window beside the kitchen door.

"What the—?" She struggles to her feet as the bloody hand blindly searches for the lock, the arm reaching deeper.

Rachel rushes to the kitchen island to find a weapon, the hand inching closer to the lock.

"Och! We don't have the time for this bullocks," Dougal grumbles, stumbling up the stairs.

Rachel finds a meat tenderizer and heads for the door, ready to break the hand if she has to. Mrs. Pearson's face appears in the window, her eyes shiny black orbs set in a too-pale face. She scans the interior and pins her unholy gaze on Rachel. The almost unrecognizable woman pulls her arm back and balls her hand into a fist, before—

"Get down!" Rachel orders as she turns her back on the

window. Glass shards fly into the kitchen, tinkling to the counters and floor. She ignores the chaos and raises the meat tenderizer into the air, aiming for the searching hand by the back door.

Three … two … one.

She brings the meat tenderizer down and hears a crunch as bones break. There's a howl of pain on the other side of the door before the hand disappears. A moment of triumph vanishes in an instant as a different hand appears, clearly belonging to someone else. She repeats the action with the meat tenderizer. Someone cries out.

"Rachel Cleary," Mrs. Pearson says in a stern voice that doesn't suit her. "I am incredibly disappointed with you. Wait until I tell your mother."

"Nan, we have a situation back here!" Dougal shouts.

Rebecca White joins Mrs. Pearson, her eyes a similar glistening black. She tuts, and says, "This simply will not do."

"Dougal, stop standing around and help me," Rachel screams, ready to continue her game of *Whack-a-Mole*. When he doesn't respond, she chances a glance over her shoulder, only to find herself alone in the kitchen. "Dougal!"

More familiar-ish faces join the two women in the window, some sneering, others smiling. None of them belong to her mother, but all of them spell doom. How smart of the Night Weaver to send her acolytes to do her dirty work for her.

Rachel expects someone else to push their hand through the broken window to get to the lock, but this doesn't happen. Instead, a great force slams against the door, rebounds, and tries again.

"Orion!" Rachel backs away from the door. "Anyone?"

"C'mon," Dougal says behind her, grabbing her by the shoulder. "We'll deal with them later."

Chapter Eighteen
When The Blood Moon Rises

At first, people assume Nancy Crenshaw is a harmless old lady who carries candy in her handbag and knits baby blankets to pass the time. She appears delicate, thanks to her petite ballerina body, papery skin, and snow-white hair. Ever since she's reached what is often referred to as the golden years, she's played the part of the somewhat senile, yet always loveable grandma to a T. However, and Rachel knows this intricate detail of her lifelong neighbor better than anyone, Nancy Crenshaw is a woman who can make grown men whimper with a mere look.

Take Sheriff William Carter, ol' Bulltwang Bill, for example: usually, he throws his immense girth around whenever he wants something, and he likes to bully those who dare to stand up against his tyranny, but not when it comes to Nancy Crenshaw ... Oh, no. Billy Boy, as she insists on calling him and who is the only person who may do so, gives her a wide berth when she's in his vicinity. If he's unable to avoid her, the Wild West show he so often puts on for others simply vanishes. Gone is the fake accent, gone is the vitriol he adds into his dialogue, gone is the holier than thou attitude. It's all, "yes, ma'am, no, ma'am, apologies, ma'am," subordination.

Seeing her walk out of the house, loaded shotgun at the

ready, and wearing an expression devoid of emotion would certainly be one of the most terrifying things to behold for any Shadow Grove resident.

For Rachel, she is a savior made flesh.

If anyone can deal with a homicidal bogeywoman with a penchant for eating children, then God help her, because Mrs. Crenshaw is made of tougher stuff than myth and magic.

While Orion is busy trying his best to talk Mrs. Crenshaw out of, in his words, "a suicide mission", Dougal and Rachel watch them get swallowed up by the persistent darkness outside the house.

"She has the home advantage," Rachel says, defending Mrs. Crenshaw's decision to confront the Night Weaver while struggling to convince herself it's a good idea. "It's not like yesterday when we were all out of our depth. Nobody knows this area better than Mrs. Crenshaw. Also, if we don't stop the Night Weaver, her acolytes are going to turn this town upside down searching for us."

"We're gonna go after her, aren't we?" Dougal says. "Even if she said we shouldn't leave the house."

Rachel pulls her pursed lips to the side of her mouth.

There's a crash in the kitchen, a breach of their stronghold, no doubt.

He sighs. "Yer a bad influence, Rachel Cleary, but I love the way ye don't cower in the face of danger."

"Thanks. Now let's go save this dump of a town," Rachel says, pushing away the smile that threatens to break free.

She follows in Orion's and Mrs. Crenshaw's footsteps with Dougal by her side, listening intently for any sign of the Night Weaver's physical presence in the claustrophobic silence, wondering where the rest of the mom club is hiding. All she can hear is Orion telling Mrs. Crenshaw to retreat, saying he'll take care of the dangerous Black Annis himself. It's not the most convincing speech.

"He's a persistent bastard, eh?" Dougal says by her side.

"He's not too bad."

"I can't figure out why he seems to care so much about people he barely know."

"I could say the same thing about you. Apart from your grandmother, you have no reason to risk your life," Rachel responds gently, smiling at him.

"Aye, but I have nothin' better to do with my time 'til Joe Farrow calls me back to work," he whispers. "Yer light's goin' out."

Rachel looks at the Fae light, which grows dimmer as they walk across the lawn—probably no more than a few feet behind Orion and Mrs. Crenshaw. "It happens, unfortunately," she says.

"If I couldn't defeat the Night Weaver with an entire army at my disp—"

"Oh, keep quiet already," Mrs. Crenshaw interrupts Orion. The *click* sounds as she chambers a shell. "Help me aim this thing in the right direction."

"You're just going to piss her off more," he retorts.

"I can't see a thing," Dougal says softly.

The shotgun cracks and an earsplitting shriek fills the air.

"Sounded like a hit to me," Mrs. Crenshaw says, followed by a double tinkling sound as, Rachel assumes, the spent shells fall onto the asphalt road. A second *click* sounds, signaling the new shells being loaded in the chamber.

Another crack, another hit. The Night Weaver's haunting

wails go on for a good long minute before they abruptly end.

"And those shells are filled with ...?" Orion asks, almost impressed.

"An old family recipe," Mrs. Crenshaw says.

All of a sudden, a large piece of fabric slithers around Rachel's body and tightens around her waist. Air is expelled from her lungs with a *whoosh*. Rachel is plucked off her feet. She finds her voice and screams, flailing as she reaches out to grab onto something—anything. Flying backward into the darkness, unable to see how high or how far she's traveling, Rachel thrashes wildly, calling out to Orion and Mrs. Crenshaw and Dougal. She comes to a stop, her limp body suspended by the single binding around her middle. She hangs in the air like a rag doll, her hair tickling her cheeks as the strands wave around in the breeze, waiting to be shaken or dropped by her demented captor.

"Annoying girl," the Night Weaver hisses in her ear. "I've been looking for you."

Rachel can't come back with a snarky response, can barely breathe thanks to the constricting, thick fabric—probably the Akrah's doing—squashing her insides, but she does find the strength to look up. The Night Weaver's blue face, illuminated by some unseen light, is in full view. Her black eyes glisten with malice as her nostrils flare and her teeth grind together.

"Pathetic child," she says, sneering. "Your suffering will be my privilege."

"You sure like the sound of your own voice, don't you?" Rachel says, narrowing her eyes in defiance. "I'm not afraid of you."

"You will be." The Night Weaver's sneer turns into an ugly smile as she bares her needle-like teeth. One metallic claw runs down Rachel's cheek, a dangerously sharp caress that sets her nerves on fire. If the Night Weaver wishes to harm Rachel, she can easily cut her into ribbons. Instead, her gaze lowers, piercing the darkness as she glares at something Rachel can't see. "Foolish." She clucks her tongue before turning her attention back to Rachel. The Night Weaver tilts her head, studying her prey. "I'm at odds at how I should proceed," she says. "Do I break you, cut you, or eat you? There are so many possibilities."

"Rachel," Mrs. Crenshaw's voice reaches them from far below.

The Night Weaver grins, the sight making Rachel's stomach churn.

"Perhaps … Oh, perhaps I shouldn't begin with you at all. Instead, I can start my revenge by making you watch as I slowly flay that old woman who shot me. I could turn your mother into one of my darklings in front of you and make her do the most ghastly things. Yes." She grins. "Yes, your eyes reveal true fear now, girl. How noble you are." The Night Weaver cackles. "Then, I can move on to the boy. He's such a big boy for his age, strong and healthy. He'll take a while to break, but I'm sure it'll be an enjoyable experience for at least one of us."

"You truly are a monster," Rachel growls.

The Night Weaver beams with pride, almost as if Rachel's given her a compliment. Another claw runs down her cheek, too gently not to be considered intimate. Rachel shivers in response, pulls her face away from the cool metal, and squeezes her eyes shut.

"Hold on, I'm coming to get you," Orion's shout interrupts her terror.

The contents of Rachel's stomach shoot into her throat as

she drops, though the binding around her waist doesn't release. She gasps when suddenly she halts again.

"No," she shouts back. "Get back inside the house!"

"Please come, *Prince*," the Night Weaver laughs. Another deafening crack sounds, one that doesn't belong to the shotgun, as an invisible force moves through the air and collides with the barrier encircling the forest.

It hits Rachel then. This whole display of the Night Weaver, trying to break into the forest under the cover of darkness, isn't because her friends are waiting for her on the other side. It's because she wants to get out of Shadow Grove and return to Orthega. Why now, though? Why is she so desperate to go home after centuries of living in the forest where she has an all-you-can-eat buffet?

Her eyes widen as she realizes the truth.

Fear.

The Night Weaver is afraid.

Rachel rakes her mind as she searches for an explanation for the sudden onset of fear. What can possibly make a predator scared? Mrs. Crenshaw, bless her soul, may be a force to reckon with for the residents of Shadow Grove, but Rachel isn't delusional enough to believe the old woman is the reason for this frantic attempt to get back to Orthega.

Orion.

"Of course," she whispers, connecting the dots.

The Night Weaver was initially banished from Orthega by the Prince of Amaris, and up until yesterday, she hadn't known he was in town. Rachel figures his showing up out of nowhere, creating all kinds of havoc in her lair, might be the reason why she's gone mental.

Before she can shout her current theory to her companions, who are presumably still somewhere below her, she's jostled around in the air as the Night Weaver crisscrosses the night sky with unnatural speed. Rachel's teeth chatter as she's shaken around from side to side.

A golden bolt suddenly flashes past Rachel's face, narrowly avoiding hitting her. She gasps, watching the arrow of light disappear into the nothingness behind her.

The Night Weaver cries out in delight, clapping as if she's just watched a magician do a trick.

"Try again, Princeling. Maybe next time you'll hit her," the Night Weaver jeers.

Rachel's heart drops to the pit of her stomach as the Night Weaver gains altitude again, carelessly pulling her along for the ride. The air becomes thinner, but the darkness doesn't disappear. There is, however, a reddish ball hanging just above the horizon. It's too early in the year for the Harvest Moon to make its appearance, too early in the month for a full moon, too. It's most likely the sun, she decides, seen through a veil of night. A Blood Moon of a different kind.

Rachel reaches around her so she can grab onto the Akrah Cloak's hem for extra support—falling from this height, even if she can't see how high she truly is from the ground, will be fatal. She twists her right hand around the piece of elongated fabric which had wrapped around her waist, and somehow manages to hoist herself to take some weight off her midsection. She breathes easier, giving her abdominal muscles a well-deserved reprieve. She climbs higher, feels her biceps and triceps burn.

Her life is hanging by a thread …

I hope I live long enough to use that saying without it sounding like a stupid cliché.

Rachel has no other option than to come up with a plan to get the situation under control. If she falls, she's dead. If the Night Weaver takes her away from here, she's dead. If Orion's aim is off by an inch with his Fae light bolts—*Do you want to get me killed by throwing more of those things, Faerie Boy?*—she's dead.

Before she can implement any sort of plan, a golden angel of destruction appears in her peripheral vision. Rachel turns to face the glint of danger hovering behind the Night Weaver and her breath hitches. Orion, or some heavenly creature resembling him, stares with supernova eyes at his foe. He bares elongated canines at the Night Weaver's back, while Fae light drips like molten lava from his body and fades into oblivion as it falls. There's something animalistic about the way he looks, about the way he calculates, about the way he moves to stay out of the Night Weaver's sight.

She watches as he raises one hand and Fae light forms in his palm. It's not the bouncing, happy Fae light she's seen in the past. This is a ball of pure solar rage, radioactive and blinding.

Her heart races as she looks between him and the nothingness below. One wrong move on his part and they'll have to scrape her remains off the road with a trowel.

With the ease of a gymnast, graceful and almost too beautiful to watch, Orion pitches the Fae light directly into the Night Weaver's back.

Light will always defeat darkness.

The Night Weaver screeches as the Fae light hits, searing away a gaping piece of the Akrah Cloak and part of her leathery skin and flesh. She spins to face her attacker, throwing Rachel around from the force.

The Night Weaver hisses like an angry cat. "*You.*"

Orion grins at her, showing off his new, fearsomely elongated canines. "A surprised Miser is a dead Miser," he growls, irises dancing with spite. A second Fae light forms in his hand and his grin grows broader, deadlier. "Run."

The Night Weaver doesn't dally around to make conversation this time—she sets off in the opposite direction.

They fly so fast, Rachel can hardly fill her lungs with the thin air which howls in her ears. Her eyes sting from the cold, but she can't close them. Instead, she turns to look over her shoulder and sees Orion in the distance, catching up with ease before he backs off again. The idiot plays with her like this for a good few minutes, while Rachel dangles helplessly.

The second ball of Fae light suddenly crashes into the Night Weaver's back, dripping down the smelted matter onto the Akrah Cloak and slowly destroying the integrity of the fabric. A deafening ripping sound echoes in Rachel's very bones. She looks up, eyes widening as she sees the tear growing larger with each twist and turn and stomach-churning flip. Rachel reaches up and pulls herself even higher up the Akrah Cloak, while her palms sweat and her heart pounds and her body aches.

"Ak-k-krah," Rachel says, bouncing from the persistent movement through the air. "Akrah-h-h," she repeats louder as she tugs at the fabric around her hand and elbow now.

The Night Weaver's movements slow somewhat and the fabric seems to come alive by itself, curling around her for more support and hoisting her higher until the wrinkly hag's face appears in front of her again. They continue to move despite this, to dodge the onslaught of lava balls being catapulted their way.

"Yes?" The Night Weaver says in a voice that doesn't belong

to her. It's a reasonable androgynous voice, ancient and somnolent.

Rachel gulps, her ears popping from the altitude. She'd gotten the cloak's attention, but now what?

"Hi," she begins, trying to buy some time while her thoughts struggle to organize themselves, so her mouth doesn't get her killed. She had come up with a proposition for the Akrah Cloak earlier, one she'd hoped it would find intriguing enough to, at least, consider. Without the Akrah, the Night Weaver wouldn't be so powerful, which might help them beat her once and for all. "I was wondering why you put up with the Night Weaver," she continues. "It seems to me like you gave up one crappy life in the dark for another crappy life in the dark."

"I feed on darkness," the Akrah says in its monotonous and sexless voice.

"Yes, but there are different types of darkness, aren't there?" Rachel says. "How I understand it, up until now everyone's just been feeding you the literal stuff. Not to mention, you're living a half-life, spent in the confines of caves and vaults. Shouldn't your glory be celebrated?"

"Indeed."

"What if I told you I can give you all that you crave?"

The Night Weaver's eyes narrow in question, but *she* isn't in control of her own body in that instant. There's a curiosity there, a glint in her bottomless gaze.

Rachel holds her head high, beaming with confidence, and says, "What if I can give you an endless supply of the most delicious darkness in existence, while you're living it up to the fullest in the light?"

The Akrah Cloak, wearing the Night Weaver's face, seems to

consider the offer for a nail-biting moment, before the voice asks, "What do you want in return?"

Now we're getting somewhere.

"Swear your allegiance to the MacCleary and Fraser bloodlines and promise to answer our call if your assistance is required for some reason or another. Simple."

Without warning, the Night Weaver—or rather the Akrah—dives straight down to avoid another one of Orion's attacks. Rachel screams, grappling for something more substantial to hold on to, tears running down her cheeks from this ungodly rollercoaster ride.

They level out again, giving her an opportunity to catch her breath, before she shouts at Orion, "Can you stop already?" Rachel hopes he will let up so she can talk to the Akrah before all deals are off and death is the only option left on the table, but from the precision movements he's making there's no telling if he will.

"You're wasting your breath," the Akrah says. "A Fae doesn't simply *stop* when they are asked nicely. They enjoy the kill too much." There is no fear or anxiety in the Akrah's tone, which is oddly soothing under the circumstances.

"Well, how do we stop Orion from hunting you?" she cries out, digging her nails into the Night Weaver's shoulders. "Do we submerge him in liquid nitrogen?"

"I don't understand what you mean."

"Of course, you don't," Rachel says, laughing hysterically, although there's nothing humorous about the situation. "How do we stop him?"

"*We* can't stop him," the Akrah says in a matter-of-fact tone. The Night Weaver's gaze meets Rachel's. The emotionless expression no longer has a calming effect; instead, the coldness makes her dread what might happen next. “If you survive, I may feel inclined to revisit your offer. Goodbye.”

The fabric suddenly unwraps itself from around Rachel’s waist, retreating to the cloak’s hem. It releases its hold on her completely, allowing gravity to have its way with her.

Chapter Nineteen
Supernova

She grasps at nothingness as she falls back to Earth, her deafening scream lost in the high winds that rush past her ears. The darkness makes it impossible to calculate how far she is from the ground, and there's no way to estimate at what velocity she's free-falling. She can't do anything to save herself from imminent death, not this time.

Meanwhile, Rachel simply cannot comprehend why she *ever* wanted to sacrifice herself in the lair. It must've been temporary madness; a brief affliction of the Superman complex. Here she is, flailing, literally falling head over heels, waiting for the inevitable end to this tumultuous journey, and she doesn't want to die. Not now. Not like this.

"*Orrrrriooooon!*" His name tears from her throat in a final, desperate attempt to avoid a grotesque death.

Topsy-turvy, down she goes, seemingly faster and faster. Where she'll land, nobody knows … *How* will she land, she wonders, butter-side up or butter-side down? It probably doesn't matter. As long as it's swift and painless, she decides. There's not more she can ask for, considering her light's going to be snuffed out whether she likes it or not.

There's an unexpected jolt interrupting the fall, like a bungee cord pulling her back from certain death. Her organs jerk, too, shocked by the sudden change in direction. She gradually slows, as if the laws of physics have done a one-eighty, and the wind dies down around her. Her scream grows louder now, a raw cry for help, which she cuts off when she comes to grips with the fact that she's not plummeting at high speed to meet the unmoving ground anymore. She drifts weightlessly like a snowflake, gracefully swaying hither and thither.

"Miss me, Clarré?" the calm, familiar voice says from somewhere below her.

Rachel drops into his waiting hands. He moves her around so her feet can touch the glorious ground without it ending in a *splat.* She holds on to her rescuer, shaking from head to toe, afraid if she lets go she'll continue falling to her death. It's only then that she realizes she's bawling her eyes out. Big, ugly tears roll freely down her cheeks. Rachel sobs as she slams one of her fists into his shoulder in frustration. Feeling the solid body underneath her hand is heaven, so she does it again, and again, crying harder. Gratitude and joy intermingle with rage as she goes limp. It'd been a close call—too close.

"You're all right," Orion says, still holding her up. "You're alive."

Rachel hides her face in his shoulder and continues to cry, inhaling his scent with every sob. She's enveloped by a heady mix of warm cinnamon and grapefruit, with blood mandarin and minty citrus notes, along with masculine leather—he's a safety blanket of smells.

"You could've killed me," she says through her tears.

"Yes," he answers. "But I didn't."

"That's not—" She pulls away from him, almost goes down

thanks to her uncertain footing and jellylike legs, before grappling at his shirt to keep upright. "You could've lied to make me feel better."

"Lying to one's allies sets a bad precedent," Orion says, pushing a strand of her hair out of her face. The intimate action doesn't correspond with his indifferent words. "I have to go after her. She's up to something and I don't like it." He opens his hand and a Fae light forms in his palm. Orion hands it over to her, whispering, "You're close to home, but don't try to make your way back until the darkness dissipates." He releases her from his hold, holding out the Fae light.

"She's afraid of you," Rachel says quickly, accepting the light source. "The Night Weaver doesn't want to break through the barrier to let something into Shadow Grove. She wants to get back to Orthega. She wants to get away from *you*."

"I'm aware, Clarré, which is why I'm going to give her what she wants," he says, a sly grin developing as he speaks. He reaches out and touches her cheek, gently trailing his fingertips across her skin. "If I don't return, don't come looking for me."

"That sounds like a goodbye," she says, eyeing him suspiciously. "Becoming a martyr isn't worth it, Orion. Believe me—"

Orion places his hand behind her neck, leans closer, and presses his soft lips against her forehead. "If I do this, the Night Weaver's influence over the townsfolk disappears. Everything will be back to relative normalcy as soon as she's crossed over into the Fae Realm."

"You're going to do something stupid, aren't you?" Rachel says as he pulls away, even though she knows it's all for naught. "I'm not going to see you again, am I?"

"You'll see me again, I'm sure," he says.

Rachel shakes her head, new tears threatening to fall. She watches through blurry vision as golden flames ripple across his body, encircling him in an enigmatic, almost heavenly, glow. Orion glances up into the pitch-black sky, donning a mischievous smile, one that spells danger. Then he's off, without giving her so much as a second look. She watches him fly away—*fly!*—until he's only a bright, moving pinprick in the sky, looking like a satellite entering the atmosphere.

Golden lightning streaks across the artificial night sky, no more than a flash to brighten the gloom. It is answered by a blaze of violet and blue, which outlines the clouds above. A sound akin to thunder rolls across the town, rumbling violently. Another sickly violet vein of light cleaves the ether, followed by the signature cackling of the Night Weaver.

"Damn you, Faerie Boy," she whispers, angrily brushing her tears away with her free hand whilst clutching the Fae light against her chest with the other. "You're going to get yourself killed."

Against his advice, Rachel walks up Griswold Road with only the Fae light to guide her. She keeps an eye on the ongoing battle overhead, even if all she can see is multicolored flashes, and the most she can hear is the dominant claps of power and the haunting laughter or hysterical wailing of the Night Weaver.

There's absolutely no way for her to gauge who's winning this fight.

Determined not to wander off into the darkness where darklings undoubtedly lurk, she walks slowly. The last thing she wants is to get killed by one of the Night Weaver's strays.

The battle rages on, with no sign of stopping in the

immediate future. The Prince of Amaris and the Night Weaver are, after all, evenly matched in this world, thanks to the Akrah Cloak's impressive power.

What a moron, she thinks, sniffing. *Did you even think your plan through, Orion? How are you going to cross the border if it's still up?*

"Next time, use your brain," she shouts up to the sky, not knowing if he'll be able to hear her, before she puts some speed into her movements. Soon, Rachel is jogging up Griswold Road, listening to her soles slapping against the asphalt underfoot to make sure she stays on track. She keeps the Fae light extended, which slows down her progress, but at least it's better than being stuck in the middle of nowhere with only a freaky lightshow for company.

Her thighs begin to burn from the effort of running uphill, her calves quickly joining in to make the jog especially unpleasant. She doesn't stop. She *can't* stop. Instead, she pushes herself into a full run.

Ten minutes later, she finds herself in front of the Fraser house, where Mrs. Crenshaw and Dougal watch the spectacle from the porch.

"Ye're alive," Dougal says, sounding unsurprised. "Gotta hand it to the Fae for keepin' his word."

"We've got to … bring the border … down," she says, running up the steps.

"Over my dead body," Mrs. Crenshaw says.

Rachel points toward the sky as she catches her breath. "He's going to … force the Night Weaver … back to—"

"The Fae Realm?" Dougal says, ending her sentence for her.

Rachel nods, grateful to use the time to suck more air into

her lungs.

"How far did you run, child?" Mrs. Crenshaw asks, grimacing. "Never mind. Look, if I open the border, it's a free for all at this point. Anything hiding in the forest can sneak into Shadow Grove while the barrier's down. What about when he wants to come back? That means the barrier will drop twice, which gives the nasties two chances to sneak in. It's too risky."

"Too risky?" Rachel asks in a higher-than-normal tone. "I'm sorry, Mrs. Crenshaw, but Orion is risking his life for human beings, people he's never met, because there won't be a town left if he doesn't." She looks up at the sky as another clash of gold and violet power lights up the sky, and a deafening rumble shakes the ground beneath her feet. "If you don't bring the barrier down, there's a good chance we'll all live in perpetual darkness."

Mrs. Crenshaw stubbornly huffs and crosses her arms.

"Nan, ye must admit, Rachel has a point," Dougal says. "He hasn't asked a thin' for helpin' us."

"Please, Mrs. Crenshaw?" Rachel presses. "Orion helped to save Dougal, he saved me twice, and he's—"

"Okay, okay, I'll do it," Mrs. Crenshaw interrupts Rachel's speech. She shuffles across the porch and toward the front door. "Just remember the three of you are responsible for whatever gets into Shadow Grove once this barrier goes down. Is that understood?"

"Yes, ma'am," Rachel says.

"Aye," Dougal concurs.

"Stay here," the old woman says, disappearing inside the house.

Rachel turns her attention back to the riotous sky, sees color slicing through the night. Suddenly, a golden ball grows larger as it heads straight down towards them. She gasps, expecting the worst, but as it approaches, she notices it's too small to be Orion. In fact, it's only one of those lava balls dropping to the ground—*Thank the stars*. The lava ball winks out of existence as it touches her mother's hydrangeas across the road.

"Ye like him," Dougal whispers beside her.

"What? No, I don't," Rachel says, folding her arms. "I've just got high stakes on the outcome of this fight."

"If ye say so," he mutters. "I hope ye ken what yer doin'. The fair folk are renowned tricksters."

"Stop mothering me, Dougal," she says, annoyed.

He shrugs. "Fine, but don't come cryin' to me when yer up the duff and he's nowhere to be found. They do that, ye know? Fae loves to leave when trouble's at its worst."

She blinks slowly, turning to face him. "I can't figure out half of what you said, but I still feel like I should punch you."

Dougal considers her words and then nods. "I would probably deserve it, too, but my warnin' stands."

"The barrier's down," Mrs. Crenshaw announces from inside the house. "Keep an eye out and let me know immediately when they're inside the forest."

"Aye," Dougal calls back, gaze swiveling to the forest.

An indigo-colored ball with sickly purple veins careens from the air and crashes onto Griswold Road, rolling to a stop between the Fraser and MacCleary houses. Rachel watches as swathes of black fabric, glowing with blue and purple power, unfold to reveal the beaten and bruised Black Annis within. The Night Weaver stumbles out of her makeshift cocoon, black blood dribbling from the corner of her mouth. She sways from side to side, her shoulders slumped over in defeat.

Orion, in all his golden glory, lands on his feet some fifty yards away. Rachel notices four scratches running the length of his upper arm, blood pouring from the deep gouges and dripping onto the ground. His hair is a disheveled mess, his eyes the color of supernovae. He doesn't show an ounce of discomfort or a trace of weakness in the way he prowls toward his enemy.

Rachel takes a step forward, wanting to assist the Fae, but Dougal holds her back by placing an arm in her way.

"Don't distract him," he says seriously.

The Night Weaver glances in Rachel's direction. "I accept your offer," the Akrah Cloak's androgynous voice says.

Rachel grimaces. "I'm pretty sure my offer expired when you dropped me. Sorry."

The Night Weaver looks back at Orion, who's stalking closer with a couple of flaming balls of molten lava in his hands that drip thick drops of light onto the asphalt road alongside his blood.

With her hands up in surrender, the Night Weaver takes a step back, toward the forest.

"A Prince of Amaris is obliged to show mercy if his opponent is—" the Akrah Cloak's voice is cut off as Orion hurtles one of those lava balls her way, striking the Night Weaver in her chest. She shoots back from the force, falls onto the road, and lies still for a moment. Her finger twitches, the blue glow emanating from her very core dulling slightly.

"I am the disgraced Prince of Amaris, lest you forget," Orion booms in the ominous voice from earlier, a commander's voice. "On your feet, Miser."

The Night Weaver struggles back to her feet, leaning precariously to the side. The Akrah Cloak dangles limply around her as if it has also lost its will to fight.

"You are not your brother, Princeling," the Night Weaver wheezes the words, sidestepping a rosemary hedge at the edge of the MacCleary's lawn and almost toppling over a second time.

"That's what everyone tells me," he growls back, lifting his hand as he readies to throw the next ball of lava.

The Night Weaver takes another step back, her blue glow dimly bouncing off the ACCESS PROHIBITED sign of the forest. She glances at the sign, her eyes widening before she takes another tentative step back. A few more steps and she'll be in the forest once more.

Rachel watches her with keen eyes, waiting for the Night Weaver to realize the barrier is down, hoping Orion has the rest of his plan figured out.

"You are *not* a coldblooded killer," the Night Weaver and Akrah Cloak's voices shriek in unison. "Not like dear *King Nova* ..." They laugh when he seems to flinch at the words.

Orion smirks, forging another ball of lava in his free hand. "No, but I am a born and bred warrior. Your life means nothing when weighed against your crimes." He tosses the next ball of lava at her, purposely missing her person but singeing the Akrah Cloak's hem.

"*Mercy!* Show us mercy," the double voice screeches. The Night Weaver takes another step back, chest heaving with exhaustion and fear. Her eyes roll wildly around in her head, searching for an escape. The Akrah Cloak, rendered powerless after its run-in with its previous owner, keeps on playing possum.

"Take off the Akrah Cloak and I may reconsider killing you," he says in an utterly emotionless tone.

The Night Weaver narrows her eyes. "You mean to leave me

defenseless in this world, while an Aurial Prince lives a stone's throw from my domain? Have you seen what these ... *creatures* ... do to one another?"

Orion stalks closer, clearly deeming her questions beneath him. The Night Weaver stumbles backward again, falls into the lush brush spilling out of the forest's opening, and Rachel sees her face change. Hope shows in her pained expression, the chances of her survival are improved. The Night Weaver scrambles back to her feet with the assistance of the Akrah Cloak before she turns and runs into the dark forest.

"Close the barrier when I'm through," Orion barks the command over his shoulder, absorbing the lava balls back into his body. He sets off after his enemy, a beacon of light moving quickly past the ACCESS PROHIBITED sign and beyond the visible tree line.

"Now, Nan," Dougal shouts an instant later.

"Now!" Mrs. Crenshaw repeats the command from somewhere inside the house.

Pitiful screams resound throughout the town, coming from everywhere and nowhere as the deep nocturnal heavens begin to dissipate. The shadows retreat, taking the Night Weaver's darklings along with them. The azure sky with its spectacular diorama of clouds and bright yellow sun breaks free of its supernatural bonds, revealing a beautiful mid-morning scene. Slowly, the screams die down and are replaced by the birds greeting the new day with song.

Rachel stares at the forest entrance, the ACCESS PROHIBITED sign remaining untouched even after the Night Weaver's violent attempts at escaping Shadow Grove.

Come on, Faerie Boy. Make quick work of her.

She watches and waits for him to return, but the interior of the forest remains unchanged. Not a single leaf rustles in the slight summer breeze, nothing creeps across the forest floor, not a tweet or a hoot resonates from within. It's deathly still. No more than a graveyard of trees nobody wants to acknowledge exists. The forest is normal again—or whatever passes for normal in this town.

Rachel forces herself to look away from the forest's entrance, pushes her worries for Orion away—she'll deal with them later—and turns her attention to Dougal. "Care to give me a ride to my car? I need to go find my mom."

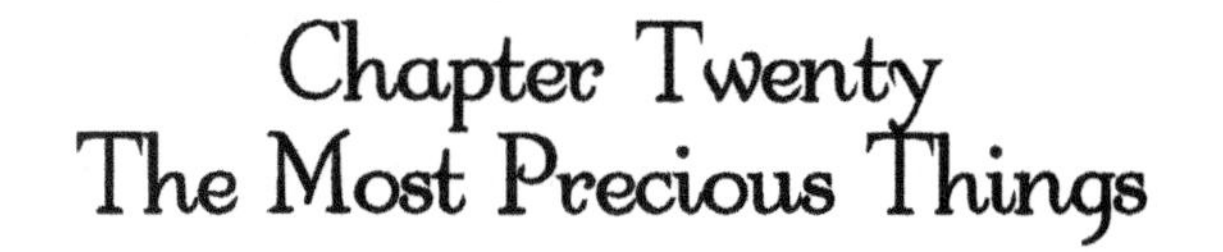

Chapter Twenty
The Most Precious Things

Within a few days, the residents of Shadow Grove have all seemingly forgotten about the nocturnal anomaly that had affected the town. They hardly acknowledge hearing bloodcurdling screams as the darklings burned alive when the sun erupted from its prison in such a spectacular manner. There's no mention about the strange colored lightning which had filled the skies when Orion and the Night Weaver battled in the heavens, no talks about anything suspicious happening near the Fraser and MacCleary houses on Griswold Road in the days preceding the peculiar event that's been emblazoned onto Rachel's mind.

Those people who'd been lured into doing the Night Weaver's bidding have apparently lost their memories, but Rachel doesn't believe anyone could go on normally if they have so much time unaccounted for between the first kidnapping and the Night Weaver's expulsion.

That being said, Rachel does suspect the Night Weaver's influence isn't strong enough to stretch beyond realms.

There wasn't a big homecoming party for the missing kids when they returned to their families. People went on as if they'd been around the entire time, four-year-old Eric Smith's mother included. So, the children who'd been kidnapped simply followed in the adults' footsteps, either by truly forgetting about their ordeal in the Night Weaver's lair or merely by saying so, in order to avoid being branded as insane by Shadow Grove's oh-so-sensible residents. Whatever the reason for the so-called collective memory loss amongst those who were involved, it worked in everyone's favor and none more so than for Sheriff Carter—the man who abducted Dougal and somehow coerced her mother into joining the Night Weaver's cult.

How much of her mom's behavior was directly related to the Night Weaver's influence? Was she capable of kidnapping children just to spend a few precious moments with someone she's lost?

Probably. Everyone has a price. What had been the sheriff's price? Human beings are capable of heinous things if they can convince themselves it's worth the consequences …

Bulltwang Bill went on the record with a made-up story of what had happened to the children—*Well, folks, we had a regular ol'* Lord of the Flies *situation with these scoundrels. They ran off to live on the rundown dairy farm near the highway. Yes, the one between Shadow Grove and the city. Scavenged for food like little beasts, I hear. But they're safe now; safe and sound.*

Nobody contradicted his statement. Not a single soul, Mrs. Crenshaw included, held him accountable for his role in the Night Weaver's plan.

Repeat a lie long enough and loud enough and eventually everyone starts believing it.

There's still no word on Astraea Hayward's location, though. Rachel and Dougal had gone back to the Night Weaver's lair and searched every part of the tunnel for the missing teen, but there was no sign of her ever having been there. Perhaps the rumor of her literally vanishing into thin air in front of witnesses isn't a rumor at all. Maybe, for once, the truth is actually being spread?

In Shadow Grove anything is possible.

As Dougal climbs into the passenger seat of her Hyundai, Rachel turns to look at the forest entrance, searching for the Fae prince who'd saved her hometown from a tyrannical overlord with a thing for black décor. When nothing stirs within the forest, Rachel sighs and climbs inside.

"It's been a month," Dougal says, strapping into the seat. "At some point, ye need to realize he may not come back."

She turns the key in the ignition, ignoring Dougal's relatively sound logic. Still, it doesn't make her feel any better about leaving the heavy lifting to one person. Fae. Whatever. The last Fae light Orion had given her hadn't faded like the others. It's in her bedroom, usually hovering above her desk or bouncing up and down on her bed. The Fae light is the only way she knows he's maybe still alive.

Rachel reverses out of the driveway and onto Griswold Road before pulling away.

"How's yer ma?" he asks. Dougal knows the answer full well, seeing as he's almost always over at their house when Rachel's not over at his.

Rachel shoots a look his way. "She's exactly how she was this morning."

"Still freakin' out about her missin' clothes?" He chuckles.

"Yes," she says, exhaling through her nose.

Rachel suspects her mother's so-called memory loss is a farce. She doesn't spend her time filling the gaps in her foggy memory. Instead, she's obsessed with figuring out who screwed with her wardrobe. On the bright side, at least things at home are systematically returning to normal—they eat dinner together every night now, *without* Sheriff Carter's eau de ugh filling up the space, and they've started to talk again. It's not like old times. There's still a barrier between them, one Rachel can't figure out how to cross. But at least she's home again.

Dougal fumbles with the radio. "No other kids have gone missin', yeah?"

"Nope," Rachel says. "Greg would've texted me if there'd been any news of more missing children. Don't worry about it."

"Ye two have gotten pretty cozy, eh? Always textin' and chattin' ..."

"Are you jealous?" Rachel grins, glancing his way.

"No! Ma's made it perfectly clear we're not to become kissin' cousins. She showed me the family tree and told me about the discrepancies in it. Then she went on to say she doesn't want her grandbabies to have webbed feet." He grimaces and visibly shudders.

Rachel laughs. "Aye, I was wonderin' if they'd told ye."

"Are ye mockin' my accent now, Rachel Cleary?"

"You bet I am," she says, giggling. "As for Greg, you don't have to worry. We're just friendly."

"Friendly?"

"He's a good kisser," Rachel says and shrugs. "Maybe you've not realized it, but Shadow Grove is a small town and the pickings are slim. You take what you can get."

"Yer such a romantic," he says, sarcasm dripping off his words as the car passes the Eerie Creek Bridge, heading toward the farmlands.

Rachel reaches up to her necklace and takes the umbrella pendant between her index finger and thumb.

"Yer ma invited us over for dinner tomorrow night. Said she had some news to share. Any idea what she's on about?"

She releases the pendant. "It's the first I'm hearing of it. Sorry."

Dougal sighs and sits back in his seat.

Rachel looks over to him. "What?"

"This town is dull, ye know? Since the Night Weaver's left, nothin' interestin' has happened. I'm … bored."

"I did warn you when you first came to Shadow Grove, didn't I?" She purses her lips in thought, wondering how she can cheer him up, before she says, "At least we have the barn bashes to look forward to, the Fourth of July is around the corner, and if you want to get a little exercise, there's always the End of Summer Fun Run."

Dougal grimaces.

"Jeez, fine, we'll go into the city one day and watch a movie or something, but you're paying for the popcorn," she says. When he doesn't respond, she continues, "*Maybe*, while we're there, we can go check out the all-ages nightclub."

His expression smooths out. "Now yer talkin' my language, Rach."

By the time they reach Berfield Farm's rustic barn, painted in bright red with white trimmings, the barn bash is already in full swing. Loud beats and electric screeches fill the night air. Through the open doors, colorful lights spill out onto the grassy field in rapid succession. Students from Ridge Crest High stand outside in clusters, talking amongst themselves near their cars or beside the barn, each holding a red plastic cup in hand, some sucking on their vapes and blowing large puffs of white, sweet-smelling smoke into the air.

"This is what I call a party," Dougal announces as she parks the car in an open space near the barn's doors. He loosens the seatbelt, eyes sparkling with excitement.

"Want me to show you around and introduce you to some people?" Rachel asks.

"No, I don't want to put ye out. I already see Joe Farrow Jr.," he says. "Meet ye back here at eleven-thirty?"

She nods. "Have fun."

Dougal smiles as he heads off to join his employer's son, Ridge Crest High's first-string fullback.

Whatever happened to shite football? Rachel wonders, pressing the key fob to lock the car doors. She watches him go, and as he nears Joe Jr. the rest of the football team surrounds him. They slap him on his back, make jokes, and almost instantly he's part of their fold.

Some people just have it easier than others when it comes to high school.

"Hey," the familiar voice says, startling her out of her thoughts. Rachel turns and sees Greg standing there, dressed in what goes for semi-casual around these parts—jeans, button-up shirt, and a pair of designer sneakers. "I didn't think you'd come."

"I'm always fashionably late," she says, leaning back against her car. She studies him and says, "Shouldn't you be inside mingling?"

He takes a step closer. "I mingle early, before our peers can get wasted and pass out."

"Clever."

"I've been known to have my moments of brilliance." Greg leans against the car and towers over her.

Rachel tilts her head back to gaze into his eyes. Does he know what Orion is, or care that the Fae prince has gone missing?

Maybe Orion isn't gone. He could be lying low, especially since Mrs. Crenshaw caught sight of him.

"Have you seen Orion Blackwood around?"

Greg seems taken aback by the question. "No. I haven't seen him. Sorry."

His expression is full of confusion, much to Rachel's amusement.

"I thought …"

"You thought?" she repeats.

He hesitates, and says, "I just thought only cheerleaders liked pompoms."

Rachel glances down at her hippie-chic outfit, one of Mrs. Crenshaw's revamps, and grins. "You thought wrong."

He chuckles as he inclines his head closer to hers. "Well, the pompoms suit you. You look amazing tonight."

"Thank you."

She averts her gaze, and her heart skips a beat when she sees a twinkle of naughtiness in his eyes. Before Rachel can get drawn into whatever mischief he has planned, she looks around and sees a few partygoers staring at them. She turns back to him.

"People are going to talk, I hope you know that," Rachel says, using his own words against him.

"You're far too worried about what people say," he responds and leans even closer.

Rachel smiles up at him and pats his chest gently, feeling the muscles hidden beneath his shirt. Her gaze moves to look over his shoulder, to where there's movement. Of course, Eddie Roberts is lingering nearby with yet another girl on his arm. Holland Keith, captain of the cheer squad, is also far too interested in what's happening with Rachel and Greg.

"We have an audience," she says.

Greg glances over his shoulder and says loud enough for all the nosy eavesdroppers to hear, "Don't mind the gossipmongers, Rachel. Their only purpose is to spread juicy news because they're too bored with their own lives."

"Shhh," Rachel giggles, pressing her hand over his mouth. She feels him grinning against her fingers and palm as he slowly turns back to look her in the eyes. She removes her hand and her humor evaporates. "This is still just a summer fling, right? When school starts in the fall we'll go back to normal?"

"Yeah," Greg says, his smile faltering. "Unless—?"

"No, we're *way* too competitive for this thing between us to become serious. We'll destroy each other the first chance we get."

Greg leans closer to her again. "So, what's the problem?"

She pushes herself onto the tips of her toes and whispers against his lips, "Just making sure, Greg. Just making sure."

Rachel and Dougal make their midnight curfew with mere minutes to spare. She rushes up the porch steps because Dougal insists on making sure she's safely inside before he heads across the road and waves goodbye before closing and locking the door behind her.

Her mother had been nice enough to leave the porch and living room lights on, but there's no sign of her having waited up for Rachel's return.

Change is gradual. Give it time.

She takes off her shoes and quietly makes her way upstairs.

Once she's on the landing, Rachel looks toward the main bedroom, the door having been left wide open, and sees her mother sleeping on the bed. She listens for any weird noises, residual influences from the darkling that had briefly taken refuge in the MacCleary house. Nothing.

Mom's safe. Relax.

Satisfied, she heads to her bedroom. As she opens the door, the Fae light flies closer, acting like a happy puppy that hasn't seen his master the whole day, and hovers near her shoulder.

"Hello again," she whispers to the sphere of light, raising her free hand to tickle its surface in greeting. "I told you I'd be back soon, didn't I, Ziggy?"

Her Fae light, which she'd named Ziggy, responds by moving away from her in zigzag motions.

"Someone's in a bad mood," she mutters, heading toward the wardrobe. Rachel opens the doors, sets her shoes on the floor, and pulls out a pair of pajamas from a shelf. Unlike her mother, she still has most of her clothes thanks to Mrs. Crenshaw. Ziggy returns to her side before it flies back to the bed. "Make up your mind or I'm switching on the light."

She changes clothes in the gloom, the music from the barn bash still fresh in her mind. Rachel hums and sways to the song playing in her head, her muscles remembering the way she'd danced until she couldn't dance anymore. She turns in place to see Ziggy bobbing over a box on her bed, neatly placed in front of her pillow.

Rachel's hand moves up to her umbrella pendant, which she closes in her fist. She walks closer to her bed, studying the ivory-embossed box tied with a golden ribbon to embellish the gift. Her eyes narrow in suspicion. Nobody comes into her bedroom, not even her mother unless they're arguing. She glances at Ziggy.

"Is this your doing, Ziggy?" she asks, turning her gaze back to the box.

Ziggy simply bobs in place, gravity-defying magic at its best. It moves out of the air and nests on top of her pillow.

She takes a deep breath as she pulls the box closer to the edge of the bed and lifts the lid. Golden tissue paper protects the contents within, which she slowly pulls aside to reveal the lilac silk beneath. Rachel covers her mouth, stifling a gasp or a sob or some other surprised sound from escaping into the night. She sits down on the bed, gently running her fingertips across the brocaded bodice, tracing the familiar golden thread. Her heart beats with indescribable joy as she carefully lifts the dress from the packaging.

"How?" she breathes the word, inspecting the exquisite craftsmanship that had gone into creating this glamorous 1950s evening dress.

A golden envelope flutters down as the layered skirts of the dress unfold, drifting to the carpet on a nonexistent breeze. Rachel stands up from the bed, gently spreads the dress—the exact garment her father had gifted her mother on their ten-year wedding anniversary—across her mattress before she turns around to pick up the fallen envelope.

Beautiful cursive letters in black ink spell out the word *Clarré*, making her heart race faster. She turns the envelope over and removes the ivory card within, reading and rereading the words written in the same elegant handwriting until her vision blurs with fresh tears.

I saw this magical dress and it made me think of you.

About the Author

Monique Snyman's mind is a confusing bedlam of glitter and death, where candy-coated gore is found in abundance and homicidal unicorns thrive. Sorting out the mess in her head is particularly irksome before she's ingested a specific amount of coffee, which is equal to half the recommended intake of water for humans per day. When she's not playing referee to her imaginary friends or trying to overdose on caffeine, she's doing something with words—be it writing, reading, or fixing all the words.

Monique Snyman lives outside Johannesburg, South Africa, with her husband and an adorable Chihuahua. She's the author of MUTI NATION, a horror novel set in South Africa, and Bram Stoker Award® nominated novel, THE NIGHT WEAVER, which is the first installment in a dark fantasy series for young adults.

www.MoniqueSnyman.com